"Corazon's a hell of a place," Henry said thoughtfully.

"All raw worlds are hell—but we could sure have ourselves some fun taming her down a little . . ." the old man's eyes hazed wistfully. "One last go-round before the Big Dark. Remember, Cap'n, how it feels to have a deck under your feet, and the whole universe on the other side of the hull, waiting to be tamed?"

"Damn your hide, Amos," Henry said softly. But the decision was made: there would be one last

# PLANET RUN

# PLANET RUN

## KEITH LAUMER AND GORDON R. DICKSON

Plus Two Bonus Stories

"Once There Was a Giant," by Keith Laumer
"Call Him Lord," by Gordon R. Dickson

**TOR**

A TOM DOHERTY ASSOCIATES BOOK

A TOR Book

First printing, May, 1982

ISBN: 48-525-5

Cover art by: Thomas Kidd

Acknowledgements:

Planet Run, © 1967 by Keith Laumer and Gordon R. Dickson
"Once There Was A Giant," copyright © 1968 by Mercury Press, Inc. Reprinted from *The Magazine of Fantasy and Science Fiction*.
"Call Him Lord," was first published in Analog Science Fiction Magazine, copyright © 1966 by The Conde Nast Publications, Inc.

Printed in the United States of America

Distributed by:
Pinnacle Books, Inc.
1430 Broadway
New York, New York 10018

## TABLE OF CONTENTS

# I

The sun was warm on his face. Through his closed eyelids, it gleamed a hot orange—like a sunrise fog on a world called Flamme, long ago. And Dulcia, the first Dulcia, came toward him, smiling through the wreaths of mist . . .

Something tickled his cheek; he brushed at it. Damned flowerflies! He'd have to start up the repellor field; didn't like the damned thing. Made a man's bones itch, like a couple of hours under high R, de-leading tube linings . . . . The glory of his memory dimmed. A grim little note of uneasiness struck discordantly through the dream. There had been something he had been trying to put out of his mind, lately . . .

The tickle came again, and the dream vanished. His eyes flew open and he squinted up at a slim, blond, long-legged young girl in a brief pink sunsuit, leaning over his garden chair with a long, feathery grass stem in her hand.

"Dammit, Dulcie, you're getting too old to go around like that," he growled.

"No, I'm not, Grandpa, I'm just getting old enough. You should have seen Senator Bartholomew's face when I went to the door—"

"Is that fool back again?" Captain Henry closed his eyes. But the feeling of uneasiness was stronger, suddenly. Fat Bartholomew—*Senator* Bartholomew now—was not quite a fool. Or at least he had not been a fool forty years ago as a young man. Henry, already aging at that time, had almost liked him then—sometimes.

Now of course he had become a "Senator"—and taken up the prissy modern manners of movement and speech that went with the political image. Still . . . the uneasiness moved stronger than ever in Henry.

"Send him on his way, girl," Henry said. "You know better than to interrupt my nap—"

"He says it's awfully important, Grandpa."

"Important to him, not me! I've already told him what I think of his politics, his business methods, his brains, and his taste in liquor . . . "

There was a sound of affected throat-clearing. Henry looked around. A tall, broad-bellied man with a now-flaccid face, but with the same angry black eyebrows Henry remembered from forty years ago, had come up behind the girl.

"I thought I'd better make my presence known, Captain," the Senator said.

"You wouldn't have heard anything I haven't told you to your face, Bartholomew," Henry snapped. "What's it this time? Not the same old proposition?"

Bartholomew grunted, took the chair Dulcie offered him. For a moment the girl moved between Henry and the sun—and for a second he was back in the dream of her great-grandmother and the lambent mists of Flamme. Then she moved out of the light and he was back in the present of hard reality—and Senator Bartholomew.

Henry looked at the middle-aged man with harsh distaste. Bartholomew was perspiring in a fashionable narrow-shouldered jacket of shiny green material with short sleeves showing elaborate cuffs with large, jeweled links. A three-inch campaign button lettered ELECT THE STATISTICAL AVERAGE was pinned prominently to his breast pocket. His lower lip was thrust out aggressively, frowning at the old man.

"I was hoping you'd reconsidered, Captain Henry. Since you didn't answer my call—"

"If I'd had anything new to say I'd have managed to dodder to the phone. I'm not bedridden—yet!"

Bartholomew pulled off his maroon beret, fanned at himself with it. "This is matter of planetary importance, Captain! Corazon is a promising world. Surely you're not going to allow personal considerations—"

"Like hell I'm not!" Henry growled. "I've put in my time on the Frontier Worlds, one hundred and fifteen years of it! I've had ten good years of retirement—up until you started pestering me . . ."

"Pestering is hardly the word, Captain Henry! I'm offering you a magnificent opportunity! You'll have the finest of equipment—"

"I prefer the sunshine—I know, you've put a

roof over your town to keep the fresh air out, but I like it—"

"All I'm asking is that you take the Rejuve Treatment just once more—at *my* expense—"

Henry looked across at the plump citizen.

"Your expense, eh? Hah! I've had the treatment three times. I'm a hundred and thirty-five years old—and I feel every month of it. You know what a fourth Rejuve would do to me."

"But I've seen your last medical report. You're in excellent condition, for your age! The treatment wouldn't make you an adolescent again—but it would restore you to full vigor . . . "

"I'd look young—for a few months. I'd fade like yesterday's gardenia after the first year, and I'd be senile in three. After that, it wouldn't matter whether I made the fourth year or not." He leaned back and closed his eyes. "That's it, Senator. You'll have to find another errand boy."

"You're not considering this matter in depth, Captain! A new world to be opened for homesteading—the first in sixty years! This errand, as you call it, would require only a few months of your time, after which you'd not only have the satisfaction of having made a valuable contribution to the development of the frontier, but you'd bank a tidy fortune as well!"

Henry opened one eye. "Why not send that Statistical Average candidate of yours? If he's good enough to be a Planetary Delegate to the council, he ought to be able to handle a little assignment like this."

"You're speaking frivolously of grave matters. Our candidate, as represenative of the median of

Aldoradon society, is an eminently suitable choice, embodying the highest concepts of democratic government.''

"You can skip the campaign speech. I don't vote the Average Man ticket . . .''

Bartholomew's veined nose darkened. He drew in a breath through flared nostrils. "As to the venture we're discussing," he said harshly, "your . . . ah . . . specialized knowledge will outweigh other considerations." Bartholomew's shifting gaze fixed meaningfully on Henry.

Henry looked at him through narrowed eyes; for a second he caught sight of his own face reflected in a polished metal chair-back. It was like a battered carving in ancient oak. "Just what specialized knowledge do you have in mind?''

Bartholomew twisted his mouth in a smile-like grimace, spread his hands. "Why, Captain, you're an old-timer, you know the space lanes, the curious mores of distant worlds. You could face up to the ruffians one would encounter out on Corazon, brazen it out, and take what you wanted. And I think you'd know what to go after," he added, eyeing the toe of his sandal.

"You do, eh?" Henry studied the other's face. "I've got twenty good years left to sniff the flowers; what would make me leave that to get my neck broken in a Run?''

"Are you interested in aluminum oxide, Captain?" Bartholomew asked casually.

The uneasiness was suddenly back—but not just uneasiness any longer. It was like an ice-cold cramp in his stomach.

"—In the form known as corundum," Bartholomew was adding.

"Just what're you getting at, Senator?" Henry said harshly.

It was Bartholomew's turn to sit silent. His glance went to the girl sunning herself by the poolside a few yards distant. Henry grunted softly.

"It's time for my lunch, Dulcie," he called. She looked up, glanced at Bartholomew's face, then rose and went off across the lawn.

"All right," said Henry, without inflection.

Bartholomew hitched his chair forward, got out a dope stick, and—as an afterthought—offered one to Henry. Henry waved it grimly aside.

"Ever since its discovery over a century ago, Corazon's been a closed world, Captain." The visitor puffed perfumed smoke past Henry. "Under close quarantine. But you were there once . . ."

"Sure. On a free-lance prospecting trip—before the Quarantine Service ever heard of the world. What about it?"

"Why . . ." Bartholomew's eyes fixed on the glowing tip of his dope stick, "just that your trip may or may not have been legal. You spent several months on the planet."

"So?"

"And you found something."

"You asking me or telling me?"

"Telling you, Captain," Bartholomew said flatly. "And I'll tell you something more. Corundum takes many forms. It makes an excellent commercial abrasive; it also appears in more attractive guises—known as ruby—emerald—sapphire, oriental topaz, amethyst, and others." Bartholomew's voice was a purr now. "There's an excellent market for natural gemstones, Captain; stones like the ones I saw your great-granddaughter wearing last month when my boy Larry took her to the graduation ball . . ."

He paused. Henry looked back at him expressionlessly, waiting. Bartholomew's voice held a rasping note now. "I know a great deal about your career, Captain—everything, in fact. I've made it my business to find out, these last few weeks." He puffed out smoke, enjoying the moment. Henry watched him, waiting.

"You've always lived modestly here—" Bartholomew waved a hand at the garden, the pool, the old-fashioned glass-walled house—"But you were a wealthy man once. And 'once' is the word."

"Is it?" asked Henry, completely without inflection.

"That's right," said Bartholomew briskly. "You lived off your principal instead of your interest, Captain. Any businessman can tell you what a mistake that is. Now what you've got left is this property, barely enough income for an old man sitting in the sun, and the credit backed by the assessed valuation of those gemstones you were incautious enough to let the girl wear. I know to the penny what that assessed valuation is."

"What's this got to do with the price of wambapears?" growled Henry.

"Just—that those gemstones represent your great-granddaughter's inheritance," said Bartholomew.

"What's it to you? I won them free and clear."

"Did you?" said Bartholomew. "I agree you

don't owe a cent—if you did I'd know about it. But *own* them—" His eyes narrowed in their folds of fat. "I happen to know you went back to Corazon at least twice—after the planet was placed under quarantine."

Henry did not move. He smiled a wintry smile.

"That was quite a while ago—if I did. Over a hundred years."

"There's no statute of limitations where possession of contraband is concerned. Your later Navy service won't affect it, either. And that last visit's essentially a matter of record. A hundred and four years ago, wasn't it, to be precise? And you got back just one week too late to be there when your wife died—"

Henry sat suddenly forward in his chair. His eyes locked with the Senator's.

"Never mind my wife, Bartholomew," he growled.

"What's the matter, Captain?" Bartholomew spread his white, slablike hands. "You couldn't have known she needed you. Or could you? Of course it was a pity, your getting back with the gemstones that would have paid for the operation that might have saved her—just one week too late. But there's no need to let your conscience bother you . . . though I suppose it's hard, having a great-granddaughter around who's the image of the wife you let die—"

Henry moved. It was a small move—simply a little shifting forward of his weight onto the left elbow and the right fist as they rested on the arms of his chair. But Bartholomew shut up suddenly. His sagging face had tightened.

"Easy, Captain . . . ." he muttered.

"Never mind my wife," repeated Henry, tonelessly.

"Of course . . ." Bartholomew wet his lips. Henry sat slowly back in his chair. Bartholomew breathed deeply once more and his voice strengthened.

"It doesn't matter, anyway," he said, "—about your—about anything that happened after you came back. It's Corazon, and your illegal trip there I'm talking about. You're still a hero, Captain, still the first and greatest of the old star-frontiersmen. The Quarantine Service wouldn't do anything to you, personally. But those gemstones would be confiscated, if someone whispered in their ears to run lattice comparison tests between them and other, sample minerals from Corazon itself."

He stopped speaking, flicked his eyes at Henry. Henry stared back; his upper lip twisted.

"And you'd do the whispering, is that it?" Henry said. The other man did not answer, letting silence speak for him. "I don't get it. You could hire an army of hard cases, if you wanted to back somebody in the Run on Corazon next month."

Bartholomew nodded, shortly.

"In spite of the fact that every slum in the Eastern arm has its quota of gun handlers, you want me—a worn-out old space-hulk—because you think I know something!"

"I know damned well you know something!" said Bartholomew suddenly and viciously. "My God, man, there's a fortune to be made! I'll supply everything you need. With my financing your entry, you'd be able to stake your claim successfully—and you'd legally own those deposits of stones you found more than a hundred years ago!''

Henry laughed suddenly, a mirthless, barking laugh that made the other stare at him.

"I see," Henry said. "What kind of split did you have in mind?"

"In view of the risk—and the heavy initial expense—"

*"How much?"*

" . . . And under the circumstances of my knowledge of your past—90 percent for me, and a full 10 percent for yourself." Bartholomew smiled ingratiatingly, puffed at his dope stick.

Henry gripped the arms of his chair with gnarled hands, shoved himself to his feet.

"Get out!" he said.

Bartholomew's heavy jowls paled. He dropped the dope stick, scrambled hastily to his feet.

"You don't talk to me that way—" he began.

Henry took a step forward. His throat felt as if it was on fire, and there was a gathering haze, a blurring before his eyes. The pulse of his blood pounded like a tom-tom in his skull.

Bartholomew stumbled backward. Two . . . three steps, but then he stopped. The soft fat of his face hardened. He had been a tall man in his younger years—although even then he had lacked half a head of Henry's massive height and a full third of Henry's fighting weight.

"You'd kill me if you thought you needed to, wouldn't you, Captain?" he said thinly, his eyes narrowing in their cushions of fat. Close to him, Henry checked himself, fought down the rage that burned in him.

"Don't try me on that, Bartholomew," he said hoarsely.

"Oh, I believe you." The Senator laughed harshly. "But since there's just the two of us here, let me tell you something. I'm capable of killing, too, if it comes to that. I'll go!" he added hastily, as Henry took another step forward. "But think it over," he went on, talking rapidly as he backed away. "I still know what I know about you, the gemstones, and Corazon; and the time for you to enter the Run is getting shorter every day. Think about that great-granddaughter of yours—and what it would be like for her to be just another penniless young girl, with no hope of what she's grown up to expect—except possibly a wealthy marriage—"

"Like your young whelp Larry, I suppose!" roared Henry, rolling forward.

Bartholomew turned and fled. For a few steps Henry pursued him; then he stopped, and breathing hard, let the other man go. He turned and stumped back toward the pool, stared down through the clear water at the multicolored grotto of the mineral spring that fed it.

"Gemstones," he muttered; and then—*Dulcie!*"

. . . And not even he could have said for sure if it was the girl who had left them a few moments earlier, or his long-dead love, of whom he thought as he spoke.


"You should have seen the Senator, Uncle Amos!" Dulcia said. She poured coffee into Henry's cup, passed the decanter of brandy to the small, turkey-necked man who drained his glass, exhaled noisily, refilled it.

"Huh! Wish I'd been there!" He winked at the girl, tugged at one end of a stained white mustache. "The Senator's used to getting what he goes after. Guess it's the first time anybody's ever turned him down flat."

Captain Henry grunted, took an old-fashioned cigar from the heavy silver box on the table. The girl held a lighter to it. The odor of tobacco mingled with the scent of wood smoke from the fireplace.

"The man's a damned fool," he muttered uneasily. "Rubs me the wrong way; chatters like a haki bird in molting season—and says all the wrong things."

She filled her cup and sat down. "Why does Mr. Bartholomew want you to go to Corazon, Grandpa?"

The small man cackled. " 'Cause he knows damn well he's the only man on Aldorado that can walk into that Corazon free-for-all and come out with the back of his head still on—to say nothing about grabbing off a nice chunk of real estate."

Henry blew out a cloud of smoke, leaned back in his chair, his long legs propped on a footstool carved from the wood of the Yanda tree and upholstered with the knobbed gray hide of a direbeast. It was a relaxed pose, but the tension shouted in the narrowing of his eyes, the set of his shoulders.

"The frontier's finished," he said. "Corazon's its last dying gasp. It's a hard world—rock and ice and tundra. No fit place for a man to live."

"But like you said, it's the last chance for a man

with a yen for a gamble."

"Sure—if it had been halfway habitable, it'd have been settled a long time ago—"

"I don't know—I've heard the Quarantine Service run into some funny stuff out there—that's why they set on it for a hundred years." The small man's dark, birdlike eyes were suddenly diamond sharp on Henry.

Henry met their stare, his own eyes as flat as a command.

"I remember," he said, "when there were fresh green worlds for the asking right here in the Sector. That's what's wrong with people today—all this Statistical Average horsefeathers. A man's got no new frontier to go out and fight for."

"Unless," said Amos, softly, "you want to count Corazon."

"There'll be plenty that'll be after it—but not any Average Man party Nancies . . ."

"There it is—a world for the taking." The small man put a log on the fire, resumed his seat, dusting his hands. "With the new Terraforming techniques, they'll transform her. Thirty million square miles of real estate: farms, mines, ports; land that'll have cities growing on it in a few years; open tundras where a man could run a million head of snow cattle; mountains and waterfalls, and rivers, and sea beaches—free to anybody that can grab and hold onto it. For a stake like that, every gambler, pirate, soldier of fortune, and con man in forty parsecs would sell his hope of a ringside seat in hell . . ."

"And Mr. Bartholomew wants Grandpa to go *there?*"

"Sure. I remember the first Run we was on together—out on Adobe, that was." Amos turned to the girl. "We staked our claim to our legal hundred square miles—a burned-out slab of desert tilted up on one side to where a Bolo couldn't climb it. I went into a nine-day crap game with it at Square-deal Mac's place on Petreac, and ran it up to half a continent . . ." he cackled softly. "Before I lost it all on a deck cut with Mac."

Dulcia's eyes shone. "That sounds like you. Was Grandpa ever on another Run?"

Amos nodded his bald, freckled head. "Yep—last one was right here on Aldorado. He was a little shrewder by then; grabbed off a nice piece of land backed up to a mountain range, with forests and minerals—and facing the sea, with a natural harbor that could handle any surface liner ever built."

"Why, Amos—that sounds like right here—Tivoli Harbor, and the Mall . . ."

He nodded. "That's right, girl."

She turned to her great-grandfather. "But—then you must have owned the whole town . . ."

Amos shook his head. "Nope. He was just a young fella then. It was just before his second Rejuve. There were a lot of homesteaders who lost out—left on the beach, with no money, no land, kids crying for home—all that kind of thing. He didn't want the land; to Henry, it was a game. He gave it to 'em. All he asked for was this little piece —and a house and a garden—whenever he got ready for it."

"You mean all those people—Senator Bartholomew, all of them—owe their whole old Mall, and everything, to you, Grandpa? And then they—'' she broke off.

"It was mostly their great-grandpas, girl," Henry said. "These people don't owe me anything. I got what I wanted."

"And they're all working so hard to elect their stupid old Statistical Average as Delegate! Why don't they send you, Grandpa? You've done more for them than anybody!"

"Now, why would I want to be Delegate, Dulcie-girl? I just want to sit in the sun and rest my old bones . . ."

"You know," Dulcia said. Her eyes went to him and fell.

He glanced sideways at her. Her eyes were large and dark; how much she resembled her great-grandmother, now, sitting there in the firelight . . .

"You're thinking about the Aeterna treatment," he said. "Forget it—"

"Why should I forget it! You could be young again—and stay young for years and years—nobody knows how long! If they'd only had the treatment back when you were opening up the Frontier, you'd have gotten it anyway for Unusual Service to the Race—the way explorers and scientists get it now!"

"Well," said Henry, smiling. "I missed my chance then—"

"But you can still get it! All Planetary Delegates get the treatment. And you could get elected just by lifting your finger if you wanted. People around here remember—"

"I'm no politician, Dulcie. Don't want to be. And I don't want to live forever. I've had my life—

more than enough. I've seen my friends go—all but Amos here—killed or dead of old age, or just drifted away. It's not the same universe any more I knew when I was young. It's the day of the Statistical Average—"

"Oh, stop it, Grandpa!"

"I mean it, girl. They want the man I was, not the old buzzard I am now."

"Old buzzard!" said Dulcia, fiercely. "You're still twice the man any of them is!"

"That's putting it mild, honey," Amos put in. "And in the old days he was the meanest, wildest, hardest-hitting young devil in the space service. Many's the time I tried to whip him myself. Never could though—he had too much reach on me."

"That was a long time ago," Captain Henry said. "We had our time, Amos—and we lived it to the hilt—with no regrets. Now we've got a chair by the fire. Let's leave it that way."

Amos poured again, tossed the drink back with a practiced gesture, sat staring into the fire.

"Then the war came along. Your great-grandpa'd just paid for the prettiest little fifty-ton fast-cargo cutter that ever outran a Customs Patrol; he signed it up for the duration. They made him a Reserve Battle Ensign; two years later he was a Battle Captain—Regular—and his boat was a burned-out wreck."

"Grandpa—you never told me you were in the war . . . !"

"Ask Amos to show you his medals some day. He forgot to mention that I was in the wreck when it was hit; he got me out."

"Oh, Grandpa—wouldn't it be exciting if you did—I mean if you took the Rejuve, and showed them all . . ."

He looked at the glowing end of the cigar. "You mean you want me to go along with Bartholomew's idea?"

"No—of course I don't! I want you to stay here —and live a long, long time. I just meant . . ."

"Oh, well; I was exaggerating a little. If I took another Rejuve, I'd still have maybe as much as five good years—" He broke off, glanced at the radium clock on the wall, a relic of Old Mars. "Say, it's getting late. What about that big dance you're going to with young Bartholomew?"

"I'm not going," she said shortly.

"Eh? Why this afternoon, it was all you could do to eat your lunch before you dashed down to the Mall to buy a dress . . ."

"I don't want to go."

"Now, wait a minute, honey. Just because old Bartholomew's Average Man party doesn't want me as a Delegate's no reason to miss your party—"

"It isn't that . . ."

"Hmm. How much of my talk with the old man did you 'overhear' today, girl?"

"I heard him say—you stole something! He ought to be ashamed of himself."

Amos cackled. "He called Henry a thief and got away with it? Say, I'd like to back the Senator in a crap game, with *his* luck . . ."

"So you think seeing the boy would be disloyal to the old man?" Henry shook his head, smiling at the girl. "Don't visit the sins of the old on their offspring. You go put that fancy dress on and go on to the dance; have a good time—"

"That Bartholomew boy's not good enough for a gal like Dulcie, Cap'n," Amos cut in. "Always got his hair combed and not a scar on his knuckles—"

"Shut up, Amos. Larry's no worse than any other young fellow with a delicate upbringing—" Henry frowned. "And what other kind is there these days?"

"A ribbon counter boy—" jeered Amos, "and a girl like Dulcie? Why, you ought to—"

"You go ahead, Dulcie-girl. Amos and I want to talk a while." Captain Henry paused to bite down on a fresh cigar and puff it alight. He blew out smoke, winked grimly at the girl. "Leave the fighting for the older generation; I think I can handle Bartholomew Senior."

The sound of Dulcia's Turbocad faded in the distance. Captain Henry looked into the fire, drawing on his cigar. Abruptly, he took the cigar out of his mouth, scowled at it, tossed it into the fire.

Amos looked sideways at him.

"What kind of bribe's the Senator offering, Henry?"

Henry snorted. "Ten percent of a jewel mine— that I've got hidden up my sleeve."

Amos whistled. "Who's he been talking to?"

"I've been wondering about that."

"So the Senator thinks you know something, hey?" Amos cackled again. "Say, now, that's an idea, Henry . . ."

"You're too damned old to be getting ideas,

Amos. Fill your glass and prop your feet up in front of the fire—that's our speed."

"Is it, Henry? There might be something in what the Senator was peddling. These young squirts nowadays—they ain't got what it takes. Look at that boy of his—a tennis-playing, baby-faced greenhorn. He wouldn't last a week on a Run. But you and me, Henry . . ." Amos leaned forward, his eyes sharp in his gnome-like face. "We could walk in there and skim the gravy off Corazon like a bar-man cutting suds."

"How old are you, Amos?" Henry asked abruptly.

"Huh? I'm lesee, a hundred and fifty-two."

"How long since your last Rejuve?"

"Forty-five, forty-six years." He leaned forward, his old eyes bright.

"What do you say, Henry? We never were the kind to go to bed while the party was still on. This setting around counting down to a funeral—that's no fun. I want to go one more time, Henry! Sure I won't last—but I want to be hungry again, and kiss a girl again, and pick one more fight in one more bar—"

"Forget it, Amos. You're too old. The Rejuve would kill you."

"Forget it, huh? Too old—!" Amos came out of his chair like a jack-in-the-box. He tossed the cigar over his shoulder. "I ain't too old to have one more try—"

"Calm down, Amos. If guts were all you needed, you'd live forever. But it's a little more compli-cated than that. Rejuve won't work at your age.

You can't change that."

"So you're just going to sit here and let a bunch of fuzz-cheeked Johnnies walk off with Corazon?"

"Talk sense, Amos. I don't need a piece of Corazon; I've got enough to last me."

"Yeah—but what about the girl? How's she going to be fixed?"

"Dulcie'll be all right. She's a smart girl—"

"Sure, she's smart—and purty. Purty enough to marry some lightweight like Master Bartholomew and spend the rest of her days hand-washing his silk socks while he's out campaigning for the Territorial Statistical Average. That what you want?"

"I was wondering what brought you over here today, Amos." Henry glanced across at him; their eyes caught and held level, and a near-forgotten current of danger seemed to wake the drowsy air of the garden.

"Cap'n, I get around." Amos's voice was different, suddenly, harder and more deliberate. "I pick up all kinds of conversation. I heard the Senator had a bug in his bonnet to talk you into Rejuve so he could hire you on for the run."

"So?" Henry's voice was equally flat and deliberate.

"So, Old Man Bartholomew's got some kind of a Nancy working for him—a private secretary. He likes to drink. I bought him a few, and he got to talking—"

"You wouldn't have put a few drops of something pink in his glass, would you, Amos?" The irony in Henry's voice was heavy.

"That ain't the point, Cap'n," the little man said grimly. "I told you—the Nancy talked."

"Whatever he said," Henry's voice marked the words like the slow beat of a hammer on a forge, "it doesn't change anything."

Their eyes met and locked again. Amos drew a deep breath. "Henry," he said, "what's on Corazon?"

Henry did not answer for a long moment. Then he picked up another cigar and savagely bit off the end of it.

"Go to hell!" he said.

"All right," answered the little man, still steely-voiced and undismayed, "I'm headed there anyway. Meanwhile I won't go away—and neither will whatever the Senator's holding over you, Cap'n. Now if it was just you, I'd say damn your worthless old hide and Bartholomew's welcome to it. But according to that Nancy, it's something to do with Dulcie—"

Henry jerked the cigar from his teeth and hurled it into the fire.

"That's a lot of good imported smoking you're making kindling out of tonight," said Amos. "All right, I won't say any more. Only as I remember, you used to be able to dicker a deal a bit. But I don't recall it ever doing you any good until you started to talk trade."

Henry glared across at him.

"Bartholomew's not invulnerable, you know," said Amos, mildly. "If he's got a hook on Dulcie, maybe I could cook up something about that lace-britches son of his—"

Henry sat up suddenly. Amos abruptly stopped talking, watching him with bright, old eyes.

"Corazon's a hell of a place, Amos," Henry said thoughtfully.

"Sure," said Amos, "all raw worlds are hell—but we could have ourselves some fun, you and me, taming her down a little . . ." for a moment the small man's eyes softened and became wistful. " . . . One last go-around before the Big Dark. Remember, Cap'n, how it feels to have a deck under your feet—going for broke against all the odds there are . . ."

"Damn your hide, Amos," Henry said softly. There was a new light in his eyes. He got to his feet, grunting a little as he straightened his back. "Maybe I've got things to say to old man Bartholomew at that!"

Amos jumped to his feet and laughed aloud, slapping Henry's shoulder.

"That's the idea, Cap'n! He can hum the tune—but we'll put the words to it!"

Henry scribbled a brief note to Dulcia, propped it on the table; then the two went out through the kitchen entrance to the garage of the antique-style villa. Captain Henry slid behind the wheel of a low-slung black Monojag, started up, gunned it out along the drive. It was a clear night with Hope, the bigger moon, riding high in the sky, and the pale disk of Dream just peeping above the tops of the imported poplars.

He took the shore road toward the lighted towers of the Mall, driving fast on the empty tarmac.

Senator Bartholomew stood in the doorway in his sequinned dressing gown, blinking from Captain Henry to Amos.

"What's this all about?" he blurted, staring at the tall old man with the leathery face and the white bristle of cropped hair. "Why, it's the middle of the night—"

"You were out at my place today, Senator, asking me to do a job for you. I'm here to call your bet."

"You'll . . . you'll go?" The Senator stepped back, inviting the callers inside. He ran his fingers through his thin hair. "Why, that's wonderful! Marvelous! But why in the name of order didn't you say so today . . ."

Henry glanced around the dim-lit, luxuriously furnished lounge room. "I'm not doing this in the name of order. I'm doing it for the hell of it. I guess maybe I've had enough naps in the sun to last me for a while—or maybe the prospect of seeing your long face every time I came down to the Mall for supplies was too much for me. What difference does it make? I'm here."

"Yes . . . " Bartholomew was nodding his head. He rubbed his hands together. "Wonderful news, Captain. I was sure you'd come to your senses—that is, I knew you had a sense of community spirit—"

"Community bath water! Now, before we go any further, let's get a couple of things straight. First —the split will be fifty-fifty."

Bartholomew jumped as though poked by a sharp instrument.

"Here—that wasn't the understanding—"

"Half to my great-granddaughter," Henry went on, "and half to your son."

Bartholomew's heavy eyebrows went up. "To Larry?" He looked dumbfounded.

"I don't like the idea of working for you, Senator —and your bank balance is top-heavy already."

Bartholomew breathed heavily through clamped jaws. "It's the boy's future I had in mind from the beginning—but why *your* interest . . . ?" he broke off, eyed Henry sharply, then nodded wisely. "Aha, I think I understand. Your great-granddaughter—and—Larry—"

"Maybe you'd better drop that line right there," Henry said in a steely tone.

Bartholomew tugged at the lapels of his dressing gown. "Very well; far be it from me to quibble—but the profits will be calculated after expenses, mind you!"

"All right; that's agreed then."

Bartholomew pulled at his lip. "You surprise me, Captain; I never knew you to be partial to my boy . . ."

"He deserves his share, Senator; he'll earn it."

"Hey, Henry!" Amos started.

"Shut up, Amos; I'll handle this."

Bartholomew gaped at Henry. "Look here," he blurted. "You don't mean—"

Captain Henry nodded. "Sure I do, Senator. You don't think I'm going out there alone, do you?"

"What is this—some—some sort of elaborate and reprehensible joke . . . ?"

Henry's eyes were sharp under white brows.

"You want me to go to Corazon. Sure, I'll go—but not unless your Statistically Average son goes with me."

Bartholomew was mopping at his face with a large flower-embossed tissue. He flung it to the floor, faced Captain Henry.

"No! I've told you ten times! You can have any other man you want—but not my boy . . . !"

Captain Henry turned to the door. "Come on, Amos. I'm going home to bed, where I belong—"

Senator Bartholomew pushed before him. His face was red. He raised a finger and wagged it.

"Do you mean, with the wealth of a planet at stake, you'd make a game of setting up fantastic conditions? What kind of insane prankster are you, you . . . you . . . "

"A minute ago it was a noble undertaking— now you're calling it a crazy prank."

"I didn't mean that! You're twisting my words!"

"Well, don't twist mine, Senator. Let's get it straight and clear. You're risking your capital; I'm risking my neck. I'll come back—and so will the boy—with a slice of Corazon that will make us all too rich to talk to."

"I think I see; you want a hostage! You don't trust me!"

"That might be a point—in case you were thinking of cutting any corners."

Bartholomew took out another tissue, wiped at his face, patted behind his ears.

"My boy's not prepared for this sort of thing," he said. "He's not strong; he's overworked himself on behalf of his Territory—"

"I know: a politician never sleeps; he also never breathes fresh air, feels the unfiltered sunlight on his skin, eats raw meat, or sleeps in his socks. He'll do all those things on a Run."

"Captain Henry, you're jeopardizing a golden opportunity for a vindictive whim! There'll never be another Run in this Sector! The nearest uncolonized worlds are a hundred years away—!"

Captain Henry looked at Senator Bartholomew, the long, pale, soft face, the extra chins, the damp, pudgy hands, the paunch straining under the tightly buttoned weskit.

"Your son, Senator," he said flatly. "Or it's no go . . ."

Bartholomew stared at Henry, his jaw muscles jumping.

"Very well, Captain," he said in a whisper. "My son will go."

"Now," Henry said briskly. "I want a brand-new scout boat—a Gendye, *Enamorata* Class; and I want it trajectoried in here as hold cargo, regardless of expense."

"But—that will cost thousands—" Bartholomew swallowed. "Agreed," he said.

"The same goes for our outfitting; I'll supply the list—no questions to be asked."

The Senator nodded.

"No need to look like an old maid agreeing to lose her virginity," Henry said. "It's for the good of the mission. Call your lawyers in and we'll get the papers signed now. And you can call the Rejuve Clinic and tell 'em I'm on the way over."

"Oh, yes, certainly. First thing in the morning. I'll call Dr. Spangler as soon as his office opens—''

"Tomorrow be damned! I'm here now—ready. Tomorrow I may be dead.''

"Dead? You're not feeling ill . . .?''

"Don't worry—I'll last out the night.''

"But—it's after midnight—''

"Sure,'' Amos put in. "And in Antipode it's quarter after nine tomorrow morning. When the Cap'n wants to do something, he wants to do it *now!*''

"Very well . . .'' Bartholomew tugged at the violet lapels of his dressing gown. "You enjoy an advantage, but that's no reason to bully.''

"Sure it is,'' Amos barked. "We've got to maintain our reputations as a couple of ornery old buzzards. It's one of the few pleasures we got left.''

Back in the car, Henry swung out onto the third-level interchange, gunned toward the glittering spire of the Medcenter.

"All right, Henry,'' Amos demanded. "What's all this Young Bart business? What do we want with that panty-waist?''

"Simple, Amos—I need a crewman—''

"What do you mean?'' Amos's voice was hoarse with indignation. "Ain't I—''

"No. You know damned well you can't go through another Rejuve; I'm not too damned sure I can.''

"Now, wait a dad-blamed minute, Henry! I was in this all the way—''

"Sorry, Amos,'' Henry said more gently. "You

know I want you—but facts are facts . . . And maybe the trip will do the boy good," he added.

"Hummph!" Amos sat silent for a moment. "So that's why you was so easy to convince all of a sudden," he said. "You figure you can make a man out of a boy."

"Maybe; it won't hurt for a handpicked sample of Aldorado's ideal average manhood to find out what it's like outside a climate-conditioned city."

"You're making a mistake, Henry. Young Bartholomew spends all his time playing tennis and reading statistics; he'll cave in on you the first time the going gets rough."

"I hope not, Amos—for a lot of. reasons." The image of the first Dulcia rose to shimmer before him. She seemed to be weighing his motives in the balance with her clear, gray eyes.

Under the blue-white lights of the Rejuve Clinic, Captain Henry watched as the doctor nervously laid out equipment.

"This is the most ridiculous thing I've ever heard of," he snapped. He was a tiny, birdlike man with overlarge eyes behind tinted contact lenses. "A man of your age—and at this time of night. Why, there are dozens of tests, measurements, bio-chemical analyses; you need at least three weeks on a special diet—and I haven't so much as checked your pulse, Captain Henry! And you expect me to put you in a regeneration tank and subject your metabolism to seventy-two hours of profound shock—"

"I have three months to get ready and get to that staging area, doctor," Henry said. "I'll need all my horsepower to make it; I don't have three weeks to waste."

"I have a good mind to refuse . . ." Spangler winked owl eyes defiantly at Henry. "There is the matter of professional ethics to consider . . ."

"I've signed the release," Henry said. "It's my neck."

The medic picked up a hypospray angrily, took Henry's arm. "Very well—but I wash my hands of responsibility; I won't guarantee an L.P. of even twelve months . . ." He pressed the plunger, tossed the instrument on the table, wiped his hands nervously.

"Kindly stretch out on the table here, Captain," he said. "You'll feel the effects of the shot in a moment now. You're committed; it's too late to turn back . . ." His voice seemed to come from far away. " . . .I hope you know what you're doing . . ."

*There were sounds that approached and receded, the booming of cannon, cries, voices out of the past . . . . There were moments of sharp pain, and he fought, striking out at an enemy that fled always before him. Light glared, blindingly; then there was darkness through which he swam alone, suitless, in the emptiness of space and in his body a terrible sickness flooded in relentless waves . . .*

*Later, he seemed to float, drugged, aware of an ache all through his body like a gigantic throbbing tooth. Under him, hardness pressed; his arms and legs tingled now. He tried to remember the accident, but there was nothing; only the irritating voice that probed, prodded, forcing itself into his awareness . . .*

" . . . up! Wake up! Wake up!"

He opened his eyes. A vague face floated over him. It was not a pleasing face, like some of those he had seen—or dreamed about . . . . He closed his eyes to the grateful darkness . . .

"He's coming out of it!" The voices were sharp now; they rasped his nerves like files.

"Go 'way," he muttered. He was abruptly aware of his tongue in his mouth, a vile taste, dryness . . .

"Water . . ." he croaked.

Arms lifted him, hands fumbled over him. He felt straps being released, the cold touch of a hypospray. He was sitting up now, dizzy, but awake, looking around a small, bright room.

"You had us worried, Captain," a thin voice was saying. Captain Henry concentrated. He knew the man . . .

"One hundred and eight hours," the voice went on. "For a while there it was touch and go."

He was remembering now. Amos had been with him—

"Where's Amos?" Henry's voice boomed loud in his ears. He took a deep breath, felt sharp pains that faded quickly. He shook his head. "I want Amos . . ."

"He . . . ah . . . isn't here, Captain."

"He didn't wait . . . ?" Henry asked.

"Mr. Able . . . didn't make it . . ."

"Make what?" A feeling of immense irritability rose up in Captain Henry. "What kind of a pal is he? Get him—now!"

"You don't understand, Captain. His system wasn't able to endure the strain . . ."

"Where is he—" Captain Henry got to his feet, weaving. "Strain, my elbow!"

"He's dead, Captain," the thin-faced man said. "The Rejuve treatment—it was too much for him. He died four hours ago. I did all I could . . ."

"You gave Amos a Rejuve? Why, you damned fool!"

"But—he said those were your orders—" Spangler gestured to a sheet-covered table. "I haven't even had time—"

Henry stepped to the table, reaching out a hand for support, flipped back the sheet. A waxy face, thin-nosed, sunken-cheeked, stared up at him with eyes as remote as a statue of Pharoah.

"Amos . . . " Captain Henry looked around blankly at the other two. "He was my partner . . . ever since the beginning . . ."

"He . . . left this for you." The medic offered a white envelope. Henry tore it open.

*If it works, I'll make you a better partner than six green kids. If it's no go—then happy landings, Henry. I wish I could of been with you.*
                                        *Amos Able.*

Henry put a hand on Amos's shoulder, felt the bones through the skin and the sheet.

"You didn't wait," Henry said. "You went ahead without me . . ."

An hour later, Captain Henry stood in the UV filtered light of the Mall, flanked on one side by

Dulcia, trim in a close-fitting suit of pale green that accented the gold of her hair, and on the other by Dr. Spangler, his hand under Henry's arm, chattering nervously.

"A fine recovery after all, Captain. Frankly, I'm surprised at the outcome; I think I'm safe in saying we've achieved a Senility Index of around .40—"

"Grandpa, I've been so worried," the girl almost wailed. "You're so weak . . ."

"He'll recover his strength quickly," Spangler bobbed his head reassuringly. "In a week he'll be his old self again. That is—his *new* self." He beamed at his jest.

A wide low car, gleaming with pale gray porcelain and bright chromalloy, swung up to the entry. A tall, slender young man with short curly dark hair, clad in stylishly cut sport togs, jumped out. He came forward, took Henry's elbow.

"Certainly fine to see you looking so chipper, sir," he said. "Dulcia's been beside herself . . ."

"That was mean, Grandpa, to go off and just leave me a note!" the girl put in.

The lad went through a gesture of assisting Henry into the car, went around and took a seat in front; he turned, a polite smile on his regular features.

"I was certainly pleased when I heard you'd agreed to let me go along on the cruise, Captain; I'm sure I'm going to enjoy it immensely. I'm quite looking forward to it."

Henry leaned back, feeling the sweat of exertion trickling down behind his ear. He stared hard at the youth.

"I doubt that all to hell, son," he said. "A better man than either of us has already died in the name of this caper. Maybe before it's over you'll wish you had, too."

The smile dropped from the young man's face.

"Grandpa!" Dulcia said. "What a terrible thing to say to Larry."

"I know," Captain Henry said. "This is the time for a pep talk about how teamwork pays off. I'm not in the mood. I'm going home and sleep for forty-eight hours—and then we're starting to work."

"Very well, Captain," young Bartholomew said. "I fully expect—"

"It's what you don't expect that hurts," Henry cut him off. "Pull in your belt, youngster. You've got a tough sixty days ahead—and after that it'll get tougher."

Senator Bartholomew hurled the machine listing to the table before Captain Henry, waved his dope stick wildly.

"This equipment list is fantastic!" he stormed. "You're spending thousands—thousands, do you hear! For what?" He slapped the paper with a damp palm. "A battery of three-centimeter infinite repeaters; a demi-total all-wave detector screen; a fire control board designed for a ship of the line! Have you lost your mind? This is a peaceful home-steading venture you're outfitting for—not a com-mando raid—"

"Uh-huh . . ." Henry grinned cheerfully at the paunchy financier. "I intend to keep it peaceful, Senator—if I have to gun my way through an army to do it. By the way, I've got a new list of stores for you somewhere . . ." He slapped pockets, went to the desk, tried drawers.

"Dulcie!" he called out. "Where's that list we made up this morning?"

The girl put her head in the door. "Larry took it down a few minutes ago—Oh, good morning, Senator Bartholomew."

Bartholomew grunted. "Now you're employing my boy as a common messenger, eh? I suppose this is your idea of getting back at me for some fancied slight."

"Why, Senator," Dulcia said. "Larry volunteered to go; he was going over to the Mall anyway—"

"Never mind the Senator's cracks," Henry said. "His indigestion's probably bothering him. Let's go over and take a look at the ship; I want to show you something."

"Look here, I came out here to talk to you!" Bartholomew barked.

"Come around when you feel better." Henry took the girl's arm, escorted her out to the Mono-jag.

"Really, Grandpa, you shouldn't goad him that way—"

"To hell with him. It's too nice a day to breathe second-hand dope." He wheeled the car out across the ramp toward the silver lance-head of the ship.

"She's really beautiful," Dulcia said. "Have you decided what to call her yet?"

Henry pulled the car up in the shadow of the fifty-foot vessel, poised on four slim vanes among stacked crates and boxes. Men in coveralls paused in their work to eye the girl appreciatively. Henry reached in the back of the car, brought out a tissue-wrapped bottle.

"In answer to that last question," he said, "I have." He stripped the paper from the heavy bottle, held it up. The label read "Piper Hiedsieck —extra brut." "So if you'll kindly do the honors . . ."

"Oh, Grandpa . . ." Dulcia took the champagne. She giggled. "It seems funny to go on calling you Grandpa; you look so dashing . . ."

"Don't get flustered, girl. Smash it over her stern pipes and give her her name."

"Do you really want me to? Now? With just us here? Can't I call Larry?"

"Sure; go ahead."

The girl went excitedly to the field screen, located the youth at an office across the field. A minute later his scarlet sportster headed across from the Admin building, squealed to a halt beside the Monojag. Larry Bartholomew stepped out, greeted Henry, beamed at Dulcia.

"Well, this is quite an occasion; real champagne, too . . ." He frowned slightly.

"Don't worry," Henry said. "I paid for it myself. Go ahead, girl, let her have it."

Dulcia took up a position by the stern tubes. "Grandpa," she said. "You haven't told me her name yet."

"*Degüello*," Henry said.

"*Degüello?*" Dulcia repeated.

"Ah, a charming choice," Larry commented, nodding. "An old Spanish word, isn't it?"

"That's right."

Dulcia took a breath, gripped the bottle by its neck. "I christen thee *Degüello!*" she cried, and swung the bottle. Wine foamed as the glass shattered; a splash of gold ran down across the bright hull plates. The workmen raised a cheer in which Henry's bellow joined. Larry clapped.

"Well, Captain, I suppose I'd better be getting back to my ah . . . duties," he said, when the broken glass had been swept up.

"Not a bad idea, Larry. You're due at the gym now."

"Yes," his smile was a trifle strained. As he turned away, he waved at Dulcia almost as if signaling her, and Henry, turning aside, later thought he had caught sight of a small lifting of her hand in return. But when he turned back to her, there was no sign of it in her face or manner.

"Larry looks so much better, Grandpa, since you've had him working out," she said, "and getting out in the unfiltered sunlight. I really think the trip is going to be good for him." She looked at her great-grandfather with a sudden, unusual seriousness. "—It isn't really going to be as . . . dangerous as Amos made out? Is it?"

"It'll be a picnic," Henry said breezily; he ran a finger under her chin. "A couple more weeks and we'll be out of your hair."

"I keep telling myself . . . the sooner you go, the sooner you'll be back."

"That's the spirit; now, what do you say to dinner at the Fire Palace and a swim under Castle Reef afterward?"

Dulcia hugged his arm. "Wonderful! And I've got something to talk to you about, anyway."

"Something?" He stared at her. "What, girl?"

"Oh . . . something. I'll tell you later." She let go of his arm, danced away. Wondering a little, he followed her to the Monojag.

The dinner at the Fire Palace was all that anyone could have expected of it. They sat on the terrace afterward, watching the twilight deepen over the sea, then changed and went down on the beach.

There, as the night closed down, they swam—and then, afterward, Henry, out of sheer high spirits, built a roaring fire of driftwood. His strength was back on him and it felt good to lay arms once more around some log two ordinary men could barely lift, and heave it, crashing, in among the crackling flames and glowing sparks. He was half drunk with his return to an age of vigor; and in his exuberance, he did not notice Dulcia's quietness until he dropped down once more on the sand beside her and saw her sitting silent, hugging her knees, pensively.

He looked at her sharply; and she turned her face away from him, but not before he had seen the sparkle of tears on her lashes.

"Dulcie-girl . . ." he put out a hand to her, but she shook her head.

"No, Grandpa," she said, "I'm all right. Really, I'm all right . . . It's just that you look so happy. Grandpa . . . tell me about her . . ."

"Her?" He scowled at the girl.

"You know . . . my great-grandmother. Was she really so much like me?"

In spite of himself his voice thickened in his throat as he answered.

"Haven't I told you a thousand times, she was?"

"It must . . ." still she would not look at him, "have been terrible for her. Having you go off that way . . ."

A sudden deadly coldness moved in him. All the guilt that had lain hidden in him all these years leaped snarling from the dark parts of his mind to tear at him. But Dulcie—this Dulcia, the young girl of now—was talking on.

"Grandpa, I told you I wanted to tell you something." She turned finally to look at him. "It's . . . about Larry. I love him."

The coldness moved out to encase him complete, like a block of ice.

"Love?"

She nodded. "So now you see . . . . There are only two people I love anywhere—now that Amos is dead—and the two of you are going off on this Run."

"Dulcia . . ." his tongue felt clumsy in his mouth, "I told you there's nothing to worry about. Nothing . . ."

"Isn't there? Really, isn't there?" She searched his face with her gray eyes. "You've always told me the truth, Grandpa. But you tell me there's nothing to worry about; and then you tell Larry something different. Do you know why he's going on this trip, Grandpa? *Do* you?"

"Why, his dad's sending him—"

"Oh, Grandpa, stop and think for a moment!" Her tone was almost exasperated. "Larry may be just a boy to you, but to himself and the Senator and everyone on this planet, he's a man—man enough to run for high political office. Larry's father can't send him any place he doesn't want to go! Larry's going because he *wants* to go—and you don't even know the reason!"

Suspicion stiffened Henry.

"What reason?" he said, sharply.

"What do you think? *You!*" She stared at him with an expression caught between affection and frustration. "You don't know—you've never known how people think of you. Don't you know you're a living hero, a living *legend* to the people my age and Larry's, on this planet? To their folks, you may still be just a man—but to my generation you're a walking, breathing piece of a history book. Now, do you understand why Larry never even thought of hesitating when his father told him you wanted him to go with you to Corazon and the Run?"

Henry grunted, off-guard.

"But you scare him half to death!" said Dulcia. "According to you, he can't do anything right, and all you have to do is look at him, to make him so self-conscious that he trips over his own feet and starts talking twice as foolish-stilted fashionable as he would ordinarily. But he'd give his right arm to please you. Grandpa, I *know!*"

Henry stared fiercely at her. A small door somewhere in the back of his mind where the memory of her great-grandmother lived, wavered half-open, wanting to believe what she had just told him.

But then, unbidden, an image of the Senator rose in his mind's eye. The fat, flabby man with the ruthless core. The boy was blood and bone of his father. If there was something worthwhile in him, it would show itself when the Run had ground the fancy manners and nonsense off him. Until then— the small, half-open door in the back of his mind slammed shut.

"All right, honey, I'll bear it in mind," he said, patting her shoulder gently. He rose to his feet like a spring uncoiled. "Now, we better be getting home. Tomorrow's a large day."

They picked up their towels and climbed the beach back to the Monojag. Driving home, Dulcia suddenly broke the silence.

*"Degüello . . ."* she said, unexpectedly. "Larry said when I christened the ship that the name was an old Spanish word. What does it mean, Grandpa?"

Henry was suddenly conscious of her staring across at him, her face white in the moonlight coming through the windscreen of the car climbing the steep and winding road.

—And even as he spoke, he realized how his lips thinned at the word, and he heard, like an echo, the grim, harsh note of hungry violence in his voice as he answered: "Cutthroat."

From the window, Henry's eyes followed the white strip of beach that curved along under the cliff-face, widening to the distant glistening bubble of the Mall and the rectangle of the port, where the ship threw back a blinding glint of reflected sun. Tiny figures swarmed around its base; by now, Senator Bartholomew and his committee of Averages would be getting impatient at the delay.

He turned, looked into the long mirror. The narrow-cut, silver-corded black trousers fitted without a wrinkle into the well-worn but brightly polished ship boots. He plucked the short tunic from the bed, slipped it over the white silk shirt; the silver buttons, the swirl of braid on the cuffs gleamed against royal blue polyon. He buckled on the broad woven-silver belt with the ebony-gripped bright-plated ceremonial side arm; he smiled, and a lean, bronzed face with blue-green eyes and short blond hair touched with gray smiled back. He opened the door and walked along the hall, down three steps to the lounge room.

Dulcia turned; her eyes widened. "Oh, Grandpa . . .!"

He grinned. "Come on, honey; takeoff in forty minutes. Let's go give the natives a treat."

They took the Monojag, howled down the winding cliff road, along the beach, cut across the Port Authority ramp, screeched to a halt beside the ship. A crowd of stylishly dressed citizens waited behind a red plush guard rope. On a platform beside the service gantry, a cluster of officials stood.

"Everybody's here," Dulcia said breathlessly. "Look, there's the Council Monitor . . . and—"

"Uh-huh; they'll have speeches planned, but I'm

afraid I won't be able to wait around for 'em."
Henry stepped out, offered Dulcia a hand. The
babble of the crowd rose higher. Fingers pointed;
strobe lights flashed.

"You were late on purpose," she whispered.
"That's mean, Grandpa; I wanted to see everybody
cheering you."

"Where's young Bartholomew?" They crossed
the open space, mounted the steps to the platform.
A short, narrow-shouldered man stepped forward,
offered a hand, adjusted a microphone.

"Mr. Mayor," he began, his amplified voice
echoing, "honorable guests, citizens of Aldorado—"

Captain Henry gently plucked the microphone
from his hand.

"We're lifting off in twenty-one minutes," he
said briskly. "Everybody back behind the yellow
safety line. Where's Mr. Bartholomew?"

There was a surprised stir in the crowd. Larry
pushed through, mounted the platform. He was
strapped and buckled into an expensive ship suit
hung with bright-colored emergency gear.

"Ah, Captain, I was just saying good-by to—"

Captain Henry put his hand over the mike.

"Get aboard, Larry. Start the countdown clock.
You know how to do that—"

"Of course, I do," Larry said urgently. His eyes
went past Henry to Dulcia. "But I don't see—"

"That's an order, Mister!" Captain Henry said
softly.

Bartholomew reddened, turned abruptly, and
stepped into the entry port. Captain Henry faced

the open-mouthed officials beside him.

"All right, gentlemen; everybody clear. The killing radius of the drive is a hundred yards." He turned to his great-granddaughter, put an arm around her, kissed her casually on the forehead.

"Better beat it, Dulcie-girl. Drive up to the cliff-head and watch from there. You'll get a better view."

She threw her arms around his neck. "Be careful, Grandpa—and come back safe . . ."

"Nothing to it," he said. He chucked her under the chin, steered her to the stair, waved cheerfully to the assembled crowd, then keyed the mike:

"All right, you gantry crews; pull back there; disconnect all and make secure . . ."

Inside the vessel, Henry climbed a short companionway in a smell of new paint and insulation, emerged into a handsomely appointed control center. Larry lay strapped into the right-hand cradle, watching the blink of red, green, amber, and blue lights on a console that rimmed half the chamber. He turned a resentful glance at Henry.

"Captain, I didn't have an opportunity even to wave to Dulcia—"

Standing in the winking multicolored glow of the panel lights, Henry stripped off the braid-encrusted tunic, dropped the heavy belt with its decorative weapon into a wall locker.

"Let's get a couple of things straight, Larry," he said evenly. "Up to now it's been fun and games . . ." He took a plain black ship suit from the locker, began pulling it on. "But the games are over. You're signed on for the cruise—and maybe, if we're very careful, and very lucky, we'll get home again some day. Meanwhile, we'll concentrate on the job ahead with every ounce of brains and guts we've got—and hope it'll be enough."

Bartholomew looked at Henry doubtfully.

"Surely you're exaggerating, Captain. This is merely a matter of selecting a suitable area and establishing our claim . . ."

"There's more to it than that. There's money at work in this Run. From what I've been able to find out, some of the toughest operators in the Sector are staking outfits. New land's hard to come by these days; we won't get ours without a fight." He took a second suit from the locker, tossed it across to Bartholomew. "Better get that Mickey Mouse outfit off and get into this. You've got about five minutes till blastoff."

Bartholomew climbed out of the couch, began changing suits. "This is a very expensive suit," he said, folding it carefully. "A gift from the Sector Council—"

"The shoes, too," Henry said. "Save those fancy ones for cocktail parties after we get back."

Larry looked indignant. "Now, Captain; my father had these boots specially made for me; they're the finest that money can buy. He particularly insisted that I wear them—"

"All right; they're your feet, Larry; and they'll be going into some pretty strange places."

"You make this sound like—like some sort of crazy suicide mission!"

"Sure . . ." Captain Henry settled himself in his

couch, clamped in, snapped his lifeline connection in place. "All suicides are crazy. Buckle in now and get set for blastoff."

The ground-control screen glowed. "Zero minus one minute," a voice said. "Ramp clear, final count." There was a loud click.

"Minus fifty seconds," the voice said. Henry adjusted the clock, watched the sweep hand.

"Forty seconds. Thirty seconds. Twenty seconds. Ten seconds . . ."

Bartholomew cleared his throat. "Captain—"

"Too late now for second thoughts, Larry."

" . . . eight . . . seven . . . six . . ." the voice droned.

"I have an important primary in the fall," Bartholomew said. "I just wanted to ask when we'd be returning?"

A whine started up deep in the ship. Relays clicked.

"If we're lucky—three months," Henry said.

" . . . three . . . two . . . one—"

Pink light winked in the rear visiscreen. A deep rumble sounded. Captain Henry felt the pressure, gentle at first, then insistent, then fierce; crushing him back as the roar mounted to a mighty torrent which went on and on. The weight was like an iron mold now, pressing over his body.

"What if . . . we're not lucky . . . ?" Bartholomew croaked.

Captain Henry smiled tightly. "In that case," he said with difficulty, "the question won't arise."

"I'm going to be sick again," Bartholomew

gasped.

"Sure," Captain Henry said absently, studying instrument readings. "Just be sure you clean it up afterward."

"That's what makes me sick . . ."

"Your stomach ought to be empty by now. Why didn't you take the Null-G shot?"

"I heard—they made one . . . ill."

Henry tossed a white capsule over. "Swallow this. You'll be all right in a few minutes. I'll put a spin on the ship in another hour or so, as soon as I've finished the final tower check." He spoke softly into his lip-mike, jotted notes on a clipboard.

An hour passed. Captain Henry made adjustments to the controls; a whining started up. Under the two men, the cradles pressed faintly, then more firmly.

"That's a standard G," Henry said cheerfully. He unstrapped and swung out of the cradle. "You'll feel better in a few minutes."

"The pressure was bad enough," Bartholomew said weakly. "It seemed like a week—"

"Only nine hours. I didn't want to put you under more than 2G—or myself either." He took equipment from a locker, set about erecting a small unit like a twelve-inch tri-D tank at one side of the twelve-foot room. He buckled on a plain gun belt, fitted a pistol into the holster, took up a stance, then drew suddenly, aimed, and pressed the firing stud. A bright flash showed at the edge of the screen, faded slowly. He holstered the gun, drew, and fired another silent bolt.

"What are you doing?" Bartholomew craned from his cradle.

"Target practice. Two hours in every twelve—for both of us—until we're scoring ten out of ten. Better get out of that cradle now and get your space legs. I'm upping the spin one rev per hour. It's a twenty-nine-day run to Corazon. By the time we get there, we'll be working under a G and a half."

"Whatever for?"

"Good for the muscles. Now hop to it. When you finish cleaning up in here, we're going down to the engine compartment and I'll show you your duties there."

"Good Lord, Captain! I'm not a . . . a grease monkey!"

"That's all right; you will be."

"Captain, I'm a trained Administrator. I thought that on this venture my executive abilities—"

Henry turned on him. "Start swabbing that deck, Mister. And when you're finished, there'll be other duties—none of 'em easy and none of 'em pleasant!"

"Is that my part of the mission?" Bartholomew's cheeks were pink. "To do all the menial work?"

"I'll navigate this tub. I'll be on the board twelve hours out of every twenty-four, and I'll spend another four getting my reflexes back in shape. If I have any time left over, I'll do my share of the shipboard routine. If not, you'll do it all."

Bartholomew looked at Henry. "I see," he said. He got out of the cradle and silently set about cleaning up the compartment.

Coming up the companionway, Captain Henry

paused, hearing a voice above. He came up quietly, saw Bartholomew, tall and thin in the black ship suit, standing across the room, his gun belt slung low on his narrow hips.

"Very well, you scoundrel," the youth murmured. He whipped out the training pistol, fired; a flash of greenish light winked in the gloom of the control chamber.

He holstered the gun, half-turned, then spun back. "Aha!" he muttered. "Thought you'd slip up on me unawares, I see . . ." He yanked the gun up, fired—

There was no answering flash.

"Drat it!" Bartholomew adjusted the gun belt, took a turn up and down the room, spun suddenly and fired, was rewarded with a flash.

"Ha!" he said. He blew on the gun barrel, jammed it in the holster.

"Not bad," Henry said, stepping up into the room. "You may make a shooter yet, Larry."

Bartholomew jumped. "I was . . . ah . . . just practicing . . ." He unbuckled the belt, tossed it in the locker. "Though I confess I can't imagine any occasion for the exercise of such a skill."

"Oh, it's handy," Henry said, "when scoundrels sneak up on you."

Bartholomew blushed. "One must have *some* amusement to while away the hours."

"Call it an amusement if you want to—but keep practicing. Your neck may depend on it in the very near future."

"Surely you're exaggerating the danger, Captain. All that talk of hired killers and opportunists

was all very well back on Aldorado, when you
were dramatizing the perils of the undertaking—"

"If you've got the idea a Run is something like
bobbing for apples, forget it. We're going to be in
competition with men that are used to taking what
they want and worrying about the consequences
later—much later."

Larry smiled patiently. "Oh, perhaps in the old
days, a century ago, lawless characters perpe-
trated some of the atrocities one hears of; but not
today, Captain. These are modern times; Council
regulations—"

"Council regulations are dandy—to start a fire
with when your permatch goes dry." Henry
settled himself in his couch, swung it around to
face Bartholomew.

"Corazon is a holdover from an earlier era. She
was held under quarantine for an extra seventy-
five years, because of some funny business with
disappearing viruses combined with bureaucratic
inertia. The day of frontiering in the Sector is past;
this is a freak, a one-time opportunity—and every
last-chance Charlie in this end of the Galaxy who
can beg, borrow, or steal a ship will be at that
staging area, ready to get his slice of Corazon. It'll
be every man for himself, and the devil take the
slow gun . . ."

"But the Council Representatives—the refer-
ees—"

"How many? A hundred men? And no fonder of
getting killed than any other salaried employee.
Sure, they'll be there to take your claim registra-
tions, hand out the official map, run a scintillo-

meter over you to make sure you aren't packing a fission weapon in your hip pocket—but out of sight of the Q. S. Tower at Pango-Ri, it will be up to you and your handgun and your bare knuckles and your brain."

"But, Captain, a few sane-minded claimants could easily band together, form a common defense, and set about organizing matters as reasonable men."

"You won't find any sane-minded claimants; the sane people stay home and buy their minerals from the developers after the gunsmoke has blown away."

Bartholomew pursed his lips. In the past two weeks aboard ship his black hair had grown; it curled around his ears, along his neck.

"Then—how are we going to invade this hotbed of criminal activity and establish our claims?"

"That's a fair question. I'm glad to see you taking an interest in these little matters. It gives me hope you may wake up at some point before it's too late and start taking this thing seriously." Henry crossed to the chart table, flipped the switch. A map appeared on the screen.

"The big thing is to know what you want. Now, the official throwaway charts give you continental outlines, and mark a few hot spots such as deserts, active volcanoes, and so on. The rest is up to the customer—"

"Why, that's ridiculous! Surely the officials have detailed knowledge of the terrain—"

"Yeah—but that would take all the romance out of it. The idea is for all parties to have the same handicap: ignorance. But the result is that line-jumpers have been going in to Corazon for the last thirty years, making up aerial surveys, taking harbor soundings, doing minerals exploration—"

"Impossible! The Quarantine Service—"

"—is made up of people. Funny, fallible—cor-ruptible—human beings. Not all of them, of course. Not even most of them. But it only takes one bought Quarantine Warden to let a man in—and out again, with the dope."

"But—we won't have a chance against anyone armed with that kind of data—"

"No, we wouldn't—if we didn't have a good bootleg map of our own."

Bartholomew looked at the map on the screen. Henry twisted the magnification control; details leaped out; mountain ranges, contour lines, no-tations of temperature, humidity, air pressure readings.

"You mean—" Bartholomew gasped, "this is an illegal instrument? We're smuggling contra-band?"

"Uh-huh. You remember the special appropri-ation of twenty thousand credits I asked for—for navigational equipment?"

"You're saying that—this map—"

"That's right. It's the best there is. I've spent a lot of hours studying it. I've picked our initial target point—and you can count on it that the same spot will have been pinpointed by others."

"You paid twenty thousand credits of my father's money for this—this stolen information?"

Henry nodded.

"Why—we don't even know if it's accurate! It could be some sort of counterfeit, constructed out of whole cloth—"

"Nope. I got it from a friend of mine—an old space hand—too old to make the Run himself."

"But how could he be sure it was authentic—even if he believed in it?"

"Easy; he made it. He always intended to use it himself, but the Q. S. held off a little too long for him. So he let it go to me."

"This is—unheard of! Good Lord, Captain Henry, do you realize what the penalty for possession of this document is?"

"Nope—but I know the penalty for *not* having it."

"You talk as though this were some sort of military campaign!"

"Right. Now, the ground rules of the Run are simple. All entrants report in to the staging area—that's a ten-mile radius around Pango-Ri—and register. Then we wait for zero hour and hit the trail. There's no restriction on the kind of equipment you use. We've got a nice converted Bolo Minor in the hold. There'll be heavier equipment than that up against us, but not much. There'll even be a few old-time hill runners going in on foot; men who've spent their last credit on a space lift in to Corazon. Believe me, there'll be dirty work in the underbrush when they start to clash over who grabs what."

"Surely there's enough for all—"

"You tell that to a man who's walked day and night for a week to stake out a mining claim that some tipster's sold him on—and finds three other customers on the same spot. Now, all entrants depart at dawn—that's oh—six hours, Pango-Ri mean time—from the staging area. They're allowed to carry all the food they want, four issue markers—a special self-embedding electronic model—communications gear, and light hand-weapons—for hunting, it says in the Prospectus."

Bartholomew shook his head. "This is a pathetically ineptly organized affair. Why, it would have been simplicity itself to survey the planet, set out markers on a grid, and assign areas by lot to qualified entrants."

"Face it, Larry. New land on virgin worlds isn't doled out like slices of cake at a church social. They can make all the rules they want, back at Galaxy Central—but on Corazon, it'll be nature's old law. It's not the Statistical Average that survives—it's the son-of-a-bitch that's tougher than the hard case that's hunting him. Maybe the Survey Authorities don't know that—or maybe they're smarter than we give them credit for. You don't tame alien worlds with busloads of bureaucrats."

"But this arrangement is an open invitation to lawlessness."

Henry nodded. "And you can count on it there'll be plenty of takers."

"But—what can we do against men of that sort?"

"Easy," Henry said. "We'll do the same thing—only we'll do it first."

It was the seventeenth day in space. Captain Henry sat at the plotting table. He lifted his head,

sniffed the air, then rose, went to the companionway, sniffed again. He grabbed the handrail,
leaped down, dived for the power compartment.
Dense fumes boiled out from a massive grilled
housing. Coughing, Henry fought through to the
emergency console, hauled down on a heavy circuit breaker. A sharp whining descended the scale.
The smoke churned, trailing toward wall
registers. Henry retreated to the corridor,
coughing violently.

"Are you all right, Captain?" Bartholomew's
strained voice sounded behind him.

"I don't know yet; we've got gyro trouble,"
Henry snapped, and plunged back into the smoke.
The haze was thinning quickly. The whine had
fallen to a growl, dropped lower, clicked to a stop.

"Bearings gone," Henry snapped. "Maybe we
can replace 'em, and maybe we can't. Let's jump,
Mister. Every minute counts! Grab that torquer—
get that housing off!" Henry sprang for the parts
index, punched keys. A green light winked. A
clattering came from behind the panel. He lifted
out two heavy, plastic-cocooned disks, eight
inches in diameter and three inches thick. The
*ping!* of cooling metal sounded in the room. Bartholomew's wrench clattered against metal.

"It's awfully quiet, suddenly," the boy called.

"I've shut down the air pumps." Henry ripped at
the plastic covering; polished metal emerged from
the dull brown casing.

"We'll choke," Bartholomew said. "The room's
still full of smoke."

"Feel that faint surge underfoot, every five
seconds or so . . .?" Henry snapped.

"Yes, but—"

"Keep working!" Henry ripped into the second bearing, "This ship isn't a statically balanced unit. It's spinning a little over one revolution per second. The axis of spin and the centroid of mass don't coincide. There's also a matter of fluid inertia; the air, the water in the tanks, lubricant reservoirs. I shut the pumps down to minimize the eccentric thrusts as much as possible—but it won't help much. The wobble will increase—and the worse it gets, the faster it will build. It's a logarithmic curve; we'll go into a tumble in a few minutes, then she'll start to break up. Got the picture? Now fumble that damned housing out of the way, and I'll find out if we're going to live another hour . . ."

Bartholomew, white-faced, worked frantically at the fasteners; Henry cleared the second bearing, leaped to help the younger man lift the housing aside. A cloud of smog churned out from the uncovered gyro chassis. Henry fanned it, peering down at the blackened shafts.

"No wonder she burned," he said harshly. "The bearings were running dry . . . !" He turned to Bartholomew. The younger man swallowed, stared back wide-eyed.

"When's the last time you made your maintenance check, Larry?"

"I . . . ah . . . this morning—"

"Don't lie to me! There's been no lubricant on these bearings for at least thirty-six hours!"

"How was I to know this would happen?"

"Your orders were to take your readings at four-hour intervals and maintain one hundred and

twenty pounds oil pressure! I said orders, Mister
—not suggestion! Sometime in the past day or so a
blockage developed in the feed line; the pressure
dropped. And where were you, Mister?"

"I thought it was just a—a drill!" Bartholomew
burst out. "I got tired of dragging up and down
those stairs! I didn't know—"

"That's right. You didn't know . . ." Henry
slapped the blackened shaft of the main gyro.
"Let's get this bearing changed!"

The floor lifted, tilted to the right, fell, slanted
to the left . . .

"Brace your feet, and when I give the word,
guide that end out." Henry grasped the control of
the cable hoist, waited while Bartholomew
fumbled for a grip.

"Up—and over—" Henry grunted. His biceps
bulged; his straining shoulders straightened. The
shaft cleared the edge of the casing, teetered, then
swung over the side. Henry lowered it to the deck.

"It's getting worse—rapidly . . ." Bartholomew
said.

"Yeah."

One of the old bearings, loose on the floor,
bounded past, crashed against the bulkhead.
Henry hauled at the cable hoist; the servomotor
groaned under the unaccustomed load as the
swing of the ship pulled at the heavy shaft. At the
other end of the shaft, Bartholomew clung, green-
faced.

"Steady as she goes, boy . . ." The walls seemed
to tilt crazily now, whirling. The loose bearing

slid, bounced off a heavy casting, clattered across the room.

"We should have tied that son-of-a-bitch down," Henry grated. "Don't let her swing!"

The surge of the floor threw Henry sideways. He grabbed, raised an arm to fend off the swinging shaft. The bearing, bounding across the room, cannoned against Captain Henry's hand, where it gripped the housing.

Bartholomew straightened, breathing noisily. His eye fell on Henry's hand. He yelped at the glimpse of bloody flesh, exposed knuckle bones; he started toward him.

"Belay that, Mister," Henry ground out between clenched teeth. "It's now or never . . ." He hauled at the cable; the wounded hand slipped; he cursed, fought the hoist savagely. Bartholomew hung on the free end of the shaft; his feet swung free of the deck for a moment. He oofed as he slammed against the housing. Then the shaft dropped a foot, another, clanged as it seated. Henry held on for a moment, breathing hard.

"All right, Larry. Cast off and button her up . . ."

Two hours later, stretched in his cradle, Captain Henry laughed shortly, holding up his bandage-encased hand.

"Nice," he said. "We don't happen to have a depot handy to calibrate the gyros again, so I'll be on the board, manually balancing her, watch on and watch on, for the next six days."

"Are you in much pain, Captain?" The young man's face was white.

Henry shook his head.

Larry swallowed. He took a deep breath and stiffened, seeming to brace himself. His face became, if possible, even a bit whiter.

"It's my fault, Captain," he said stiffly. "My fault entirely."

Henry looked at him grimly and a little curiously. By the boy's standards, at least, it had taken a certain amount of guts to say that. For a moment Dulcia's words about Larry on the beach the night before they had lifted ship, came back to him. But he shoved them aside once more. Larry might be showing something—it was too early to tell.

"Ever hear of shipboard responsibility?" said Henry harshly. "It's the Captain's fault if he trusts a man who can't be trusted. Only a damn fool would go on to Corazon now. You know that, don't you? We're asking for trouble, going in like this."

"I'll not let you down again, Captain." The young man's jaw muscles were knotted at the angle of his sharp face on each side. The sweat stood in little beads on his pale forehead. "You'll see. When we get there, you'll see that my knowledge of administrative routine will be a help to us. As an official—"

"I don't know about that part," Henry cut him off roughly, looking at his bandaged hand. "But you stitch a nice seam, I'll say that for you."

Larry flushed, opened his mouth as if to say something, then clamped it determinedly shut again and turned away. He went out without a word.

All right, boy, thought Henry, looking after him. One swallow doesn't make a summer. You've got a lot to learn yet—even if it turns out you're capable of learning, after all.

The last murmer of the pumps died away. In the groundview screen, Henry studied the massive concrete block of the Pango-Ri Port Authority building stretching to the barrier wall lining the ramp edge; beyond, a mushroom-town of flimsy prefabs, inflated domes, and low wooden shacks sprawled across the dusty plain. Farther away, clumsy structures, garish with colored plastic, loomed up into the hazy afternoon sky of Corazon.

Henry shifted the field of view; a line of space vessels appeared, parked in an irregular rank that stretched away toward the purplish line of distant hills.

"All these ships are here for the Run?" Larry stared. "There must be hundreds of them—thousands . . ."

"Yep; and every one of those tubs will be hauling anywhere from a couple of men to a platoon. I'd say we've got upwards of a quarter of a million competitors in this little rummage sale."

"All for this wasteland? I had rather pictured our wandering through unpeopled forests, surveying vast, deserted tracts, selecting our claim . . ."

"We'd better get over to Run HQ and get on the log or we'll be wandering around an unpeopled port—after the rest of the Run has left."

Bartholomew frowned thoughtfully. "I think my

informal official blazer with the Statav pocket patch will be correct; I've no desire to overawe the registration personnel." He glanced at Captain Henry. "I think I should be the one to deal with the Quarantine authorities."

"We'll both deal with 'em—at the tail end of a long line. Wear warm clothes you don't mind sleeping in—something with pockets; we'll pack some hard rations. We'll be lined up for a good twelve hours."

Bartholomew raised an eyebrow. "I don't think that will be necessary, Captain. A word from me to the appropriate individual, and we'll be whisked through the formalities."

"Try bucking the line and they'll be whisking you off the deck with a ramp broom. Let's go." Henry started past Bartholomew.

"Captain, surely you're not thinking of making your appearance in a soiled ship suit? I'd suggest the outfit you wore when you came aboard; it was quite impressive—to a layman, I mean."

Henry smiled. "You might have an idea there, Larry. It could cut down on the competition. They'd die laughing."

Bartholomew shrugged, looked at Henry's bandaged hand. "How is your hand? Perhaps I'd better call for a doctor."

Henry carefully pulled on a pair of soft leather gloves; he flexed his fingers. "The hand's not too bad. Remembering not to bang it will be the problem."

"It should be in a sling . . ."

Henry laughed. "Don't let's tip off the opposition, Larry. My little infirmities will be our secret." He took a small box from the wall locker, handed Bartholomew a palm-sized slug gun. "Keep this where you can get a hand on it in a hurry."

Bartholomew looked at the weapon, a dull gray lozenge shape like a water-worn stone. "A gun? Whatever for?"

Henry pocketed the twin to Bartholomew's gun. "That's it," he said. "Whatever . . ."

A heavy-faced man with a crooked jaw and a scar-furrowed cheek slammed a huge rubber stamp against a blue form and flipped it into the hopper. He jerked his head at Captain Henry. "Let's go, bud. Shake a leg." His voice was a blurred growl. Henry dropped the sheaf of forms before the official; he leafed through them, snapped one out, shot Henry a look.

"Where you been, *Degüello?* This is the old PC Master's ticket; they been invalidated over nine years."

Henry took a folder from an inner pocket, dropped a plastic-covered card before the man. "Maybe this will do."

The crooked-faced man squinted at the card, looked up quickly.

"Why didn't you say you were Navy, pal?" He leaned forward. "Welcome to the psych ward, brother," he said in a changed tone. "What brings you out in the hot sun with this bunch of hull-scrapings?" He jerked his head toward the crowd milling in the vast rotunda.

"Land," Henry said. He took the card, tucked it away.

The registration official nodded. "O.K., so I asked a stupid question. Say . . ." he looked past Henry's ear. "You weren't at Leadpipe with Hayle's squadron, I guess . . .?"

"Second echelon. We hit Stapp's flank element just before the old *Belshazzar* blew."

"Whatta you know? I was in Culberson's Irregulars, covering off Amroy IV. We never got close enough to pick up a ping on the IFF, but we mixed in nine days later, when Stapp pulled his Bogan reserves out of his sleeve. Let's see now . . . what was the name of his flagship . . ." The man rolled an eye toward the distant ceiling.

"*Annihilator.* A hundred and forty thousand tons, mounting six hellbores and a stern battery of ten-centimeter infinite repeaters; crew of ninety-seven, Coblentz commanding . . ." Henry leaned heavily on the table with his unbandaged hand. "Do I pass the quiz . . .?"

"You got me wrong, brother . . ." the man looked at Henry reproachfully.

Bartholomew pushed up beside Henry. "Captain, I think this fellow's hinting for a bribe," he said sharply.

The registrar's heavy brows drew down. His face folded in a pained frown.

"Back in line, buster—"

"Just a minute." Larry looked severe. "I happen to be a Designated Territorial Statistical Average; I've been standing in this line for over fourteen hours, and I have no intention of submitting to any sort of shakedown!"

"You don't, hey?" The slurred voice cut in. "I wonder if you know that guys get disqualified from registration for jumping the line—"

"You're drunk!" Bartholomew snapped. "You can hardly speak coherently!"

"Uh-huh." The official nodded. "You're right; I don't talk so good. But I'm a whiz at blackballing lightweights that talk themselves right out of the Run—"

"Mr. Bartholomew would like to apologize to you, Registrar," Henry cut in. "He had a hard trip out and he's not responsible. I'll see that he keeps his chin dry from now on."

"This kewpie is with you?" The registrar aimed a finger at Bartholomew, staring at Henry.

Henry nodded.

The registrar motioned; "Let's have the papers."

Bartholomew fumbled the documents out, thrust them toward the men, opened his mouth—

Henry's elbow stuck him under the ribs. He oofed, grabbed at his side with both hands.

"A guy's got to have a sidekick," the registrar banged the stamp down on the two sets of papers, shoved them across to Captain Henry. "But if I was you, brother, I'd sell this one and buy a poodle."

"Thanks, pardner." Henry took a firm grip on Bartholomew's arm and led him away.

The younger man caught his breath. "I'll . . . report him . . . Drinking on duty—"

"Uh-uh," Henry shook his head. "War wound. Notice the scars? On his jaw and throat? Blaster burns always leave a bluish edge."

"Eh?" Bartholomew pulled free. "You mean . . .

the way he talked . . ."

"He had half his face shot off. They did a nice job of putting it back—the tongue is tough to rebuild."

"Oh . . . I . . ."

"Forget it. We're registered. We've got a full day before the gun goes off. Let's get a meal and then take a walk around Tent Town and find out who's here. After that we'll have a better idea of what to expect—guns or knives."

They sat in a booth in a low-ceilinged, dirt-floored shack, squat finger-marked glasses before them on a rough plank table. Henry lit up a dope stick, looked over the crowd. At the bar, a small man in undersized sailing togs and a soiled white yachting cap with bristly blond hair showing under its edge lifted a glass to him in a sardonic toast. Beside Henry, Bartholomew nodded, waved. The small man rose, said something to the man beside him, slipped off into the crowd.

"I see you've made a friend," Henry said.

"I met him while you were buying supplies," Larry said.

"What's he selling?"

"Selling? Nothing. He's retired, actually. His name is Mr. Columbia. He owns a fleet of freighters. He's just here as a sort of relaxation. He agrees that if we work together—"

"His name's Johnny Zaragamosa. He's put on weight since I saw him last, but he's still wearing the same hat."

Larry opened his mouth; then he shut it with a

snap. "Oh? Just because I was the one who met him—"

Henry cocked a sardonic eye at the younger man. Larry was beginning to feel his oats and answer back, was he?

"He was a dope runner when I knew him," Henry said. "Of course, he may have quit and bought a freight line since then."

"Just—" said Larry, stiffly, "because it was my suggestion—"

"Why did he leave so suddenly, Larry?"

"How should I know?"

"Maybe he left the water running in one of those freighters of his."

"Captain, if there's an opportunity to work out a peaceable partnership arrangement, surely you're not going to spurn it?"

"The only arrangements you could work out with Johnny would be for a quiet funeral. Now keep your eyes open and let's see how many other chiselers we can spot."

They were in another dive—the tenth—or was it eleventh—of the evening. Larry leaned across the table, his eyes squinted against the layered smoke.

"It's almost three in the morning," he stated. "We've done nothing but visit unsavory bars and drink unlicensed spirits with unshaven rough-necks."

"And so far we're still unshot, unknifed, and un-poisoned. We're doing all right."

Larry gulped half his drink, made a face. "This time could have been put to good use, working out a *modus operandi* with other gentlemanly entrants."

"I agree the booze is bad," Henry went on. "And some of the boys haven't seen their barbers lately; but we might pick up something valuable talking to the old hands at the game—"

"Drunken derelicts!" Bartholomew snapped. "They look like the sweepings of prisons for incorrigibles—"

"Some of them are—and I wouldn't count on it they left by the front gate. You'll also find ex-military men, cashiered cops, former bouncers, bodyguards, and prize fighters, not to mention stickup artists, needle-men, pickpockets—"

A small, slim man with an empty glass in his hand slipped into the seat beside Henry.

"Twenty years no see, Cap," he said, bright eyes darting to Bartholomew and back to Henry. "Did I hear you mention my name?" He had a hooked nose and dense black brows, a thin-lipped mouth with a nervous smile.

"No, but I was getting to it. Mr. Bartholomew, this is Mr. Minot—sometimes known as Back Fence Louie."

"Around here, they call me Lou the Shoe; it's like old times, Cap. I heard you was here . . ." His eyes went to Henry's gloved hands. "And that you had a little trouble on the way out . . ."

"Have a drink, Lou." Henry pushed the bottle across. "What else do you know that's free?"

Minot poured, drank, sighed, refilled his glass. "You been here twelve hours. You're riding fast iron; there's a roll behind you, so the small operators are staking you out. They figure you're tracked. You're hauling green freight—" Lou glanced at Bartholomew. "But the wise money says there's an angle . . ."

Henry laughed. "You're slipping, Lou. Your curiosity's showing."

The little man leaned close, glanced around. "The word is," he said in a low voice, "you went for the big Four, you must have a wire."

"I'm afraid I'm not following the conversation," Bartholomew interrupted. "I confess this specialist's jargon is beyond me."

Lou the Shoe looked Bartholomew over.

"Your first time out, bud?"

"And my last!"

Lou nodded. "Could be," he agreed. He turned back to Henry. "They're all aboard, this cruise, Cap; mop-up boys, dozers, kangaroos. There's three backbone squads working Tent Town right now. Don't shop around, is my advice: plant your markers and get out before the tombstone lawyers dope your pattern."

Bartholomew shook his head sadly, leaned in his corner, his arms folded. Lou blinked at him, gulped down the rest of his drink, wiped his lips with a limber forefinger.

"Lou's just warming up," Henry said. "He's tossing out all the common gossip on the off-chance I might look interested—"

"Gossip nothing," Louie countered, looking indignant.

"And meanwhile, he's trying to pick up salable information from us." Henry refilled Minot's glass.

"Oh, yeah?" The small man's lips pulled taut,

showing a gap in a rank of ocher teeth. He leaned close. "Get this: Heavy Joe Saggio's in town . . ."

Henry paused in the act of pouring, then he topped off his glass, lifted it in salute, drank half. His eyes seemed brighter suddenly.

"You wouldn't kid an old pal, Lou . . .?"

Lou's face twitched. "He's holed up in the private room at the Solar Corona right now, talking business with a sandbag squad from Croanie."

"Don't tell me you leaned over Heavy Joe's shoulder and heard him mention me by name . . .?"

Lou grinned nervously. "Could be, Cap. The way I remember it, you and him had a couple of run-ins."

"That was a long time ago."

Lou nodded. He emptied the glass again. "Look, Cap," he lowered his voice, talking behind a hand with which he seemed to be rubbing the side of his nose casually. "There's dough behind Heavy Joe this trip; a syndicate, out of Aldo Cerise. The word is, it's a split-and-snatch deal, a kid-glove caper. That's all I could get. And stay away from a joint named Stella's."

Henry put his hand in a knee pocket of his ship suit.

"Never mind that," Lou said. "It's on the house. Thanks for the drink." He rose. Henry raised an eyebrow inquiringly. Lou leaned over the table.

"You got a lousy memory, Cap; I owe you a couple of favors. And take it from me—keep your screens open tonight . . ." He slipped away in the crowd.

Bartholomew shook his head. "A childishly transparent effort," he said. "I suppose later he'll be back, offering late bulletins for a price."

"Maybe—but I think maybe we'd better drift on now and see what jumps out at us . . ."

Captain Henry and Bartholomew went in under a glare sign reading STELLA'S, climbed the rickety stairs, emerged into a wide, crowded room with an uneven ceiling half-hidden by layered smoke. A short, burly waiter with a black jacket and soiled ruffles came up, offered an edge-curled menu badly printed on cheap wine-colored paper.

"What'll it be, gents?" he yelled over the blare of taped music, the surf-roar of boisterous conversation. "How about a nice algisteak with a side order of recon spuds?"

"We want steak off a cow," Henry said. "At a corner table."

"Sure—but it'll cost you . . ."

Henry fished a hundred credit token from a pocket, flipped it to him.

"Make it good," he said.

Bartholomew trailed Henry and the waiter to a table. Henry ordered; the waiter slapped at the table with a damp cloth, moved off with the gliding gait of an old Null-G hand. Two girls with dyed lips and eyelids, swirling hairdos in silver and violet, multiple necklaces, and bare breasts squeezed above dresses like sequinned corsets, appeared out of the crowd, dropped into the empty chairs.

"Hi, fellas. I'm Rennie; she's Nicki," the taller of

the two said cheerfully. "Got a smoke? Brother, what a day!"

"Yeah," Nicki agreed. "Did you see the big slob I was with? For ten cees he wanted me to stand behind him all night while he shot dice; he said I'd bring him luck. Boy . . .!"

Henry offered dope sticks. "Have you ladies dined? If not, please be our guests."

"Hey!" Rennie smiled. "A nice guy for a change."

The waiter reappeared, hovering. Henry signaled. He grinned and went away.

"What's your name, Dreamboat?" Nicki smiled warmly at Bartholomew.

He cleared his throat. "Lawrence H. Bartholomew."

"Wow! That's a lot of monicker. I'll call you Bart. What's your friend's name?"

"Why, ah, Cap—"

"Call me Henry. You girls work here?"

Rennie lit up, blew out smoke, shook her head. "Not exactly; we're free-lance. Stella's O.K., though. We get along. How about a dance?" She stood and tugged at Henry's hand. He glanced over the crowd, then rose and followed the girl out onto the floor. She moved into his arms—a strong, slender, young body with a faint fragrance of exotic blossoms.

"I don't think I've seen you around, handsome," she said. "Just get in?"

"Uh-huh." The band changed its tempo, took up a rhythmic triple-beat flamencito. The girl moved with a smooth, sure rhythm, following Henry's lead.

"Say, you're good," she said. She glanced toward the table. "Your partner's pretty young, isn't he?"

"You've got to start some time."

"Sure."

The beat changed again. "My God, it's great to find a real dancer, after these cargo-sled operators that have been trampling me." Rennie executed an intricate maneuver, looked at Henry with shining eyes. He grinned back, made a sudden graceful move, twirled her to the left, then to the right, let her fall almost to the floor, caught her up on the beat. She laughed aloud. "Hey, Henry, you're the greatest! How about this one . . . ?"

The band played; the crowd milled and chattered. Against the backdrop of people, the girl's face floated, a disembodied smile, her eyes on Henry's.

A heavy body slammed against Henry. He caught himself, turned to look into a wide, broad-nosed face with scarred lips and a half-closed eye.

"Blow a whistle next time and I'll get out of your way," Henry said. He half-turned away, turned back quickly and knocked aside a hand that had reached for his shoulder. Rennie pushed in front of him, facing the intruder.

"Get going, you big ape!" she spat. "Fade. Take the air!"

The scarred lips pulled back to show a chipped tooth; a square hand with hair on the back reached for the girl. Henry eased her aside, stepped close, grabbed the thick wrist. Over the man's shoulder, Henry caught a glimpse of Bartholomew, nodding across the table at a man in a too-tight uniform blouse; it was the man he had called Mr. Columbia and he leaned toward him, talking earnestly. Nicki was gone. Then the crowd closed in, shutting off the view.

The scar-faced man struggled to free his arm. Henry smiled tightly, face to face with the other.

"Go play some other place, stranger," he said easily. "This spot's taken."

The wide face grew dusty red. "Don't get in my way, Mister." His voice was a bass wheeze. "The doll is with me."

"Anybody can make a mistake," Henry said. "But only a damned fool insists on it." He pushed the man from him; he staggered back a step, then growled and moved in. Henry blocked a low punch with his left forearm, set himself, and slammed a short right that smacked home just below the ribs. The man oofed and leaned on Henry as the waiter appeared, fumbling at his hip pocket. Henry passed the man to him.

"He got hold of some bad lobster; help him outside." He turned; the girl was gone. He pushed through to the table where he had left Bartholomew. It was empty.

The waiter came up with a tray; he dumped it on the table, slid two plates off. He looked past Henry's left ear.

"The ladies ah . . . run into an old customer," he said. His tongue touched his upper lip. He reached over, dropped a used napkin in front of Henry, tossed another before Bartholomew's empty chair. He stared at Henry's napkin, then picked up the tray and slid into the crowd.

Henry prodded the napkin, palmed a slip of paper from under it.

DON'T EAT ANYTHING. WATCH YOUR-
SELF. SORRY TO CUT OUT, BUT I'VE GOT
MY OWN PROBLEMS. RENNIE.

Henry turned away from the table. The headwaiter appeared, blocking his way.

"Anything wrong, fella?" His thick lips twitched
in a sick smile.

"I just got a good offer from a Mr. Columbia,
and I'm hurrying to take him up on it," Henry
said. "Which way did he go?"

The man's hand strayed toward his pocket.
"How about the bill?" His voice was thin and high
now. There was a scar down the side of his face
like a seam in a football.

"There was a mistake on the order," Henry said.
He looked into the man's small gray eyes, set deep
under meaty brow ridges. "The wrong kind of
sauce." There was a sudden shout outside. Henry
turned, looking down the stairs. He pushed past
the headwaiter, went down into a rising clamor of
voices.

The crowd on the boardwalk was a dense-pack-
ed, pushing, bottle-waving, curse-shouting mass of
glassy-eyed, open-mouthed men in use-worn ship
suits, odds and ends of uniforms, patched
weatheralls. Heavy guns were strapped to swag-
gering hips; massive boots clumped; hoarse voices
bellowed greetings, snarled threats, blasphemed
the gods of a hundred worlds under the flashing,
multicolored glare signs on bars, joy houses, game
rooms. Across the narrow strip of mud that served
as a street, massed backs formed a dense ring.
Henry shouldered his way through, reached the

front rank. Half in a narrow alleyway between two shacks built of packing case boards stamped KAKA, a body lay sprawled, face down.

" . . . turned around and there he was," another voice said plaintively. "I always gotta miss the action . . ."

Henry stepped to the body, turned it over. The big-nosed face was a mask of mud. A six-inch length of fine-gauge steel wire projected from just below the left collarbone. It was Louie Minot, dead.

Henry looked across at a heavy-featured man who plied a toothpick on large square teeth, looking down on the body.

"Did you see it?" Henry asked.

"Naw." The man smiled. "I'm ankling along, minding my own business, and a guy shoves me. I damn near swallow my toothpick. I turn around and there he is."

"Who shoved you?"

"What's it to you?"

Henry moved close. "You sure you didn't see it?" he said softly.

The bland expression changed. "Listen, you—" A fist started up in a short, vicious jab; Henry's hand shot out, grabbed the other's wrist, wrenched it behind him. The wide mouth opened; the toothpick fell. Henry drew the man close.

"What's your name?"

"Pore Scandy. What's it to you," the man blustered.

"Give, Pore," Henry said.

"Hey, that hurts," the wide-faced man was on

tiptoes. All around, the crowd watched, suddenly quiet.

"It was a guy with a mustache," the man blurted. "He had a pot belly, and warts, and lessee —yeah, he had a game leg."

"You forgot the long red beard." Henry reached across, lifted a small handgun from the man's side pocket. He put the muzzle against the straining chest beside him.

"Your gun?" he inquired conversationally.

"Somebody planted it on me."

"A wire-gun. A torturer's rod. I ought to feed you one through the knee."

"Look, what's the beef—" the thick man grimaced.

"Where's the kid, Pore?" Henry asked softly, his face close to the other's. The man's mouth went slack.

"Gimme a break," he hissed. "I don't know nothing."

Henry twisted the arm; the joint creaked. "Where's the kid?" he repeated tonelessly.

"Look, it's all my neck is worth—"

Henry gave the arm another half turn. "Don't let's waste time; talk it up, fast."

"Look, if I knew, I'd spill—but who tells me anything?" Sweat was running down the heavy cheeks. "All I know is, it was a fifty-credit caper. An old guy with a bad hand, Joe said—"

"Joe won't like you with a broken arm. Funerals are cheaper than doctors."

"O.K., O.K.," the man whispered hoarsely. "Go to the Solar Corona. That's where the stakeout was—I swear that's all I know . . ."

Henry shoved him away; he turned and dived into the crowd, which was breaking up and moving off now. A moment later, Minot's body lay alone in a ring of trampled mud. Henry looked down at the crumpled corpse.

"I should have listened closer, Lou," he said softly. "And so should you."

The Solar Corona was a blaze of garish light from the writhing lines of neon radiating from the wide door cut in the corrugated metal front. Inside, Captain Henry bought a drink at the bar, looked over the crowd.

"You have somebody special in mind, or will I do?" a voice rasped at his side. A woman's face, haggard under uneven paint, looked up at him. A thin hand tucked back a wisp of dead hair.

"Brother, what a night," she focused with difficulty on a jeweled finger watch taped to a bony finger. "Two hours to go; three weeks I been here —and I hardly made expenses . . ." She leaned on the bar, hitched onto the stool.

"Seen Johnny Zaragamosa around?" Henry asked idly.

The woman leaned closer. Henry caught a whiff of stale face powder.

"Friend of yours?" Her voice was scratchy, like a cheap tri-D.

"A friend of a friend."

"Then your friend better keep his hand in his pocket, or Johnny'll be in there ahead of him . . ." She showed her false teeth, swallowing half the contents of the glass the barman had thrust in front of her. Henry glanced sideways at her.

"My friend's got a strange sense of humor," he said. "But sometimes he carries a joke too far."

The woman fumbled out a dope stick, drew on it, puffed out violet smoke.

"As far as Heavy Joe Saggio's rooms at the Dead Dog?"

"Maybe," Henry said. "He's a pretty funny guy."

The woman turned toward him, opened dry, crimson lips to speak—

She stared at him for a long moment. The dope stick dropped to the bar, rolled off on the floor. She stooped swiftly, came up with it, leaned on her elbows, staring at the ranked bottles on the back bar.

"I got a message for you from a girl named Rennie," she said rapidly. "Your pigeon's in deep. Johnny used the pink stuff—too much. The kid folded like a pair of deuces to a ten-cee raise. They're trying to bring him out now. After they milk him—" She finished the drink in a gulp. "If he's a friend . . . well, you'd better hurry . . ."

"Where's this Dead Dog?" Henry snapped out.

"A flop, a couple blocks from here—but some rooms fixed up in back."

"Show me." Henry slid a hundred-credit token along the bar. The woman's thin hand went over it, whisked it out of sight.

"Listen to me," the woman said urgently. Her fingers dug into Henry's arm. "The run starts in less than two hours. Leave the poor crut—there's nothing you can do."

"Just a call on an old associate," Henry said. "I wouldn't want to leave town without dropping a card."

"Don't be a fool! What can one man do—" she broke off. "Hey—your boat; is it a Gendye fifty-tonner, a new job, plush . . . ?"

Henry nodded.

Her clutch on his arm tightened. "My God, listen! They're pulling a hijack on you! Get back to your boat—fast! But watch it; there's a stakeout on the gate . . ."

Henry peered at her in the darkness. "Who are you? Why are you helping me?"

"They call me Stella. Rennie said you were a right guy; let's let it go at that." She plucked at his sleeve. "If you go in there alone, you'll only get yourself killed. Play it smart! You've got a boat to save."

Henry took her hand from his arm gently. "I'd have to give it a try, Stella—wouldn't I?"

She was a shadow against the faint glow from the crosswalk.

"Yeah, you would, wouldn't you?" Her voice caught. "Come on. I'll show you . . ."

Captain Henry stood in the dark courtyard, scanning the barely visible alleyway which ran along the left side of the ramshackle two-story building. A cold rain was falling steadily now; Henry's left hand ached inside the tight glove; he cradled it in his right, listening. The silence rang in his ears. Far away, a drunken voice called; faint footsteps hurried, faded. A night lizard scuttled in

the shadows. Somewhere behind the sagging
facade of the Dead Dog, Bartholomew would be
coming out of the drug now, blinking at hard
faces, feeling the smash of heavy fists. Henry
smiled tightly, hefted the wire-gun, then started
forward, hugging the wall. Skirting the yard, he
moved quietly to the back of the building. The
alley ended against a sheet of perforated metal.
Above, he could see a glassless window opening
overhung by a crude awning. He listened for a
moment, then tucked the wire-gun into the thigh
pocket of the ship suit, started up.

The reach from the metal wall to the windows was
a long one. He pulled himself up and in, ducked
under the header, stood in an unlighted room.
From somewhere, a murmur of voices sounded. A
damp odor of moldy wood hung in the air. He
crossed the room, brushed aside a coarse hanging,
felt his way along an uneven floor to the wall
against which two vertical rails ran up, with heavy
cross members spiked against them at eighteen-
inch intervals; the grand staircase of the Dead
Dog.

The voices came from the other side of the par-
tition. Henry felt along the wall to the left, reached
a blank corner. There was no door.

He went to the ladder, tested the rungs, then
climbed carefully. His outstretched hand touched
the ceiling. He pushed; the cover lifted. Cold, wet
air blew in. He went up, emerged on a sloping
roof. Rain drummed aginst plastic roof panels;
through wide gaps, lines of light glared. He moved
softly to the nearest aperture, knelt, looked down

into an empty room with a sagging cot, a rough pallet with a snarl of dirty blankets, a table with glasses, an empty bottle. The voices were louder now.

He went on across the roof, following the line of the bearing wall. Before him, a thin, translucent roof panel glowed softly; below, a thick voice was talking in a monotone, not quite loudly enough to be understood. Henry crouched, brought his face close to a quarter-inch crack.

A tall, heavily built man with a bald head fringed by curly black hair paced under him, turned, waved a hand on which four rings winked against sallow skin. A small man with bushy hair followed nervously, staying at the bald man's side. Beyond, Larry Bartholomew leaned forward in a chair, his hands tied behind him. The square-toothed face of Pore Scandy was visible behind the captive. A pair of feet showed on the right.

Henry put an ear to the crack.

" . . . only got an hour; this punk's dry. We got to cut for it—now!" The voice was Scandy's.

"When I need your mouth, I tell you, O.K.?" Heavy Joe Saggio's voice was the growl of an old and ill-tempered grizzly.

"Maybe he got a point, *capo*—"

There was a sound like a dead fish hitting a side-walk.

Saggio was standing, feet apart, a gun in his hand. The bushy-haired man was dabbing at his cheek where a line of red showed. Scandy shrugged; his mouth twisted. He came around Bartholomew, reached out. Saggio threw the gun toward him; his hands curled lovingly around it.

Henry took the wire-gun from his pocket, flipped the safety off; he rose to a kneeling position, aimed carefully through the crack, centered the sights on Scandy's neck just below the hairline, squeezed the trigger. As the gun barked, he shifted to the bushy-haired man, fired again. A gun fell from the small man's hand. Scandy leaned, fell against Bartholomew, slammed the floor. The small man was bent over, clutching his side. Henry swung the sights to Saggio as the big man ducked back, out of sight. The fourth man crossed Henry's field of vision in a jump. The lights died.

Henry pocketed the gun, moved back quickly, got to his feet. He took three running steps, crossed his arms over his face, jumped, landed squarely on the thin panel that had glowed on the roof; sharp edges raked the tough ship suit as he slammed through, hit the floor in a shower of broken plastics. He rolled, came to his knees with the gun in his hand. There was a tinkle as a final fragment dropped from the smashed panel; then silence.

Across the room, Henry could see a thin line of light around the door in the opposite wall. Against it, something moved, down low, coming between Henry and the light—a man on all fours.

There was a sound of movement near the middle of the room. A groaning sigh came from Bartholomew.

"One more move and the pigeon gets it," Saggio's deep voice rumbled. Henry crouched motionless, silent. The crawling man came closer. Henry could see his hands now, feeling over the

floor. It was the fourth man, searching for one of
the dropped guns.

"I'm covering the pigeon," Saggio said from the
darkness. "I know where he is, O.K. I'm going out
now—I leave him to you, nobody shoots. Deal?"

Henry breathed slowly, with his mouth open,
not moving.

"I'm making my move now," Saggio said. "Hang
loose . . ."

The crawling man turned suddenly, moved
across the room, careless of noise now. His
breathing was fast and shallow. A board cracked;
a doorknob rattled, hinges squeaked.

"It's all yours-su—" Henry fired at the same
instant that Saggio's needler spat, heard Saggio's
words break off into a snarl of pain. A door slammed back against the wall. Henry fired again,
dropped and rolled, fired, heard a shrill ahh! that
choked off. He fired again as running feet pounded, receded into silence.

He got to his feet, flicked a permatch alight.
Scandy lay crumpled by Bartholomew's chair, a
length of wire bright against the pale, coarse skin
of his neck. The small man lay against the base-
board, his toes in neat shoes pointed like a diver in
free-fall, his arms hugging his chest, his mouth
open, the cut on his cheek purple against green-
white skin. In the wood frame of the door an eight-
inch length of wire stood, still quivering.

Henry wedged the match in a crack in the wall;
by its feeble light took out a pocketknife, cut
Bartholomew free, hauled him to his feet. The
younger man sagged. Blood dribbled from his cut

mouth. Henry shook him, then slapped his face with his open hand. A dim light seemed to focus in the vacant eyes.

"Let's go, Larry. Make your feet work."

Larry groaned, tried to pull free.

"Before Mr. Columbia gets back," Henry said. Bartholomew's eyes steadied; his feet groped, found balance.

"Come on . . ." Henry helped him to the door, plucked the match from the wall. The narrow, unevenly floored hallway was empty, dark. They went along it to a well with a ladder. At its foot, a man lay, face down. A length of wire protruded from his back under the right shoulder blade. Bartholomew shied when he saw the body.

"Don't worry about the dead ones," Henry said softly. "Heavy Joe's down there somewhere—and he's alive, with a piece of wire in him. He'll be in a bad mood about that. We'll take the back way. Can you stand now?"

Bartholomew nodded vaguely. "Mr. Columbia," he said thickly. "He took something out of his pocket . . ."

"Sure, we'll chew over that later. Now let's see you work those legs."

In the alley, Henry helped Bartholomew to his feet. There was a sound from the darkness. An unseen door creaked. A tall, wide figure eased out awkwardly, one hand clamped to his shoulder, throwing a long shadow across the muddy yard. He paused, reached for the light switch on the wall—

"Hold it right there, Joe," Henry said softly.

Saggio bared his teeth in a mirthless grin. He had large, dark eyes, a shapeless nose, a square jaw, blue-stubbled. His hand was clamped to his shoulder.

"Enrico, baby," he growled. "Someplace I heard you was old, you lost your steam, got a bum hand. Ha! I should have knowed better . . ."

"Rumors get around, Joe—don't feel too bad. Turn around now, and head back inside. Do it real nice."

Saggio started into the shadows. A thick tongue moved over his lips that were black in the dim light.

"What you waiting for, Enrico? Maybe you never get me under your iron again, eh?" He straightened. Some of the tension went out of him. "You don't like to kill me, and maybe a couple of my boys mark you—"

Henry squeezed the trigger of the gun in his hand. A length of wire spanged into wood. Saggio's head jerked convulsively; his eyes widened. He stood very still.

"Better move, Joe," Henry said.

Saggio grinned suddenly, nodded. "O.K., Enrico baby." He turned away, then paused, looked back.

"It's like old times, hey, Enrico? I see you again sometime, huh?" He moved off, walking briskly like a man who had suddenly remembered an errand.

Inside the wide rotunda of the Port Authority Building, Henry walked Bartholomew to the processing line. A familiar scarred face frowned up at him from behind a desk, glanced at Bartholomew.

"Hi, *Degüello*. What happened to Junior?"

"He had a fall," Henry said. "He'll be O.K."

The scarred man leaned forward, sniffed. He cocked an eye at Henry.

"The pink stuff, hey? He spill his guts?"

"They overdid it. He slept through the proceedings."

"Some smart guys outsmart themselves." The scarred man stamped papers, waved toward the far side of the hall.

"You cut it close, bud. You got about thirty minutes before the red rocket goes up. You played it smart, getting the extra crewman. He went aboard the car half an hour back."

Henry looked at him. "Was he alone?"

"You ain't expecting to get a whole platoon into that Bolo Minor, I hope. You'll be squeezed with three."

"Yeah. Thanks for everything."

"Good luck, bud—I'd still ditch dreaming-boy, if I was you."

"I can't. He owns the outfit."

Henry pushed through the turnstile, walked Bartholomew across toward the high glass wall, with the sweep of flood-lit ramp beyond where the massive armored ground vehicle unloaded from *Degüello* squatted, dwarfed by the looming silhouettes of converted freighters, ancient destroy-

er escorts, battered short-run liners. Bartholomew staggered, breathing noisily.

"How's your head now, Bart?" Henry asked.

"Ghastly. My legs—like lead. I don't remember—"

"Forget it. Try to stay on your feet long enough
to get aboard. Then you can go to sleep."

"I guess I made a fool of myself . . ."

"You had lots of help."

Faint gray tinged the eastern sky now. A power
unit started up, stuttering. An odor of ozone and
exhaust gases floated across from the ships. Men
hurried to and fro, throwing triple shadows across
the tarmac. The dawn air was tense with expec-
tancy.

A line cart puttered into view, rounding the
flank of a space-pitted vessel. Henry hailed it; it
slowed in a descending whine of worn turbos.

"I need a Decon; how about it?"

A tired-faced man in a white coverall stared at
him from the cart.

"You birds; you drink all night, and all of a
sudden you remember you got no clearance
papers. If it was left up to me, I'd say to hell with
you—"

"Sure." Henry handed him a ten-credit chip.
"Sorry to bother you. I've had a couple of things
on my mind."

He pointed toward the Bolo, parked a hundred
feet away.

"O.K.; seein' it's just a car, I guess I got
time . . ." The driver maneuvered his cart into

position, attached hoses. Henry lowered Bartholomew to the ground, went to the panel set in the
flank of the heavy machine. There were tool marks
around it; it opened at a touch. Fragments of the
broken lock lay inside. The button marked PORT
—UNLOCK was depressed. Henry pressed the
LOCK button, heard the snick of the mechanism
above.

The Decon man started up the blower. Its hum
built up to a sharp whine. Minutes passed. Bartholomew had stretched on his back, snoring.
Henry lifted him to his feet, walked him until he
could stand alone.

The driver shut down the blower, disconnected
the hoses, reeled them in. He revved up his turbos,
wheeled off.

Henry helped Bartholomew to the car.

"Going to be ill . . ." the younger man said.

"Let's get aboard; then you can tell me all about
it." Henry cycled the hatch open; the two men
climbed inside. A faint odor of Cyanon still hung
in the air. Bartholomew gagged.

"Why . . . another Decon . . . ? We did that . . .
before . . ." He broke off, staring at the body of a
man, lying head-down in the short companionway.
The eyes of the inverted face were open; the mouth
gaped, showing a thick tongue. The thin features
were a leaden purple.

"G-good Lord . . . !" Bartholomew groped for
support. "There was . . . man inside . . . when—"

"Yeah; let's get moving."

Henry hauled his sagging shipmate past the
corpse, settled him in his cradle, buckled him in.

He flipped the countdown switch, set the clock.

"You knew . . . that man . . . was aboard," Bartholomew gasped out.

"Go to sleep, Larry," Henry said. He strapped himself into his gimbaled seat before the Bolo's panel, punched buttons. A ready-light glowed on the panel. The countdown clock ticked loudly.

"Attention!" the ground-control screen said. "Zero minus two minutes . . ."

There was a sudden loud snore from Bartholomew.

Henry started the engine, glanced over instruments, flipped on the specially installed wide-vision screens.

"Ten . . . nine . . . eight . . ." the screen said. Henry slipped the clutches, revved the mighty Bolo engines.

". . . three . . . two . . . one . . ." The Bolo moved out of the shadow of *Degüello*.

"It's all yours," the speaker said. "Go and get it!"

They were ten miles into the rough country east of the port, slamming ahead, over and through obstructions like a charging bull-devil. On the screens, the clustered blips of other vehicles had fanned out now, spreading to all points of the compass from the starting point. The port IRAD showed a massive vehicle—a ten-tonner—pacing the Bolo at one mile. To the right, two smaller vehicles raced, on courses converging from two miles. Henry's glance went over the fire-control panel. Green GO lights glowed cheerfully at him.

He smiled to himself, added another five hundred meters per minute to his speed. It was time to thin out the opposition.

Beside him, Larry slept, strapped in his padded couch.

At twenty miles out, the ten-tonner—a Gendye Supreme, Henry guessed—still held position at half a mile, matching his speed. The two smaller shadowers had fallen back, were mere bright specks on the screen astern. Henry flicked a switch; a pink light winked on the panel—the BATTERY ARMED telltale from a salvaged destroyer. He boosted his speed another half kilometer per minute. The Bolo bucked, slamming through tangled desert scrub.

Forty-six minutes and forty miles from Pango-Ri, Henry adjusted course to the south, punched a random evasive pattern into the course-control monitor. The couch rocked under him as the Bolo curveted in a spiral reverse. The escorting vehicle tracked him, holding interval. Henry whistled. The boy was good—and riding good iron.

Abruptly the alarm bell clanged. Henry read dials. A forty-kilo mass, closing at a thousand feet per second; a light missile. He keyed the intercept-response circuit, felt the Bolo buck as his missiles launched. Lights flashed as new missiles slid into position in the magazines. On the screen, the two tiny rockets curved out, minute flecks of yellow-white against the blackness, converging on the attacking missile.

The screens dimmed to near-opacity as the incoming weapon detonated in a blaze of hard radiation.

Bartholomew stirred, opened his eyes. "What's . . . going on?" he managed.

"Some lawless character just took a shot at us," Henry said tightly. "Go back to sleep."

"A shot—?" Bartholomew was wide awake now. "Did you report it?"

"Too busy—"

"But that's illegal! Can't we do something—!"

"Sure; we can fire back with our own illegal battery."

"Captain, my father—"

"Shut up! I'm busy . . .!"

Ten minutes passed while the two war-cars raced northward side by side, their courses steadily converging.

"A little closer," Henry muttered. "Just come in a little closer, baby . . ."

"What are you doing?" Larry demanded.

"I'm letting him get his head well into the noose," Henry said. "If I close with him, he might spook—but since he's playing the heavy . . ."

"Perhaps he just wants to—to negotiate!" Larry said.

"We'll fool him by opening the conversation first," Henry said, and thumbed the FIRE button. A flickering glare sprang up around the Bolo. The screens flickered uncertainly as excited ions struck in uneven waves. The speeding Supreme veered away, suddenly wary too late. As it turned, its image flicked into incandescence. The screen went from white to yellow to red, faded to show long streamers trailing out to all sides in a blaze of hard radiation. Dark pinpoints of solid wreckage fanned out; a vast smoke ring shot through with bright flashes formed, grew.

The ground-control screen crackled.

"*Degüello*—what's going on out there? A while ago, I read two blasts near you—just now I picked up a two K-T flash less'n a mile abeam of you. Plenty of the hard stuff, too! It'll be raining hot iron around here for a week! Are you in trouble?"

"*Degüello* to tower," Henry grated against the slam of the speeding machine. "No, I'm having myself a time. I guess some of the boys are sloppy drivers . . ."

"If I didn't know a Minor didn't pack an armory, I might get an idea you carted some contraband in here, *Degüello*! You wouldn't pull one like that, would you?"

"Goodness, that would be illegal, tower."

"It would at that. Maybe you better call a misdeal, *Deguello* . . ."

"I hate law suits, tower. I'll take my chance."

"It's your play. But watch somebody moving in at two-seven-oh. Tower over and out."

A bell clanged. The IRAD showed a small car emerging from the dust cloud that was all that remained of the heavy Gendye. It swung toward the Bolo.

"Looks like he carried a spare," Henry muttered; he waited, frowning, his finger poised over the firing key. The car flashed past a hundred yards distant, close enough for Henry to read ISV

MANTA-II lettered on the side.

At the last instant, a bright flash winked from it. Henry's finger went down on the key. The Bolo lurched. The vision screens blacked. Henry fought the controls while Bartholomew clung to his cradle, his eyes and mouth wide.

"Tricky," Henry grated. "A gyrob—a remote job. But I think we outgunned them."

"Who are they?" Bartholomew demanded. "What does it mean?"

Henry was studying the terrain map. A long peninsula stretched north from Pango-Ri, curving to the horizon and beyond—fifteen hundred miles of mountain, desert, and ice.

"It means we're in the clear for the moment," he said. "We're IRAD-negative, so maybe we've lost them for good—if we can stay ahead of them. But hold on to your hat, Larry, the next few days are going to be a little hectic."

Three days and nights had passed, Henry and Larry alternating at the controls as they raced northward. Now massive ice crags loomed on the forward direct view panel; a wilderness of broken ice was visible beyond. Strangling voices were coming from the Bolo's power compartment. Henry wrestled the wheel, attempting to brake the speeding machine to a halt.

"We can't stop here," Bartholomew yelled above the tumult. "Nothing but ice and broken rock . . .!"

"Left track's locking!" Henry shouted. "We'll settle for what we can get!"

Low, scrublike trees hurtled past the Bolo. There was a rending crash, a shock, and the car skidded wildly. The emergency retrorockets fired a brief burst; then the car was careening sideways, throwing a spray of pulverized ice a hundred feet in the air. It shot over the crest of a rise, dropped into deep snow, plowed on another hundred yards, and came to rest with a final bone-barring impact in a jumble of fallen rock and ice.

Bartholomew fumbled his way from his couch, bleeding from a cut on the side of his head. Choking, black smoke still wafted from the panel. Bartholomew coughed, groped his way to the view screen.

"Where are we?" he gasped, staring out at the bleak, white wilderness visible beyond the prow, half-buried in snow.

"About twelve hundred miles north of Pango-Ri, I'd estimate." Henry tossed a smashed ration box aside, got to his feet, cradling his left hand. There was blood on the tight black glove. "And lucky to be talking about it. That last shot must have gotten to us."

"You've hurt your hand," Bartholomew said. There were dark circles under his eyes, and his face was greenish pale.

"I'm all right." Henry looked him over. "How do you feel?"

"I ache all over," Bartholomew said. "And my mouth is cut . . . ." He explored the raw marks on his lip with his tongue.

Henry scattered gear aside, examining the panel. "Let's see how bad off we are—"

He broke off as his eye fell on an instrument on the still-smoldering panel. He swore with feeling.

"What is it?"

"Right on our tail—so much for forty thousand credits' worth of radar-negative gear. A heavy job —a fifteen-tonner, anyway—about fifty miles out."

"You mean there's a vehicle nearby?" Bartholomew babbled. "Thank heaven! Signal them. Try the communicator—!"

"Calm down, Bart. Could be it's a far-out coincidence; wouldn't bet my second-best brass cufflinks on it."

"But, Captain—it's an incredible stroke of luck—"

"The worst luck you could have would be for that car to pay us a call. We've got to get clear of here—fast. Come on; get your pack ready!"

"Leave the car? But this is our only shelter!" Henry ignored him, shoving food into his pack, checking the charge in his power gun.

"We don't need shelter, Larry," he said. "We need distance between us and them."

"But they're our only hope of getting help!"

"Don't bitch about a little thing like a twelve-hundred-mile hike back to port. We have more immediate worries. Get the first-aid kit!" Henry picked up the folding marker frame and the plastic carton containing the four official markers that had been issued to them at Pango-Ri, then cycled the hatch open, looked out at blowing snow. Icy air cut at him like a saw.

"Captain . . ." Bartholomew stood beside him,

shivering in the arctic wind. "You actually think they might *attack* us?"

"Uh-huh."

"But—they can't do this! There must be a law—!"

"Sure; the Survival of the Fittest, they call it. It may not be democratic, but it still works."

"It's madness!" Larry shivered. "This violence, lawlessness. Those are civilized men—"

"Not these boys; they intend to kill us. I don't plan to let 'em, if I can help it." Henry jumped down into the soft snow.

Bartholomew followed, then looked back at the warm cabin.

"But to leave this—to go out into a blizzard— how do we know we can even survive?"

"We don't," Henry said. "That's what makes it fun."

An hour later, Henry and Larry came down off the broken rock-slopes to a gravel-spit at the edge of a frozen river.

Larry dumped his fifty-pound pack with a groan of relief.

"Troubles?" demanded Henry, sardonically.

Larry looked over at him.

"My feet hurt," he answered. He looked at his hands. "I've already worn blisters on my palms from trying to lift the straps free of my shoulders." He stared at Henry. "How about you?"

"All right. You'll be all right, too. It's a matter of getting used to the idea a little discomfort won't kill you."

Larry bit his lower lip.

"You're in command," he said. "But it's only fair to warn you I'm not convinced of the need for abandoning the car and all the expensive equipment in it. It'll be my duty to report that fact to my father, as backer, when we return."

"Don't bother; he wouldn't appreciate the humor of it." Henry broke off, looking back in the direction from which they had come. A low rumble sounded; a flickering light winked against the lead-colored sky.

"Oh-oh; company's here." He got to his feet. "I hope this dissipates any last, lingering doubts you may have had that we're the object of someone's attentions," Henry said.

"But—if they're really after us—why aren't they following our trail? We've only come two or three miles."

"Maybe they're a little extracautious. I did what I could to discourage 'em back at Pango-Ri."

"What *did* happen there? Was there . . . violence?" Larry trailed as Henry headed upslope against a driving wind.

"I guess you could call it that."

"Was anyone . . . injured?"

"Well, you got a split lip."

"I mean, seriously?"

"I don't think so. I left a couple of lads in an alley, nursing headaches, and Heavy Joe has a piece of Pore Scandy's wire in his arm, but they'll recover."

"Well, then, why are you so sure—"

"Of course, I killed four of them," Henry added.

Bartholomew stopped dead. "You k-k-killed four m-men?"

"Remember the chap we found when we came aboard? He got an overdose of rat poison—"

"I-I seem to remember—something—a face, upside down . . ."

"That's the guy. You were coming out of the gas by then."

"But—you'll by tried for murder—"

Henry started off. "Who by?"

Bartholomew trailed him, still struggling into his pack harness. "By the planetary law-enforcement agencies . . ."

"Not here; there's no law, no cops, no murder trials."

"Then the Quarantine Service—"

"They're busy managing the Run. They don't bother much with unsuccessful entrants."

"But when we return to civilization—"

"We're outside the jurisdiction of Aldorado. The only law here is what you make up as you go along. Heavy Joe sent his boys up against me, and I outgunned 'em. It could have been the other way around."

"But—how could you do it, Captain—kill a man, a fellow human?"

"Before you see home again you may know the answer to that one."

They tramped on in silence for an hour; the probing wind bit at the exposed skin of their faces and wrists; dry snow particles stung like flying sand.

"What will we do when night falls?" Bartholomew called suddenly. "The temperature is well below freezing now; it will drop even lower—"

A bright flash glared briefly against the snow, throwing long shadows for an instant ahead of the men. Underfoot, the ground quivered. A dull *boom!* sounded, rolled, faded.

"There went the Bolo," Henry said. He stood, staring back along the trail. Across the icy rock, a few footprints showed, filling rapidly with brown snow. "She deserved better than that."

"They blew up our car?" Bartholomew's face was haggard in the fading light.

"Still think it's a detachment of the Travelers' Aid?"

Bartholomew stared around at the broken landscape of gray rock, white ice. "What if they follow us—attack us here . . . ?"

"We're dead meat if they follow up close. My idea is to reach the hills; maybe we'll find a spot to hole up."

"What then? Our suit power packs won't last forever; we'll freeze—even if they don't kill us . . ."

"We're not dead yet. Let's stay alive and wait for the opposition to make a mistake."

"Listen," Larry cupped an ear. "Isn't that the sound of engines?"

"Could be. I guess the boys plan to make sure of us."

"How—how many of them—" panted Larry, leaning against the slope and the wind, "did you say you killed?"

Henry smiled grimly. "You like the revenge motive, eh?" He shook his head. "It doesn't figure; they're spending a lot of money chasing us; sentiment isn't in it."

"Captain—do you notice anything . . . ?" Larry stopped, stood with his head up, sniffing the air. "I detect—a sort of fresh, green odor—very faint . . . " He nodded forward, toward the next line of hills. "From up ahead there . . ."

"That so?" said Henry. He turned to look oddly at the younger man. "Well, the unexpected always demands an explanation. Let's shove ahead and take a look."

Ten minutes later they topped a rise to look down across a sheltered valley that stretched to a distant, hazy line of high white hills. A dark clump of foliage showed starkly a quarter of a mile distant.

"Good Lord, Captain," Bartholomew stared at the scene. "Those are trees down there . . ."

"That's right. We'll have cover—and they'll stand out like flies on a wedding cake in all this nice smooth snow."

They tramped down across the snowy field. Ahead, the clump of trees loomed up, tapered, pale-barked tree ferns, fifty feet high. The two men circled cautiously, then came close. A breath of warm air seemed to flow upward from the shadowed grove. They went in under the trees. A gentle breeze stirred the feathery leaves on low-hanging branches.

"Captain—this is grass underfoot! And that wind! It's warm! It's coming from there . . ." Bartholomew went toward the mound at the center of the copse, almost buried under creeping vines. Henry stood watching the younger man. Larry stopped, came up with a tiny, pale yellow flower of intricate shape.

"It's incredible! This oasis—"

He broke off. There was a sudden motion; a tiny winged creature whirred from the dark mound, darted past Bartholomew's head as he ducked. It fluttered on, then fell to the snow at the outer edge of the ring of trees. It lay, beating gossamer wings, then fell still.

"Captain!" Larry looked from the vine-grown mound. "There's a light shining from here ..." Henry came up beside him. Through the blanketing tangle of fluttering leaves, a greenish glow filtered from below.

"There's sort of a crack down there—a slot in the face of the mound!" said Larry, excitedly. "The air is coming from there!"

Henry shoved past him, pulled aside finger-thick creepers, revealing a smooth, rock-like surface. It was geometrically flat, dull grayish-black in color, with a five-foot-wide, three-inch-high opening.

"Why, it's man-made," Larry said. Henry nodded. He had drawn his gun, almost absently. There was no sound but the steady sigh of air flowing from the opening.

"It looks old," Bartholomew whispered. "But the light ... Do you suppose ... ?"

"Nobody home—for a long time now." Henry holstered the gun, worked his way behind the screen of vegetation; his feet sank into a soft mulch of decayed vegetation. "Let's get this stuff cleared away and take a look inside."

Half an hour later, Henry's knife sawed through the last of the interwoven network of twisted vines; a mass of heavy foliage fell away from the opening. A warm draft gushed out, blowing fallen leaves, whipping at dangling tendrils of greenery. Henry looked down into a rectangular chamber fifteen feet on a side, bare, unadorned, its floor drifted deep with blown dust and dead leaves, dotted over with tiny green plants and the white knobs of fungus. At the far side, a slab door stood ajar; soft green light came from beyond it.

"If we pull a little more of this debris away, we can climb down in there," Henry said. "Then if we can douse the light, we'll have a first-class defensive position."

"Is that wise, Captain?" The green light cast shadows on Bartholomew's face. "It may be some sort of trap."

Henry shook his head. His eyes glittered in the eerie light. "The boys are tricky, all right; they trailed us a hundred miles off the beaten track. But I'm pretty sure they didn't rush ahead and set up a booby trap at the end of the line. Nobody's that good."

He dug into the loose-packed rubbish, cleared a trough, then turned and lowered himself down the sloping heap to the floor of the buried room. The light glowed from an open doorway. Beyond it was another room, much like the first, but longer, bright-lit by the glare from still another door. In the middle of the floor lay a pattern of small objects like scattered sticks.

Bartholomew dropped down, came up behind Henry.

"What do you suppose it is?"

Henry stooped, picked up a curiously shaped object of reddish metal. A shred of grayish fabric clung to it. He stirred the stick-like remains with his finger.

"It's a skeleton," he said.

"A skeleton? Of what?"

"Something that wore clothes."

"Clothes . . . ? But those don't look like anything human . . ."

"Who said it was human?" Henry's voice was rough; it tore at his throat. He turned toward the bright doorway, twenty feet away at the end of the long chamber. A haze like hot air rising from a blast pad shimmered in the rectangular archway. Beyond stretched a view of rolling green hills, dotted with groves of thin-stemmed trees with celery-like tops. Far away, wooded mountains reared up under a sky as deep and clear as green glass.

"What . . ." Larry's voice stumbled. "What is it? How . . ."

But Henry scarcely heard him. He was already walking toward the mirage-like scene. A steady flow of warm air pushed into his face, bringing an odor of spring.

There was a moment of pressure as he passed through the door, like the surface of a pond breaking; and he was standing among nodding wild flowers. He filled his lungs with the warm air; like a man who has at last come home, and something that had been locked inside him for so long that he had all but forgotten it was there, released.

Then he came back to the present. He made himself turn and step back into the chamber. Larry was staring at him.

"Good Lord!" said the young man, softly. His face was pale. "What is it, Captain? What does it mean? Why didn't you toss something through there before you tried stepping through yourself? Anything could have happened to you, when you stepped through that—that *hole* in the world."

"Let's get back topside and camouflage the opening," Henry said brusquely. "Then we'll come back down and you can take a look for yourself."

The distant mutter of turbos rose and fell. "They're coming up fast," Henry said. "We left a pretty good trail that last half mile or so. When they hit that, they'll be here in minutes."

"We've done all we can," Larry panted. "After we slide down, I'll pull the mat in place. Then if we close the inner door to shut the light away—"

"Yes," Henry said. His mind was only half on the defensive preparations they were making. He added, absently, " . . . and if they find us, they'll still have to come through the door one at a time . . ."

The two men re-entered the chamber, settled the mass of bundled vines firmly in the opening. Inside the inner room, they pushed the heavy door to. It seated smoothly. Henry turned to the entrance.

"—That skeleton, Captain," said Larry following him. "It must be from some non-human creature—but on all the worlds we've found yet, there was nothing higher than the insect level—"

"Martian pyramids," said Henry, briefly.

"But those were natural formations—"

"Maybe." Henry was almost to the entrance. "And on the other hand, maybe whoever built this visited a few other places, too."

Larry caught at his arm, stopping him.

"Captain! You aren't just going to walk through that doorway again without checking—" Henry shook off the young man's grasp.

"Stay behind if you want to," he growled, and walked toward the light, toward sunshine and flowers and grass. A tingling sensation washed over his face as he went through, and then the feel of yielding sod under his feet. The warm, moist odor of clean earth rose up around him. Behind him he heard the last half of a spoken word.

"—air!"

He turned; beyond the delicately carved stone of the doorframe, Larry stood in shadows, staring at him.

"Come on along, Larry," Henry said. "We've got some claim markers to plant."

"Captain . . ." Larry was staring at him strangely. "I have the impression you know this place; that you've been here before."

"Do you?" Henry said, and turned and started away across the springy turf.

On the bank of a stream half a mile from the low, stone-faced building that housed the portal, Henry set up the marker frame.

"O.K.," he said, "let's have the marker, Larry."

Larry opened a light case, took out a six-inch cylinder pointed at one end, passed it over.

"These markers are the cat's meow, Larry," Henry said. "They blast their way down about forty feet into solid rock, and fuse the hole closed behind them; and a thousand years from now, they'll still be putting out a trickle signal."

"Very interesting, I'm sure," Bartholomew muttered. He looked pale, sick. Every few seconds he glanced toward the portal as if expecting to see the enemy charging through, guns blazing. Henry ignored the boy's worried look. He fitted the marker into the slide on the light frame erected on the sod, clamping the cover tight.

"Let's get back of something; there'll be vaporized granite around for a few seconds..." He moved off thirty feet to the shelter of a fallen log. Bartholomew followed, limping on both feet.

Henry keyed the detonator. There was a spurt of white fire from the frame, a deep-toned *whoomp!* White light glared for a moment across the sunny meadow, outlining the trees in vivid relief. An odor of hot rock whipped past as the ground underfoot trembled. Dirt pattered down all around.

Henry handed Bartholomew the bright red disk of plastic he had removed from the marker before placing it.

"She's planted—but it won't do us any good unless we can produce the tabs on demand—so take care of it."

"Why me?"

"Just in case the opposition catches me. I can't give 'em what I haven't got."

"What if they catch *me?*"

"You stay out of it—don't try to help me if I'm caught. Hide; lie low until you can get clear—then try to make it back to Pango-Ri—"

"Captain, look—I've been thinking. That other car; Ground Control at Pango-Ri must have known we were in trouble, and sent out—"

"Mighty fast work; they were there within minutes. And what about that blast we heard?"

"A signal—"

"Some signal; a flare would have been more to the point."

"But things like you're talking about just don't happen. My father—"

"Look around you, Larry..." said Henry, heavily, "and tell me that 'things just don't happen...'"

Larry glanced around at the turf, the distant trees, and the green sky. He shivered, slightly.

"I... don't know..."

"It's pretty country, Larry. Go ahead and admit it."

"Yes... I'll agree with you there..." The young man's back straightened, and a faint note of an enthusiasm Henry had never before heard in Larry's voice sounded in it now. Then his gaze came sharply back to Henry. "But we can't stay here indefinitely with the crew you say are hunting for us up there and winter coming. We could be stranded here . . . maybe we could come to terms with whoever's supposed to be after us . . ."

"You're a forgiving soul, Larry—and a forgetful one. Relax. We'll get our other markers planted; then we'll wait twenty-four hours before we have a peek outside."

A blaze of stars lit the wide summer meadow like a full moon.

"That's Iota Orionis, all right," Henry said. He lay on his back, spooning omelet from a ration can. "But I'm damned if I can find any of the rest of the Orion stars from this angle."

"It's incredible," Larry said. "Why, with that much displacement of the constellation we could be over a thousand light years from the Terran Sector—but that's impossible."

"We're here," said Henry. "You'd better pretend to believe it." He was watching the younger man. With the light of the fire on his face, Larry's features showed a wonder and a kindling of excitement, an *aliveness* that was new to him. *I never meant to bring him here, Dulcia* . . . Henry thought to his long-dead wife. *I never even meant to bring myself, again—or thought I didn't* . . .

Then, suddenly, he was thinking of a duty left undone for more than a hundred years. He got up unobtrusively and left the fire. When he came back, some little while later, Larry stared at him.

"What is it, Captain?"

Henry shook his head and sat down by the fire again, dusting his hands.

"Burial detail," he said, shortly. "That's all— those bones we saw, coming in."

"You buried that alien skeleton? But—" Larry broke off abruptly, his brows narrowing thoughtfully as he stared across the flames at Henry. " . . . Of course, Captain," he wound up softly. "You know best."

He turned to look at the star-filled sky again.

"I've been watching the stars move," he went on, in a strangely quiet voice. "I've been watching the whole sky of them move as this world turns . . . and I've been thinking. You know what this means, Captain—what we've found here? We've got a universe to explore again! We've been stagnating for a hundred years now; without FTL travel, there'd never be another frontier, where a man could test himself against the odds; we'd settled down to the day of the Statistical Average —and I thought that was the millennium. But now I see it all differently! Now—we'll study this thing, learn how it works. And when we do—Captain, the whole Galaxy will be open to us!"

He swung about to face across the fire to Henry.

"Do you know what I mean?"

Henry was staring into the fire. There was a look on his face that made Larry fall silent . . .

Looking into the red embers, Henry felt the old words stirring in his mind. He had thought he had forgotten them, a century before; but now they

came back as they had rung in his head when he
had first walked this alien earth, seen this other
sky—rung in his head until he was drunk with
them and the new universe before him, until he
had forgotten his home, his race, even the first
Dulcia, waiting for him on Flamme, alone, with
the baby due and no one to whom she could turn.

Oh, Dulcia. If only I'd come back to you when I
promised you I would. But it was a whole new
world—a whole new Universe. I *had* to see. You
understand how it was with me, don't you, girl
. . . ?

—They came creakily, strangely from his tongue
at first, but they rang out, gaining strength as he
recited . . .

> There's no sense in going further—it's the edge of
>     cultivation,
> So they said, and I believed it—broke my land
>     and sowed my crop—
> Built my barns and strung my fences in the little
>     border station
> Tucked away below the foothills where the trail
>     runs out and stop.
> Till a voice, as bad as Conscience, rang intermi-
>     nable changes
> On one everlasting whisper day and night repeat-
>     ed—so:
> Something hidden. Go and find it. Go and look be-
>     hind the Ranges—
> Something lost behind the Ranges. Lost and wait-
>     ing for you. Go!
>
> So I went, worn out of patience; never told my
>     nearest neighbors—

Stole away with pack and ponies—left 'em drink-
    ing in the town;
And the faith that moveth mountains didn't seem
    to help my labors
As I faced the sheer main-ranges, whipping up and
    leading down.

March by march I puzzled through 'em, turning
    flanks and dodging shoulders,
Hurried on in hope of water, headed back for
    lack of grass;
Till I camped above the tree-line—drifted snow
    and naked boulders—
Felt free air astir to windward—knew I'd stum-
    bled on the Pass . . .

He chanted on, the fire of the old poem filling
his veins with its light and lifting him up, up and
out toward the unknown stars as he talked. He
had forgotten the past and a hundred years of
penitence and sorrow. He had forgotten even the
presence of Larry, staring silent across the leaping
flames at him. The old call—the call that had sung
him out to the worlds untrod by men ever since his
strength had first come on him, was singing to him
now. The last verse of the poem rolled like an
anthem from his tongue . . .

. . . Yes, your "Never-never country"—yes your
    "edge of cultivation"
And "no sense in going further"—till I crossed
    the range to see.
God forgive me! No, *I* didn't. It's God's present to
    our nation.
Anybody might have found it but—His Whisper
    came to Me!

Slowly Henry came back from the wild cataract of feeling and memory on which the ancient words had swung him, and how he was seeing himself clearly: for the first time in a hundred years he stood face to face with himself—and saw that the flame had never left him. It had been in him, all this time, the fire that had beckoned him onward, ever onward, always onward into new worlds. A noble fire, he'd always thought it—but crimes had been committed in its name.

"Dulcie," he murmured aloud. "Oh, Dulcie . . ." He shook his head like someone coming out of a dream; and looked across the fire.

On the other side of it, Larry still sat transfixed, staring at him, the lean young face as still as if the boy had been magicked into stone.

"It's a poem," Henry said. "—*The Explorer*. An old Terran named Rudyard Kipling wrote it back in A.D. 1800 or thereabouts."

"I think—I almost understand, Captain," Larry said.

Henry laughed harshly. "Who ever understands anything, kid?" he growled and the spell that had bound both men together for a moment was broken.—But not completely broken, for Larry still looked at Henry with eyes like those on someone who has seen a legend put on flesh and walk.

"Captain . . ." whispered Larry. "You . . . you'll never die . . . "

"Roll over and get some sleep," muttered Henry, lying down. "We'll leave at dawn."

He rolled over himself, turning his back on the younger man and what had just passed between them.

They climbed up at dawn through the blocked doorway, emerging into the sub-zero cold under an icy blue sky.

"That was a long night," Larry said. "It looks like late afternoon here."

Henry led the way across to the edge of the clearing, looked out across the snow.

"Footprints and tread tracks, but no signs of life now. It looks like they gave up and went away."

"What will we do now?"

"First, we'll reconnoiter the area; there may be a useful piece or two of the Bolo left lying around. Then we'll start walking."

"Walking?" Larry looked at him. "To Pango-Ri? Twelve hundred miles?"

"You have a better idea?"

"No. I . . ." the younger man hesitated. "I thought maybe we could signal for help. Build some sort of communicator. It wouldn't have to be a screen—even a sparkgap transmitter would do."

"No can do, boy," said Henry. "Not without the wrong people picking up the transmission and homing in on us. No," he shook his head, "that's out. We walk. Let's scout the remains of the car before full dark, and then hit the trail. We'll be less conspicuous by night."

They started across the churned snow, reached the surrounding line of hills, entered the area of broken rock.

Henry stopped, listening, looking into the early evening gloom with narrowed eyes.

"Maybe I was a little too optimistic," he said.

"Optimistic?" Larry stared at him, his thin face tense.

"Turbos!" Henry snapped. "Hear them? This is where we split up, Larry. Use your compass; head due south; I'll rejoin you as soon as I throw the hounds off the trail . . ."

"You mean I'm to go—alone—" there was a faint ring of panic in the young man's voice.

Henry nodded. "I'm sorry now I got you into this, Larry—but you're here. Take the blaster . . ." He handed it over. " . . . And remember what I said about letting me handle my own troubles. Good luck."

"Wait! I can't—"

"You'd better, Larry. Now split!" He turned, started toward the high ground at a trot. Behind him Bartholomew stood, the blaster in his hand, looking after him.

There was a sound from the direction of the slab-tilted crest ahead, a stark and ragged silhouette against the red sky of evening. Henry dropped flat. The low outline of a tracked carryall moved into view. There was a sudden crackling sound, then an amplified voice:

"Play it smart and easy, and nobody loses nothing. I'm giving you fair warning! I got twenty men. There's only the two of you. Now, you make it easy on us, we'll make it easy on you. Put your guns down and stand up with both hands in sight . . ."

Henry groped in a flapped pocket, took out a green capsule. He swallowed it, then took the slug gun from his pocket, moved off, keeping in the shelter of massive stone fragments. Harsh voices shouted. Off to Henry's left a light winked on, a dusty blue-white lance stabbing into the twilight. It reversed, playing over the rocky ground, swept up the slope, throwing red-black shadows across the ice. Henry dropped, worked his way back as the light glared just above his head. There were more yells. A second light blinked on. Men crashed down the slope, fanning out to surround his position. The light moved on; Henry rose to a crouch, his feet dashed for a dense shadow.

Lying flat among tumbled boulders heaped at the foot of an exposed rock face rising among the trees, Henry listened to the shouts behind him. If he could make it to the top of the outcropping, he might get clear . . .

Henry moved forward, keeping low; a cleft split the wall before him. He wound his way into it, braced his back, got a grip above, pulled himself up. The injured hand gave a stab of pain; blood trickled down his wrist, hot as melted lead. Henry swore, reached again . . . the blood-wet hand slipped. Henry lunged, missed, fell with a clatter. Someone yelled nearby. Feet pounded, a man burst into view.

"Hold it right there!" The voice was like a knife grating on bone. A whistle shrilled. Men closed in on either side; Henry saw the glint of guns. Around him, the scene held a curiously remote quality; the capsule he had swallowed was taking effect. There was a whine of turbos; the carry-all came up, light glared on its side. It halted; a big man jumped down and came up to Henry. He was a looming black outline against the blinding light.

"This him, Tasker?" somebody said.

"Sure, who was you expecting, the fat lady in the circus?" The silhouette had a meaty voice. A hand prodded Henry.

"Where's the kid, Rube? You boys had me worried there for a while; you dropped right off the scope. Where were you?"

Henry said nothing; silently, he repeated the autosuggestion which the hypnotic drug would reinforce. *I can't talk, I can't talk* . . .

"I'm talking to you, hotshot!" the big man said. He took a step closer. "I ast you where the kid was."

Henry watched; a heavy fist doubled, drew back—

Henry shifted, and swung a hearty kick that caught the big man solidly under the ribs; as he doubled, Henry uppercut him. The impact against his fist seemed as insubstantial as smoke. Someone yelled. A blow across the neck sent Henry to his knees. He saw a knee coming, turned his face in time to take it on the side of the jaw. The cold rock hurt his knees—but distantly the drug was working.

Hands were hauling him upright. The big man stood before him, holding one hand against his stomach, dabbing at his mouth with the other.

"I left myself open for that one," he said between clenched teeth. "Now let's get down to business. You got some marker tabs; hand 'em over."

Henry shook his head silently. There were men holding his arms. The big man swung a casual backhanded blow, rocked Henry's head. "Shake him down, boys," he growled.

Heavy hands slapped at Henry, turning out his pockets. His head rang from the drug and the blows he had taken. Blood trickled down his cheek from a cut on his scalp.

"Not on him, Tasker."

"Give, hotshot," Tasker said. "You think we got all night?"

"What's with this guy?" a small voice asked. "He ain't said a word."

"Yeah; that's what they call psychology. Guys that think they're tough, they figure it's easier that way; if they don't start talking they don't have to try to remember when to quit." He hit Henry again. "Of course, hotshot here knows better than that. He knows we got the stuff that will make a brass monkey deliver a lecture. He just likes to play hard to get." He swung another openhanded blow.

"That's O.K. by me," he added. "I kind of like it; takes my mind off my bellyache."

"Look, we're wasting time, Tasker. Where's the kid at?" someone called.

"Probably hiding back of a daisy someplace. He won't get far in the dark. After we work hotshot over, we'll have plenty time to collect the kid. Meantime, why not have a little fun?"

"Yeah; this is the punk that drilled Pore with his own iron—"

"To hell with Scandy; he was a skunk. This crut

clubbed *me* down . . ." A thick-set man with a drooping eyelid pushed to the fore, set himself, slammed a left and right to Henry's stomach . . .

To Henry, the pain of the blows seemed as blurred, as a badly recorded sense tape. His tongue was thick, heavy, responding to the autohypnotic suggestion. Something as soft as down tugged his arms over his head. The throbbing in his skull and chest was no more than a drumbeat now. He blinked, saw Tasker's heavy-jawed face before him—like a slab of bacon with a frown.

"This son of a bitch don't act right, Gus," he growled. A small man with dark lips and white hair came close, stared at Henry. He thumbed his eyelid back, then leaned close and sniffed.

"Ha! A wise jasper! He's coked to the eyebrows, boss. Some kind of a CNS damper and paraben hypno, I'd guess." He looked sharply at Henry. "That right, bud?"

Henry looked at the man. His vision was clear enough. He moved his fingers; he still had motor control. If he got a chance, it would be pleasant to kick Tasker again . . .

A pillow struck him in the face. "There's no use hitting him; he can't feel it," the small man said.

"Slip him some of your stuff, Gus," Tasker snapped. "He's clammed up; O.K.: I know how to open clams."

"I haven't got anything that will kill this effect. We'll have to wait until it wears off—"

"Wait, hell!" Tasker barked. "I want action—now!"

"Of course, he can hear everything we say." The

little man's deep-set eyes studied Henry's face. "Tell him you're going to break his legs, cut him up. He won't feel it, of course—but he'll know what you're doing—and if he tries hard enough, he can throw off the hypnotic inhibition on talking . . ."

Tasker's face came close. "You heard that, didn't you, hotshot? How do you feel about a little knifework? Or a busted bone or two? Like this—" He bared his teeth, brought his arm up, chopped down with terrific force. Henry heard the collarbone snap, and even through the anesthetic, pain stabbed.

"Careful—the shock to the system can knock him out . . ." The small man fingered Henry's wrist.

"Pulse is good," he commented. "He's a very rugged constitution—but exercise a little restraint."

Tasker wiped the back of his hand across his mouth. His eyes were unnaturally bright. "Restraint, yeah," he said. "You got one of them scalpels, ain't you, Gus?"

"Umm. Good idea." The little man went away.

Tasker came close. His eyes were slits, like stab wounds in a corpse.

"To hell with the kid," he said softly. "Where's the mine at?" He waited, his lips parted. His breath smelled of raw alcohol.

"I been over this ground like ants on a picnic; I'll be frank with you, hotshot. I didn't see no mine—and my plans don't call for waiting around . . ."

*If he'd come just a little closer . . .*

"Better give, sweetheart. Last chance to deal . . ."

Henry swung his foot. Tasker danced back. Gus came up, handed over a short knife with a glittering razor edge. Tasker moved it so that it caught the light, reflected into Henry's eyes.

"O.K., hotshot," he said in a crooning tone. "That's the way you want it. So now let's you and me have a talk . . ."

Henry hung in the ropes, his body laced in a net of pain like white-hot wires. His heart slammed against his ribs like a broken thing.

"You'll have to slack off," Gus said. "He's coming out of it; he's lost a great deal of blood."

"It's getting daylight," someone growled. "Look, Tasker, we got to round up the kid . . ."

"You think I don't know that?" the big man roared. "What kind of a guy is this? I done everything but gut him alive, and not a squeak out of him. Where's them tabs, you son of a one-legged joy-girl?" He shook the black crusted scalpel in a blood-stained fist before Henry's eyes. "Listen to me, you! I got a pain-killer; it works fast. As soon as you tell us where the tabs are, I'll give it to you . . ."

Henry heard the voice, but it seemed no more than a small annoyance. His thoughts were far away, wandering by a jeweled pond in the sunlight . . .

"All right, hotshot—" Tasker was close, his eyes wild. "I been saving the big one . . ." He brought the scalpel close. "I'm tired of playing around. Talk—now—or I'll gouge that eyeball out there like a spoonful of mushmelon—"

"You'd better let me close up a few of these cuts," Gus said. "And I need a blood donor; type O plus, alpha three. Otherwise he's going to die on you."

"All right; but hurry it up." Tasker turned to the men lounging around the clearing in the dim light of predawn. "You guys scatter and find the punk. Slim, take your car and run east; Grease, you cover west. The rest of you fan out south . . ."

Fingers fumbled over Henry; the net of wires drew tighter. His teeth seemed to be linked by an electric circuit which pulsed in time to the jolting in his chest.

Turbos whined into life; the high-wheeled carryalls moved off among the rock. A tinge of pink touched the sky now. Henry drew a breath, felt steel clamps cut into his side as broken ribs grated.

The small man whistled tunelessly, setting clamps with a bright-metal tool like a dentist's extractor. The sharp points cut into Henry's skin with a sensation like the touch of a feather. A grumbling man stood by, watching his blood drain into a canister hung from a low branch. Gus finished his clamping, turned to the blood donor, swabbed the long needle, plunged it into Henry's arm, smiling crookedly up at him past brown teeth.

"He felt that, Tasker. He's about ready . . ."

It was quiet in the clearing now. An early-rising song lizard burbled tentatively. The trees were visible as black shapes against a pearl-gray sky. Sud-

denly it was very cold. Henry shivered. A blunted
steel spike seemed to hammer its way up his spine
and into the base of his skull, driven by the violent
blows of his heart.

"Where'd you hide the tab?" Tasker brought the
scalpel up; Henry felt it against his eyelid. The
pressure increased.

"Last chance, hotshot," Tasker's face was close
to Henry's. "Where's that kid?"

Henry tried to draw back from the knife, but his
head was cast in lead. There was a snarl from
Tasker. Light exploded in Henry's left eye, a fountain of fire that burned, burned . . .

"Watch it! He's passing out . . ." Voices faded,
swelled, mingled with a roaring in which Henry
floated like a ship in a stormy sea, spinning, sink-
ing, down, down into blackness.


A veil of red-black hung before the left side of
Henry's face. Dim shapes moved in a pearly fog.
Strident voices nagged, penetrating the cotton-
wool dream.

" . . . I found him," Gus was saying. His voice
was urgent. "Right over there . . . hunkered down
back of your carryall."

Another voice said something, too faint to hear.

"You don't need to worry. We're your friends,"
Gus said.

"I've got my guys running all over the country,
looking for you," Tasker said heartily. "I guess
you was hiding out right here all the time, hey?"

"Where's the Captain?" Bartholomew's voice
almost squeaked.

"Don't worry about him none. Say, by the way, you haven't got the tabs on you—?"

"Where is he, damn you?" Bartholomew's voice burst out.

Henry hung slackly in the ropes that bound his wrists to the side of the carryall. By moving his remaining eye, he was able to make out the figure of Tasker, standing, feet planted wide, hands on his hips, facing away from him. Bartholomew was not in sight. Beside Tasker, Gus sidled off to the left.

"Hey, youngster, let's watch yer language," Tasker growled. "We're here to help you, like I told you . . ." He moved forward, out of range of Henry's vision.

"Leave me alone . . ." Bartholomew ordered. There was a quiver in his voice.

"Looky here, sport, I guess maybe you don't get the picture," Tasker chuckled. "Hell, we come out here to help you. We're going to get you back to Pango-Ri, where you can get that claim filed—"

"I want to see Captain Henry. What have you done with him?"

"Sure," Tasker said agreeably. "He's right over there . . ."

There was a sound of steps in the brittle snow crest underfoot. Bartholomew stepped into view, a tall figure wading through the ground mist under the tilted rocks. He stopped abruptly as he saw Henry. His mouth opened. He covered it with his hand.

"Hey, take it easy," Tasker said genially. "Ain't you ever seen blood before?"

"You . . . you . . . incredible monster . . ." Bartholomew got out.

"Say, I told you once about talking so damn smart. What the hell you think we're out here for, the fun of it? This boy's kind of stubborn; didn't want to cooperate. I done what I had to do. You can tell that to your old man; we went all the way. Now let's have those tabs and get the hell out of here."

"My God . . ." Bartholomew's eyes held on Henry, sick eyes in a pale face.

"Weak stummick, hey? Don't look at him, then. I'll call the boys in and—"

"You filthy hound—" Bartholomew turned away, stumbling.

"Hey, you crummy little cushion-pup!" Tasker's voice rose to a bellow. "I got orders to safe-conduct you back to your pa—but that don't mean I can't give you a damned good hiding first—"

The little man came into view, moving quickly after Bartholomew. A gun barked; he stumbled, fell on his face, bucked once, clawing at himself, then lay still.

There was a moment of total silence. Then Tasker roared.

"Why, you flea-brained mamma's boy, you went and shot the best damned surgeon that ever sold dope out of a Navy sick bay! You gone nuts or something . . . ?"

"Cut him down," Henry heard Bartholomew's voice. "I'm going to take him to your car. There'll be a med cabinet there—"

"Look here, buster," Tasker grated, "this bird alive is one little item I don't want around, get me? You must be outa your mind. Your old man—"

"Leave my father out of your filthy conversation! He wouldn't wipe his feet on scum like you . . ."

"He wouldn't, hey? Listen, you half-witted little milksucker, who do you think sent us out here?"

"What do you mean . . . ?"

"I mean our boy here got a little too sharp for his own good. He held your old man up for half a cut—and highpressured him into sending his pup along, just for insurance. The old man don't take kindly to anybody twisting his arm. He give orders to let hotshot here stake out his claim. Once he done that, we get the tabs and take 'em back—and you along with 'em . . . And I'll tell you, buddy-boy, you're damn lucky your old man's who he is, or I'd string you up alongside this jasper!"

"You're saying—my father sent you here?"

"That's it, junior. Your old man's quite an operator."

"You're lying! He couldn't have told you where to come; I didn't even know myself . . ."

"There's a lot you don't know, sonny. Like that beacon you got built into them trick boots you're wearing. The hotshot fooled the boys back at Pango-Ri, all right—but it didn't make no difference. I had a fix on the left heel of yours ever since you hit atmosphere." He chuckled. "What do you think of that, boy?"

"I'll show you," Bartholomew said. He moved into Henry's field of vision, a tall, slender figure with a gun in his hand.

"Hey—hold on—" Tasker started. Bartholomew brought the gun up and shot Tasker in the face.

Henry lay on the ground, looking up at the pale light that illuminated the eastern sky. A turbo started up, whined up to speed. Bartholomew jumped down, bent over him.

"Captain—can you hear me?"

Henry drew a breath, tried to move his tongue; it was five pounds of dead meat. Over his body, fire ants crawled, devouring. Deep inside, an ache swelled and throbbed. He tried again, managed a grunt.

"You're horribly injured, Captain. I'm going to try to get you into the car." Henry felt Bartholomew's hands under his. Red-hot knives plunged into his body. Then his feet were dragging. Bartholomew's heavy breathing rasped in his ear.

"I've got to try to get you up over the side now, Captain . . ." He felt the other's shoulder under his chest, lifting. The pain swelled, burst in a cloud of incandescent dust that filled the Universe . . .

He was on his back again, feeling the bed of the carry-all under him, jolting, jolting. The sky was a watery gray now, heavy with snow.

"We'll be there soon, Captain," Bartholomew was saying. "Not much farther now. We'll be there soon . . ." The turbos snarled, driving the heavy wagon at high speed, changing tone as the ground sloped upward.

"Only a little farther, Captain," Bartholomew said. "Then you'll be all right . . ."

The car was crawling now, wallowing along in deep snow. The turbos slowed to a petulant growling. The jolting which had filled the Universe since the remote beginning of time ceased suddenly, like a vast crystal soundlessly shattering. Pain poured into the sudden silence. Henry was aware of snow blowing against his face.

A voice dug at him like a knife. "I'll be back in just a minute, I have to clear the entry."

Cold seared his face, like frost on an ax blade. How the ax cut as it struck! But the blows were somehow less now, fading, like a pendulum on an ancient clock, running down . . .

Henry blinked. His left eye was glued shut. A heavy weight seemed to press into his brain. Far away a drumming sound started up, rose to a steady roaring. It reminded Henry of a waterfall he had seen once on a low-gravity world, far out toward the galactic rim. Galatea, that was it. A wide river had wound across a plain and spilled into a gorge, fanning out into a rainbowed curtain, and the scattered droplets fell around you, soft and warm . . .

But the drops were cold now, and they struck hard, hammering at him like hailstones . . .

Bartholomew was standing over him. Snowflakes clung to his cheeks, melting, running down to drip from his chin. His ship suit glistened wetly, its shoulders frosted.

"I'm going to lift you again, Captain . . ." Then there was movement, and pain, and a scent of growing things.

" . . . be all right, Captain . . ." Bartholomew was saying. "All right . . ."

The dream beckoned, but first there was something that had to be done. He tried to remember; his mind seemed to slip away so easily, back into the soft, distant dream ...

He tried again, rousing himself to urgency. *The carry-all—it would betray them. Get rid of it ... to the east, about three miles, there were high sea cliffs...*

*And the birds would soar there, floating effortlessly on wide wings, white and silent under the high sun ...*

"—operating off broadcast power from their ship," Bartholomew was saying. "They'll follow us —find our hideaway ..."

Henry could see Bartholomew's face, hollow-cheeked, colorless, unshaven, his lips black against the pale skin. Poor kid. He hadn't understood what he was up against ...

"Captain—I've got to get rid of the carryall. I'm going to head east. The map showed the coast— it's only a few miles. Maybe I can run it into the water ..."

Henry felt muscles twisting in his face. Good boy, he said clearly—then realized, with a sudden pang of dismay, that his lips hadn't moved. He tried to draw a breath—

The jaws of some ravening bird of prey clamped down on him, hurled him into a red-shot blackness. A rotten log made of fire burst open, and the grubs writhed there, deep inside him, while time passed like flowing wax ...

" . . . Captain . . . it went over. It hit an outcropping on the way down, and bounced out. It hit in deep water and sank. I don't think there'll be any signal from it. But they can follow the trail. The snow . . ."

The voice echoed on in the great hall. The lecture was dull. Henry tried to settle himself comfortably and sleep. But the chair was hard. It cut into his neck. And someone was shaking him. Morning already. And cold. He didn't want any breakfast, he was sick. Tell them . . . too sick . . .

"I salvaged a handgun and some cable, and a med kit, a small box of rations—and the tarp. I'm going to have to leave you here a few minutes while I try to find a spot . . ."

. . . Something moved in the blackness between the stars. It was a strange, arrowhead-shaped ship. Light winked from it—and his own ship leaped and shook. It fled. But the path of its flight was clear in his tracer tank.

He limped after it. It had homed for the desert world marked on the charts as Corazon. In the hills he located it—and a lance of light reached across to touch his ship and the metal flared and burned.

On foot, he moved through darkness, firing a handgun at a strange, long-legged shape in glittering black silks. He drove it back to its own ship, to the portal it had landed to build. The door was barred and locked, but he blasted it in. Then he was inside and it was hand-to-hand.

It was larger, but he was stronger. Finally, it lay still. He looked down at the strange, peaceful face

in the metal room. Face and body, clothing the
bones he had buried . . . when? Yesterday? Then
when had they fought?

But he bore it no ill will. They were both fore-
runners—outliers of their people, breakers of new
ground, claimers of new worlds. It had beaten him
in space, ship-to-ship, but body-to-body on the
ground, he had beaten and killed it. That was how
the chips fell.

. . . It had completed the receiving end of its
portal before he found it. Wondering, he put his
hand through, then stepped past the door into a
new world, with the green sky . . .

And he had almost forgotten to come back . . .


The music was gay. Dulcia, the young Dulcia,
was dancing with him at the Fire Palace . . . There
was no need to worry, Dulcie-girl, he was telling
her . . .

No need . . . . He would not leave her defenseless
to the wolves, that much he could still do for her.
If young Bartholomew was salvageable . . . if there
was enough in him to make a man . . . The Run
would show it up; and Henry would bring him
back. If he was not, if he was not fit to take care of
Dulcia after Henry was gone, then he would not
come back. Henry would see to that. She didn't
know. God willing, she would never know . . .

The boy was flesh and blood of his father. If he
was headed the way his father had gone, he would
never see Aldorado again. Time would tell.
Time . . . and the Run . . .

The music was gay. Dulcia smiled at him small and golden-haired, slim in a silvery dress with a long skirt, cut in the style of long ago. The cloth rustled, whispering. It was cold to the touch. Dulcia's face was cold. How still she lay, under the glaring lights. There was no smile on the dead lips.

"We tried to reach you, Captain. I didn't know if you'd want to authorize the surgery; fifty thousand credits—after all, this is not a charity—"

Blood ran out of the pale, fat face. The hands on his arms were like paper. He crushed the stones in his hand until blood ran out between his fingers, and for a moment it seemed the rubies themselves were bleeding . . .

He threw them against the antiseptic white floor; they bounded, sparkling red and green and blue. Stones . . .

"There's your damned fifty thousand credits! Why didn't you save her life!"

Under the harsh light, the jewels winked against dead tiles. How cold her face was . . . . They pulled at him, and he struck out, but someone had tied his arms now, and someone had broken his bones, and the pain was an awful reality that raked at him, roaring in fury . . .

Eons passed. Mountains rose up from the sea, streaming mud and the innumerable corpses of the microscopic dead. Storms beat about the peaks; rivers sparkled, carving gorges. The surf rolled across low beaches, flat in the white sunlight. Ice formed, broke with a booming as of distant cannon.

He lay in the icy surf, stirred by the breakers that tugged, tugged, unceasingly.

" . . . have to wake up, Captain. Don't die . . ."

His eye was open. He saw Bartholomew's face quite clearly. *If only he could explain that he was encased in ice; the boy would understand that it mustn't be broken, or the pain would flood back in . . .*

Henry blinked. He saw Bartholomew's expression brighten. The kid was having a tough time of it. Henry drew a breath; he wanted to tell him . . . . But no voice came.

His tongue—my God, had Tasker cut his tongue out . . . ? With an agonizing effort, Henry pushed, bit down—

There was a stab of pain like a candle flame against charred wood. He felt a hot tingle of reaction. His chest moved in a ghost of a laugh. What did it matter whether a corpse had a tongue . . . ?

Something fumbled at his arm.

"I have the med kit here. This is supposed to kill pain. I hope it helps, Captain."

*It's all right, Larry. I don't feel a thing, as long as I lie still. You see, I'm inside this cake of warm ice . . . .*

*No, dammit. Keep your thoughts clear. This is that last lucid spell before the end; . . . . don't louse it up with fantasies. Poor kid. How the hell will he get back? It's a long walk; twelve hundred miles, mountains, deserts, bogs—and winter coming on. He's got a year—a short Corazonian year—to file his claim . . . .*

Bartholomew's face was strained. "I'm going to try to set the bones, Captain. I can do it, all right, I think. I took a course at the State Institute . . . ."

*Don't waste time on me, Larry. Tasker's men will*

*be showing up, up above, any time now. They'll see the tracks, all right. Maybe they'll come in after us, maybe not. A shame for those bastards to get their hands on this . . . .*

*You'd be safe here—if you ran, hid in the woods —but what will you eat? Maybe, if you start back now, before the snow fills the passes . . . . But it's cold out there; the storm's just starting. It might last a week—or two weeks. There's nothing to eat here—but if you leave, the wind and snow will get you. Don't worry about the tabs, they don't matter any more. Too bad. Dulcia will be O.K.; she's a smart girl—*

*But Old Man Bartholomew; I should have figured that angle . . . a tough old pirate . . . fooled me . . .*

"All right, Captain. I'm going to start now . . ."

The real pain began then. It went on and on. After a while Henry forgot it. He forgot the broken bones and the new world, found and lost again so soon, and the storm that howled beyond the portal, and the men above who hunted them and the endless wilderness that stretched to Pango-Ri. He forgot all these things, and many more, and it was as though they had never been; and he was alone in the darkness that is between the stars.

And then he was remembering. First the pain, of course; then the reason for the pain . . . .

That was a little more difficult. There had been the order to disengage and pull back to Leadpipe. His boat had been hit . . . a rough landing, and then the fire. Amos—

Amos was changed. His face—all wrinkled, and

his red hair gone—

Amos was dead. Something about a garden, and jewels—and a girl! Dulcia—but not Dulcia. Only something in her smile, and the curve of her cheek as she sat by the fire . . .

Old Man Bartholomew. Don't trust him. He wants—

The Run. Young Bartholomew was with him; smoke, and burned bearings . . .

No. That was O.K. Just the hand. But maybe they'd piled in—

He opened his eyes . . . .

Just one eye. A knife had done that. But it was a dream. My God, what a dream. Let it fade, lose itself in the shadows of the night . . . . It was good to be back in his own bed; but the mattress was hard. Where was Dulcia?

"Captain . . . ?"

Henry made out a vague form bending over him. It was a boy—Larry . . . the name came from somewhere. What was he doing here . . .

"I've got some soup for you . . . " Larry's voice shook. He went away. The light was brighter now. Larry was back. His face was like a skull with skin stretched over it. He was wearing a false beard half an inch long. It was ridiculous; Henry wanted to laugh. The false face had fooled him for a moment.

Something warm touched his lips; an indescribably delicious flavor flooded his mouth. He felt his throat contract painfully. More of the warm fluid came. It burned its way down. Henry ate eagerly, lost in the ecstasy of hunger appeased . . .

Later, Bartholomew was back.

"I rigged a sort of bunk out of the tarp, to get you up off the ground. I was worried, Captain. Almost a week. I was afraid you'd starve. I saved the canned rations for you . . ."

Larry talked. It was a long story he was telling. Henry wondered why he talked so much. What was it about, anyway . . . ?"

" . . . I went up again, three times. I didn't see any signs of them . . . . I saw a few animal tracks. I'm going to try to hunt . . ."

Sometimes he wondered who Larry was, and he would rouse himself to ask, but always it was too hard, too hard, and he would sink back, and Larry would lean over him, with anxious eyes, and then the room would fade and he would roam again through great deserted valleys where icy winds blew without surcease, toil up lonely hills whose tops were hidden in mist, following lost voices which called always from beyond the next divide.

He was looking at a hand—a broken claw, twisted, marked across by purplish scars, vivid against the pale skin.

Gray light gleamed wanly through a narrow cleft in a wall of rock. Snowflakes blew in, swirling, to settle melting, in a long puddle. Shaggy animal hides lay scattered on the floor. A wisp of smoke rose from a heap of embers against a blackened wall. There was a stack of blackish firewood, two crude clay dishes, and a large pot, a heap of shredded greens, and a joint of purplish-black meat. It was a strange dream—almost real.

Henry moved to push himself up to a sitting position. There was a weight against his chest, pressing him back. He gritted his teeth, raised himself to one elbow. An odor of wood smoke and burned meat hung in the air, and a thick, cloying reek of uncured hides. A coarse-haired fur lay across his lap. He reached to throw it back—

His head rang from the blow it took as he fell. What the hell was wrong with him? Drugged, maybe?

His eye fell on the butt of a Mark IX pistol. Beside it was a pair of boots, caked with mud—and with a darker stain.

His boots. Quite suddenly, he remembered.

Tasker, and the little man, Gus. He had supplied the scalpel. They had strung him up, and carved him into strips. And he had died, and gone to hell.

And now he was here, alive.

Strange.

A pulse thudded like the beat of a hammer in Henry's temples. Larry Bartholomew had killed Tasker—and Gus. Some kid! Well, life was full of surprises. And he had brought him here—somehow—and kept him alive.

Henry moved then, pushed himself over, face down, got his hands under him, pushed himself up to a sitting position. His left hand—it was useless, a frozen tangle of broken fingers. But the right— it would hold a gun . . . .

No telling how long the boy had wasted here, nursing him back to a dim half life. Feeding soup to a broken body that should have died . . . .

He could reach the blaster; one quick squeeze, and the agony would be over. And Larry could make a start for Pango-Ri. Henry dragged himself, feeling the cold of the rough wet floor against his body. He rested, with his face against the stone. He had a beard, he noticed. He touched it with his left hand; over half an inch; a month's growth, anyway. Damn! A wasted month, with winter setting in. If the boy had started back as soon as he had killed Tasker . . .

He reached the plastic case by the pallet of furs, fumbled the blaster out. He set it on narrow beam, dragged it up until the cold muzzle pressed against the thudding pulse above his ear—pressed the firing stud.

Nothing happened. The blaster fell with a clatter. He lay, limp, breathing in wracking, shallow gasps.

He'd never committed suicide before. It was quite an experience. Even when it didn't work.

Larry had used the blaster for hunting, exhausted the charge. So much for the easy way. Now, he would have to crawl outside—as soon as the faintness passed.

Bartholomew was squatting beside him. "Easy, Captain. Easy. You're better! You crawled all that way—but what in the name of sanity were you doing? It's cold over here . . ."

Henry looked at Bartholomew leaning over him, draped in a long-haired animal hide. His face had aged; the skin was rough, scored red by the wind and snow, with a network of tiny red veins across the cheekbones, from frostbite. His beard was thick, black, curling around his mouth, meeting the tangle of overlong hair about his ears. There were lines beside the mouth. He was holding up two bedraggled creatures, half rabbit, half bird.

"I'll broil these, Captain! They ought to be good! You should be able to take a little solid food now!"

Bartholomew bustled over the crude pots. "You'll feel even better after you eat, Captain. I've got some plant hearts here—ice bushes, I call them—they're not bad. I've tried just about every-thing. We need some sort of fresh vegetable along with the meat. And hunting's getting harder up above, Captain. There seems to be no wildlife—out there . . ." He nodded toward the shimmering wall.

He talked, building up the fire, setting out pots, cutting up the small carcasses with a short-bladed pocketknife. He roasted the animals whole, then cut off choice bits, fed them to Henry with his fingers. Henry's mouth gulped them down like an automatic disposer, as though his appetite were a thing apart from the rest of his body.

"Captain, soon you'll be strong enough to talk; we have so many things to discuss—so many plans to make."

With a mighty effort, Henry pushed the food away, shook his head. Bartholomew stared at him, then at the bit of meat in his fingers.

"You must eat, Captain—"

Henry shook his head again, fell back, breathing hard, his eyes fixed on Bartholomew's.

"What is it, Captain?" Bartholomew put the clay pot of meat aside, crouched over Henry. "What's wrong?" His expression changed abruptly.

"Captain—you CAN hear me . . . ?"

Henry managed a nod.

"And you're strong enough—you eat easily enough. Captain—why don't you speak?"

Henry felt the pulse throb in his temples. He drew a breath, concentrated every ounce of energy on forming a word . . .

A grunt . . .

"You *know* me, don't you, Captain? I'm Larry—"

Henry nodded.

"You were injured. But you're safe here now. You understand that, don't you?"

Henry nodded.

"Then—why don't you speak?"

Henry's chest rose and fell, rose and fell. Perspiration trickled down the side of his face.

Bartholomew's face stiffened. His hand dropped from Henry's shoulder.

"Good Lord, Captain . . ." His voice broke. "You haven't spoken—because you can't! Your voice is gone; you're a mute . . . !"

"It's all right," Bartholomew was saying. "It must have been the shock; I've heard of such things. You'll get your voice back eventually. Meanwhile, I'll just ask you questions—and you can nod, or shake your head. All right?"

Henry nodded. Bartholomew settled himself, pulled his fur about his shoulders, adjusted Henry's malodorous coverlet.

"Are you comfortable? Warm enough?"

Henry nodded impatiently, watching Bartholomew's face. *To hell with that! Ask me about the weather, the mountains, the winter setting in . . .*

"Do you remember . . . what happened?" Bartholomew looked anxious. Henry nodded. Bartholomew swallowed. "You . . . were right, of course, Captain. I . . . I never dreamed such men really existed—"

Henry raised his head. *Why didn't the boy get on with it—get to the important things?*

"I've concentrated on hunting and gathering firewood. In the evening, I've been skinning animals, and trying to scrape the hides and sew them together . . ." He tugged at his cape; the green hide crackled. "I'm afraid I'm not very good at it. And I made the pots from clay—there are great slabs of it along the river—" He broke off.

"But, of course, that's not important. Captain, do you suppose they'll send out search parties from Pango-Ri?"

Henry shook his head.

"They won't find us . . . ?" Bartholomew's voice trailed off. Henry opened his eye. *Now they would be getting to the point . . .*

"I suppose I knew that . . . with a whole world to be lost in. But we're running out of food. Game is getting scarcer—the cold, I suppose. And I haven't dared try anything from—the other side . . ."

Bartholomew was getting to his feet. "You're tired, Captain. You'd better sleep now. We'll talk again tomorrow—"

Henry tried to sit up, shaking his head, watching Larry's face.

"But I'll bring you food, Captain—and I'll keep the fire up. You'll see! We'll be fine, Captain. And you'll get better—soon . . ."

There were tears on Bartholomew's face. He wiped at his eyes with the back of his hand. "You have to be all right, Captain!"

*Yeah. Otherwise little Larry Bartholomew would be on his own. So that was what was bothering him . . .*

"I think I understand, Captain. You think that you might slow me down—be a, well, burden. Nonsense! We'll wait here until the worst of the cold weather has passed, and by then you'll be—"

Henry was shaking his head.

"You're thinking of the claim? The time limit?"

Henry shook his head.

"Then you think—we won't manage through the winter?"

Henry nodded, waiting for the next question . . . .

Bartholomew chewed his lip. "Then you'll just have to hurry up and get well, Captain."

Henry shook his head wearily.

"Oh, yes you will, Captain. I'm not leaving without you."

Henry nodded angrily.

"You feel we'll have to go soon—before the weather gets even worse. Very well; I understand. We'll go as soon as you're ready—and don't bother shaking your head—I'm not going without you. So if you want me to get back and file the claim, you'll have to try very hard to get well, Captain. You see that, don't you?"

Henry looked at Bartholomew. There were fine lines around his eyes—the weeks of no sleep, overwork, and cold had left their marks. His eyes held steady on Henry's.

Henry opened his mouth; Bartholomew fed him a charred lump. He sighed and lay with closed eyes, chewing the rank, tough meat.

"You're sitting up very nicely, Captain," Bartholomew nodded and smiled. "Perhaps tomorrow you can try standing."

Henry shook his head. He laid the bowl aside, fumbled with his hands for a grip on the wall beside him.

"I don't think you ought to try it yet . . ." Bartholomew fluttered, then took Henry's arm. "But I suppose you're determined . . ."

Henry gripped Bartholomew's shoulder. It felt solid under his hand; hunting and hauling wood and rope-climbing were filling out the boy's lean frame. Then he let go, leaned against the wall.

It was a strange feeling to be standing again—or almost standing—after—how long? Six weeks now? His legs were like rotten sticks.

"Captain, that's marvelous; now you'd better lie down again—"

Henry held on, straining to move the left leg; it hung limp and dead. He clamped his teeth, heaved; the leg twitched, O.K.; at least it wasn't paralyzed. Now the right . . .

"Really, Captain . . ."

Henry struggled, concentrating on the leg. It was the bad one; the broken knee hadn't turned out too well. He leaned his weight on the left leg, the toes of the crooked right leg just touching the floor. He was already dizzy—and all he'd done so far was get to his feet and lean on the wall.

Bartholomew moved to help him. "Careful, Captain, you can't afford a fall—"

He shook his head, elbowed himself from the wall, stood teetering. *God, how the hell did a kid ever learn this balancing act!* He put the short leg forward, then hopped. His leg was like a stick of soft clay. Bartholomew was chewing his lip, getting ready to jump for him . . .

The right leg again; another hop. *Watch it; almost went over that time.*

"Wonderful, Captain! That's enough for this time. Let me help you back now." He came across, reached for Henry's arm. Henry motioned him back. *One more step first.* He took a breath, felt his heart thud. *To hell with the pain; that's nothing. Getting across the room—it just takes one more step. And another. And another . . .*

"I don't like that wind, Captain. You shouldn't try it today. Probably tomorrow it will have died down. After two months, another day won't matter." Bartholomew looked at him anxiously.

Wrapped in his stiff fur clothing, Henry pushed at the cape with the twisted left hand, gripped the stick with the right. It was amazing how much you could do with a hand, even with three fingers broken and stiff, as long as the tendons hadn't been cut.

He moved across to the entry with his hopping gait, his left elbow pressed to the side where badly mended ribs ached under their tight binding. The scars on his face itched under the two-inch beard —a tangle of gray and white. He staggered as the icy wind whipped through the opening; Bartholomew boosted and hauled him up, out into the stinging mist of blown snow. He squinted his eye

against the cold that cut at him like a great knife;
the cape lifted, slapping at his back. His breath
seemed to choke off in his throat. He took a step;
Bartholomew was beside him, his arm under
Henry's. "Watch out, Captain! That breeze is
pretty strong."

Bartholomew tightened Henry's pack straps. He
moved his shoulders, felt the dull pang from his
left side. The coat Bartholomew had stitched up
for him felt better now; and his boots fitted better,
too, with the fur linings stuffed inside.

"Captain, are you sure it wouldn't be better to
wait until tomorrow, just on the off-chance—"

Henry shook his head, started unsteadily across
toward the edge of the grove.

The prints of Larry's shaggy homemade
mukluks were bare patches of black rock through
the powdery snow. They led up a sharp incline
among tumbled boulders. Henry fought his way
up, scrabbling with one hand and an elbow, grop-
ing with feet that were like old boots filled with
ice water.

There was Larry's face, Larry's hand reaching
out to help, Larry's voice: " . . . we've made a start!
We're on our way!"

*Uh-huh. We've gone fifty feet. Only twelve hun-
dred miles to go.*

Henry ducked his head against the wind, started
off down the blizzard-swept slope. Forget about
the pain. *Walk as if you knew how. What's pain,
anyway? Nature's little warning. O.K. I've been
warned. Just make the legs work, one after the
other, and don't think about anything else.*

It was hard, counting the paces. Ten; and then fifteen. Then twenty. Five times that, and it would be a hundred. *Nine more hundred and it would be a thousand. Another couple of thousand, and I'll have walked a mile.*

*Where was I? Twenty-five? Four times twenty-five is a hundred . . . .*

*To hell with that. All right so far. Thirty paces. Thirty-one steps from the room; thirty-two crab steps away from the nest by the fire . . . God how it hurts . . . .*

Bartholomew's hand was under his arm. "You're doing fine, Captain." He had to yell to make himself heard over the shrilling of the wind, through the muffling fur turned up about Henry's ears. The boy hadn't done a bad job, making the parkas. And he'd killed the animals and skinned them out, too. Not bad, for a lad who'd never chased anything livelier than a statistic in his life. Larry might make it; stranger things had happened. If he didn't panic. If he had luck with the hunting, before he tackled the passes. If he didn't get lost. If—

If he had a magic carpet, he could fly back to Pango-Ri. Never mind the ifs.

Damn! He'd lost count again. *Call it fifty. Still on my feet. Getting a little numb, but that's O.K.; I can't feel the wind now. Frostbite is the least of my worries. Fifty-five. Thank God the ground's level here, no gullies to scramble through. Just put the foot, hop, put the foot, hop. It's easy. Just do it enough, then you can rest. Lie down in this nice white, clean stuff, and dream off into wherever it is*

*that memories go when they're forgotten, and let
Larry get on with the business of surviving....*

He was aware of Bartholomew's hand on his
arm.

"Half a mile, Captain. The going gets a little
rough ahead, I'm afraid. Broken ground, and rock
fragments—"

Henry's foot caught on an upjutting projection;
he stumbled, tried to stiffen his legs; they folded
like paper. He went down, sagging in Bartholomew's arms.

"I'm sorry, Captain! I should have stopped for a
break before now, but you were moving along so
well..." Henry slumped in the snow. His chest
burned; the right knee pulsed like a great boil,
ready for lancing. His side—the damned ribs felt
as though they hadn't even started to knit; the raw
ends were grating together...

"A few minutes' rest...you'll feel better..."
Bartholomew fumbled in his monstrous pack,
brought out something. He worked over it...

An odor of hot beef stew struck Henry's nostrils
with an almost painful intensity; his salivary
glands leaped into action with a stab like a hot
needle behind his jaws.

"I saved this, Captain...for the march."

Then he was chewing, swallowing. Food. It was
better than rest, better than warmth, better than
the most elaborate pleasures devised in the
harems of kings. He finished, pushed himself to a
sitting position, got his feet under him. Larry was
helping him up. He stood, still tasting the wonderful stew.

"Watch your footing now, Captain." Bartholomew's hand was under his arm; he leaned on it, tried a step. It worked. Ahead, the gray landscape stretched off into the mist of blown snow. It was a little like life—a foggy vista into which you pressed on, and on. And when you had gone as far as you could—and you fell and the snow covered you—the unknown goal was as far ahead, as unattainable as ever . . . .

The knee was the worst part; his face was nicely anesthetized by the cold, and the side had settled down to a dull explosion that pulsed in counterpoint to the fire in his lungs, and the drag-hop, drag-hop was a routine, like breathing, that seemed to carry itself along by its own momentum. But the knee . . . . Surely, there were bone chips grinding the flesh to shreds. The pain ran up to his hip, down to his ankle.

They had stopped. Henry looked around, saw nothing but endless snow.

"We've done a mile and a half, Captain. Shall we take a short rest now?" Bartholomew's voice was an irritation, penetrating the simple equation of agony and endurance. Henry shook his head; he took a step, faltered for a moment, then caught up the rhythm again.

He drew a deep breath; that was a mistake—the fire leaped up, chokingly, died slowly back to the cozy bed of red-hot embers. That was fine; it was keeping him warm. But the knee . . . . How long could a man walk on a broken leg? There was only one way to find out.

Later, he was sitting with his back against a

drift of snow, the bad knee propped before him, the pain only a remote thump, like a doctor's rubber mallet against a wooden leg. Bartholomew had his arm, doing something to it. He felt the brief pang of a hypospray.

The snow was red, cut by the black shadows of tall trees.

"We'll camp here, where we have a little shelter," Bartholomew said. He was roasting a curiously scaled and beaked creature with a meaty tail, over a tiny fire.

"This is some sort of relative of the rabbity things I shot, back at the portal. I'm sure it will be edible. A pity it smells so much like burning butadiene."

Henry stared into the small, bluish flames. It had been a memorable day. Walking, falling, getting up, walking . . .

"I think it's done, Captain." Bartholomew took the roast from the spit, sawed off a joint, passed it over to Henry. "I think we're going to be all right for game from now on; there are a lot of these fellows around. I shot three; I'm letting them freeze as reserve supplies."

Good boy. Hang on to the food. Twenty thousand feet; that's four miles, straight up. Figure an average thirty-degree slope . . . A squared plus B squared . . . call it a nine-mile trek to the summit of the pass. It might be possible. It depended on things like snow depths, winds, unseen crevasses, avalanches, snow blindness, or little unscalable rock faces a few inches higher than a man could jump . . .

Better tell him to rig some grapple hooks—out

of what? And how to tell him? Tramp out letters in the snow?

The meat was good—a little like turtle flesh, but tenderer. There was no salt, no melted butter, no silver and linen and thin glass and fragile porcelain, no candles and wine . . . but by God, it was as rare a feast as had ever been laid before a hungry man.

"More, Captain? It's rather good, isn't it? I wonder if the animals would be easy to raise, commercially? It's a mystery what they live on; nothing here but rock and ice . . ."

Bart rambled on. Henry half-listened, his mind drifting off on side trails. Old Man Bartholomew; would he live up to his agreement—if Larry did get back with the claim? Too bad Amos wasn't there, to look out for Dulcie's interests. He'd wanted to come pretty bad. Poor Amos. But maybe he was lucky at that. His death hadn't been an easy one, but then these last few weeks were a memory a man could do without, too . . .

"We'd better tuck in now, Captain. A long day ahead tomorrow."

Henry nodded, managed to move, crawl the three feet to the tiny tent. Bartholomew helped him inside; God, how it stank! But it broke the force of the wind, and kept the snow out of his face. He pulled his blanket of fur over him, settled himself. *So this was the way it ends; you eat dinner, and go to bed . . . .* Henry closed his eyes. *And that was that . . . .*

There was a smell of vulcanizing rubber, and for an instant, Henry was back in a town on a small, backward world called Northroyal, standing in the tree-shaded courtyard of an inn, watching the stableman weld a new set of retreads to the worn wheels of the little red two-seater that he and Dulcia had driven down from the port . . . .

"Breakfast is about ready, Captain," Bartholomew was silhouetted against the pale light that filtered through the tent flap. The cold bit at Henry's nose like pliers. He moved, felt stabs from every joint.

*Doctor prescribes long, invigorating walks in the open air for the patient; this is guaranteed to give him an understanding of how a mummy would feel, if you unwrapped him in a cold-storage vault . . . .*

He lay, listening to the thump of his heart, the rasp of breath in his throat. So he was still alive! He moved his right leg tentatively. Fresh, vivid pain flooded up from it. Oh yes, he was alive, all right! That wasn't what the program had called for. When a man—sick unto death, with more half-healed wounds than the average accident ward, undernourished and poorly clad—spent a long day overexerting in sub-freezing weather—and then went to sleep in the snow—he was expected to die of exposure, if nothing else.

But instead, he was alive—awake—still a dead weight on young Bartholomew's back—and time was running out even for a healthy man, alone, to have a chance of making it.

Henry drew a deep breath; his chest gave a dutiful stab of agony. He got his hands under him, sat up. There was a moment of vertigo; the ribs complained a little more. He rolled over, worked his

way out of the tent, feeling the icy fingers of the
fitful morning breeze nipping at him. The food
smelled better now; he was getting used to the
stink. Knowing how it tasted helped; it was like
cheese in that respect. He took a mouthful of
snow, let it melt and trickle down. Bartholomew
handed across a slab of meat. Henry bit into it. It
was burned on the outside, chilled in the center.
He ate it hungrily.

"I slept on the breakfast steaks, Captain," Bartholomew said cheerfully. "Didn't want them to
freeze. We're getting an early start; sun won't be
up for another half hour."

Life was a perverse damned phenomenon; if
there were a prize waiting for him just across the
next rise, a pretty girl, a bank account, a vacation,
all expenses paid—

He'd have dropped dead a hundred yards from
the cave.

But all there was was twelve hundred miles of
wilderness or maybe eleven hundred and ninety-
five, now. And he was good for another hour, or
two, or three, of dragging himself on, spinning out
the declining threads . . .

"The wind's behind us now," Bartholomew said.
"That will help some, of course, but I imagine it
will bring colder weather. I'd say it's down close
to thirty degrees of frost now. I suppose a little
more won't make much difference."

*No, not much; it would just freeze you, standing
up, between one step and the next; it would kill a
patch of exposed skin quicker than a dozen un-
shielded megacuries. But that might make it easier;*

*a fast death was more fun any day than this teasing along...*

Bartholomew folded the tent, strapped up his pack, hoisted it onto his back. He stood before Henry.

The damned fool was actually grinning.

"We're going to make good time today, Captain. I have a feeling." He took Henry's arm; Henry shrugged him off, got to his feet unassisted. Why the hell had he been letting the boy waste strength, supporting him, saving his own waning vitality? It was almost as though dying wasn't what he wanted at all...

Later, he was sure it was. It wasn't as though there were any hope of surcease, ever; the supply of miles was limitless; the depths of cold only skimmed so far. And if some weatherproof St. Bernard came along now, with a keg of miracles hung around his neck—

He'd still be a mute, one-eyed cripple, pitifully maimed, horribly scarred, lacking all sorts of useful parts. A man wouldn't want to live in that condition, even if he weren't a drag on the living. That was simple enough. Why, then, did he go on, head down, parka hood pulled close about his face lurching grotesquely onward, teeth clenched against the pain, while thoughts of food, and warm beds, and blessed rest tormented him like jeering imps?

Time lost its meaning. There are an infinity of infinities within infinity; and an infinity of eternities within eternity. Forever passed, while he endured; then there was a time of lying in the snow, mindless with exhaustion, and then the brief, sharp sensation of food, and then again, eternity . . .

The sun was high, a pale disk in a glaring sky; later it hung in the west, shedding its cold light without the faintest hint of heat, smaller than it should be, subtly the wrong color. Bartholomew was moving about, making a fire, chattering.

" . . . a good twelve miles, I'd estimate. And the mountains are closer than we thought. It's the misty air; it makes things look far away. We're almost into the foothills now; the ground was rising for the last hour's hike today . . ."

The voice tuned in and out.

" . . . do you agree, Captain?"

Was the boy still asking questions of the oracle —the halt, the lame, the half-blind oracle, dying before his eyes?

*Sure. Anything you say. It doesn't matter. Let's get going.* Henry swallowed, got to his feet, pulled away angrily as Bartholomew attempted to help him with his pack. The younger man started off, stamping away through foot-deep snow; and Henry followed.

The peak loomed over them, dominating the sky. The wind had shifted again, blowing across the slope from the west now, bringing a stinging hail of snow particles. The drifts were deeper here— dry, powdery drifts, that flowed underfoot like desert dust, each footprint sending down a minor avalanche. Henry's eye burned from the white glare. Ahead, Bartholomew stamped on, long-legged, tall, bounding up the slope like a deer, then waiting while Henry dragged his way up behind him.

"I don't like the look of the clouds, Captain," he called. "They have a sort of yellowish tinge; I'm afraid that means more snow . . . . And it's getting dark fast . . . ."

Henry came up, kept going; the long slope stretched ahead, white, smooth, blue-shadowed, rising in an unbroken sweep to the far heights of the pass. Why waste time talking about the weather? Just keep going, up, up, into the cold, into the thin air, thinking about nothing except the fact that it was reach the summit—or die here.

He had fallen, and Bartholomew was pulling at his arm. Henry groped, got his feet under him, struggled up. Couldn't let the boy waste his strength. Had to go on . . . as far as he could . . . walk on until the plunging heart burst. Maybe someday their bodies would be found, frozen deep inside a glacier of blue ice, preserved intact, a silent memento of the old days, long ago, when men had come, barehanded, to tame the alien world . . . .

He was down again. Bartholomew's hands hauled at him. The wind howled, drowning the boy's words. He shook his head; heavy, wet snow was caked against his lips, his eye. He thrust with his feet, found a purchase, crawled forward another foot. It was easier this way. The ground sloped steeply up here. He reached, with one hand and one crippled claw; his feet groped. Another foot. Where was Larry now? Good boy; not wasting his strength any more. Gone on ahead . . . . He could rest now . . . .

Bartholomew was back, pulling at him. Still at it . . . still determined to coax a dead man over a mountain. Couldn't let the boy wear himself out that way . . . . Go on, a little farther. Die, body . . . . Die, and let both of us rest . . . .

He couldn't remember why the operation was necessary. It had been going on for such a long time. The anesthetic was wearing off; he could feel the scalpel cutting in—cutting into his eye—

No, it was his knee. They had cut it off, and now they were welding a steel joint in place. The fools. You couldn't weld steel to flesh! And the gas he was breathing; the welding torch had started a fire; the gas was burning, and he was breathing in the pale flames, the blue fire that was burning his chest out . . . .

It was a hell of a funeral. The pallbearers were carrying him, head down—without even a coffin. A man needed a coffin. It was cold, when you were dead, without a box to keep off the icy wind. And they had stripped the body, too. And someone had cut off his hands, and his feet—

The stumps ached—but not as badly as the knee. They had tried to cut that off, too, but it had been too hard. That was because it was made of steel . . . .

The explosion jarred Henry alive. The end of the world. In a moment the other bodies which had been blown out of the graveyard would come raining down . . . .

" . . . sorry . . . Captain . . ."

There was one of them now. Not a body, though. It had spoken.

What were the words? Sorry . . .

Oh, how sorry a man was, once it was all over —sorry for all the lost opportunities, all the cruel words, all the joys untasted, all the little trusts betrayed . . . .

Couldn't be . . . much farther . . ." Henry heard. *Much farther. Much farther . . .*

" . . . a minute . . . try again . . ."

Try again. If only a man could. The awful thing about death was the barrier that stood between you and all the things that you should have done, once, long ago, when you were still alive.

But if you could push through the barrier . . .

Perhaps if you tried . . .

There had been something that someone had wanted. It had been a simple thing, if he could only remember . . .

"Please, Captain. Wake up. Wake up . . ."

That was it. He had to wake up. That meant to open his eye . . .

No, that was too hard. It was easier just to pretend he was awake—and who would know the difference? It was a clever idea. Henry wanted to laugh aloud. He would pretend to be awake. He would move his legs—that was important, he seemed to know, somehow—and his arms . . .

One arm was gone. Yes, someone had cut it off once—But the other was there. It had a steel hand at the end of it, and he would reach out, catch it on something, pull, then reach out again . . . .

The shout rang, loud and clear—cut off quickly. Henry waited, listening. He heard the screech of wind, the beat of blood inside his skull; nothing more.

He was on a mountain—he remembered that. He remembered the funeral clearly . . . .

But someone had shouted. He was alone, here, on the mountain that dead men climbed—and yet a shout had sounded just ahead . . . .

His arm was a grappling hook. He threw it out, caught it, pulled himself forward. It was not an easy way to travel, but it seemed correct, somehow. He pulled, reached again, touched nothing. Strange. He pushed with his feet, stretching . . .

The world was tilting under him. He poised for a dizzy moment, hanging in air—and then he was falling—and then a shock, an instant of wrenching pain—and a vast softness that enveloped him in silence through which, far away, a voice called.

There was an odor of wood smoke and hot food. Henry pried his eye open. He was half sitting, half lying against a fur-padded wall of rock. Overhead, a ledge slanted down to a curtain of animal hides. Beside him, Bartholomew squatted by a small fire, feeding twigs to the flames.

"Just in time for dinner," Bartholomew croaked. His eyes were bright, set deep in a weather-ravaged face above an ice-matted black beard. "I dug you out of the snowbank; it broke your fall."

Henry's hands ached. He lifted one, stared at flushed, dusky-red fingers.

"Your hands were pretty cold, Captain, but I

massaged them by the fire; I think they'll be all right. My feet were a bit chilled, too."

Henry looked, saw bloody rags of fur wrapped around Bartholomew's lower legs. He leaned back, closed his eyes.

"You understand, don't you, Captain?" Bartholomew said hoarsely. "We've made it across the mountains; we're over the pass and a couple of hundred feet down the south slope. We're going to make it, Captain! We're going to make it . . . ."

Standing in the autumnal clearing, Captain Henry pressed the stiff fingers of his right hand against his thigh; pain shot up to his elbow. He pressed harder. The knuckle joints yelled reluctantly; the fingers bent a quarter of an inch.

There was a sound of footsteps tramping through underbrush. Bartholomew came into view, black-bearded, wide-shouldered; there were half a dozen bug-eyed, thin-bodied animals looped to his belt. He tossed them down, unslung his bow and quiver, crouched in the snow by the fire with the short-bladed knife he used for skinning.

"Spider rats," he said. "No other game."

Henry picked up the bow clumsily with his stiff-fingered right hand, looked at it critically, then pointed to the game and nodded.

"I'm getting quite accurate," Bartholomew said. "I picked off that last fellow at over thirty yards."

Henry drew the blaster clumsily from the

holster at his hip, closed his thumb and little finger around it, tried to fit his forefinger around the firing stud. The gun dropped to the ground. Henry shook his head angrily, bent stiffly to pick up the weapon, holstered it, and resumed his pacing, working at the stiff fingers.

"I saw traces of another camp fire," Bartholomew said. "Not over a week old."

Henry picked up a stick, smoothed a muddy patch with his boot, scratched words. Bartholomew craned to read them:

WE'LL SET WATCH TONIGHT

Bartholomew nodded. He reached up, caught a three-inch branch, with a pull brought it crashing down. He stripped off the twigs and broke it over his knees. His leather jerkin had split up the side, days before; through the tear, Henry could see the play of heavy lateral muscles under the shirt. His face was burned dark by the weather; the powerful lines of his neck rose from wide, solid shoulders. His forearm, wrist, hand were tanned, sinewy. He had changed, these last months on the trail.

There was a flicker of motion among the trees; Bartholomew dropped, whipped his bow clear, and nocked an arrow in one motion. Henry hauled the blaster from the holster at his side. His fingers closed clumsily on the grip. A long-legged, long-necked creature bounded from a coppice, scrambled up the slope, kicking up a scatter of rotted vegetation. Henry brought the blaster up, fumbled at the firing stud. A brief glare winked against the nearby tree trunks—

Bartholomew's bow twanged; an arrow flashed.

The beast stumbled, struck, and rolled, kicking, coming to rest with oddly jointed legs atangle.

The two men moved up; Bartholomew's bolt projected from behind the left shoulder blade, the bare-scraped wood white against the smooth gray pelt. Beyond, a wisp of smoke curled up from a tree trunk, scorched by Henry's miss.

Bartholomew took out the skinning knife, set to work. Henry picked up the empty water bottle in his better hand, set off downslope. A hundred feet from the clearing he halted abruptly, peering through underbrush at a hut among the trees.

It was a flimsy construction of prefab plastic panels. Around it, nothing stirred. There were two small windows on the side facing him; dark, empty squares of translucent plastic. Dead leaves were drifted against the side of the shack; wild spring flowers clustered about a weathered refuse heap.

He moved back softly, retraced his steps to the clearing where Bartholomew was turning steaks over the fire. As the younger man looked up, Henry motioned. Bartholomew's bow leaped into his hand.

Henry turned, led the way back through the deep forest trail. They circled the hut, moved closer. A quarter of an hour later they stood by the front of the deserted structure. There was a blaster burn on the curled plastic panel. The door hung open, its lock broken. Henry stepped through into an odor of mold and decay. A badly rotted corpse was curled in a corner. Behind Henry, Bartholomew peered at the shriveled face. Henry went across to a weather-stained chest, pulled open a drawer; a twelve-legged spider leaped out, scuttled away.

"They deliberately smashed everything before they abandoned the place . . . ." Bartholomew opened a wall locker. Dusty garments dangled from hooks. He pulled out a musty ship suit, tried the control; the fabric warmed to the touch.

"Here, Captain—you'll sleep warm from now on."

Henry's scarred face twitched in a crooked smile. He began stripping away his rotted furs.

Bartholomew took a box from the shelf, opened it. "They left us a few amenities! God, won't it be wonderful to wash—and get rid of these ghastly whiskers?"

Henry looked into the mirror; under grizzled brows, a single bright eye set in a gray-whiskered face carved of scarred and ancient leather stared back at him. Lank white hair fell in tangles to his shoulders. Behind him, Bartholomew's scissors snicked. He caught Henry's eye in the mirror.

"Captain, I wonder—the scars . . . . What I mean is, your beard—I think it's quite distinguished-looking . . ."

Henry's mouth twisted in amusement. He nodded.

"I'll just trim it up a little . . ." Bartholomew snipped carefully at Henry's tangled mane, then shaped the three-inch beard before starting on his own snarled black curls.

He trimmed his hair short, clipped the beard away, then lathered and shaved with the old-fashioned blade razor.

"That's a bit better . . ." He stared at himself in

the cracked mirror. "I've changed, Captain," he said. "I don't think I'd know myself . . ."

Henry watched as Larry pulled on the ship suit, zipped it up; it was a snug fit over his solid chest and filled-out shoulders.

"Clothes make a difference," Larry said. "Suddenly I remember some of the comforts we've done without for a hundred and ninety days."

He threw a sharp look Captain Henry's way. "We've come over eleven hundred miles, by my reckoning. We can't have much farther to go."

Henry nodded briefly. He went outside, picked a spot where soft ferns padded the ground, stretched out. Bartholomew followed.

"That's the idea, Captain; get some rest." Larry took a spot beside Henry.

"It's been over six standard months since we left Pango-Ri," he said thoughtfully. "They'll have forgotten all about us by now. When we reach the port, suppose you go along to arrange for our passage out, and I'll register the tabs . . . ."

Henry glanced at him.

"It's in both our names, of course," Larry added. "Either of us can file it. If one of us is killed, the survivor gets it all."

Henry's eyes narrowed. His glance held on Larry's face as the sunlight struck across it, highlighting the new muscle of the jaw, the squareness of the features. Henry frowned. Larry frowned in response.

"What's the matter? You think there'll be trouble?"

Henry smiled faintly. The eyes of the young man were seasoned now, and wary. As Henry watched, they grimmed and harshened. For the first time Henry noticed how the black eyebrows above those eyes had thickened and begun to resemble the dark and angry eyebrows of Bartholomew senior.

The Run would toughen a man—but a toughened man could go either to the good or the bad. Larry had yet to show which way events here on Corazon had turned him—toward someone who would be good for Dulcia—or toward being his father's son. If he was his father's son, it would be the worth of their claim that would be filling his mind now . . . .

"Well, never mind now," said Larry abruptly. "Let's get a good night's sleep. We'll talk about it in the morning."

The sun woke Henry, shining in his eyes. A piece of paper was pegged to the ground beside him with a rusted kitchen knife from the cabin. He unfolded it.

I'M GOING ON AHEAD TO PANGO-RI. ALONE, I CAN TRAVEL FASTER. IF THERE'S TROUBLE, I'M IN BETTER SHAPE TO HANDLE IT THAN YOU. BY THE TIME YOU GET TO PANGO-RI THE CLAIM WILL BE FILED. AND A WORD TO THE WISE—WATCH YOURSELF COMING INTO TOWN.

LARRY

Henry crumpled the paper savagely, hurled it from him. He caught up his pack, stuffed it hastily with what provisions Larry had left him, pulled it onto his back, glanced at the sun, and set out southward.

Two days later, he struck a raw, unpaved road, rutted and potholed, slashing through the dense timber like a wound.

After an hour, a heavy truck came into view from the north, its air-cushion jets spattering wide sheets of mud. It halted, settled into the muck; a red-faced man opened the cab, leaned out.

"You got a long walk ahead of you, pal, if you're headed for Pango; it's a hundred and thirty miles. You better hop aboard." He looked at Henry, lowered his voice. "What happened to you, brother?"

Henry swung aboard, flashed the driver a quick smile.

"Cautious, too, hey? Well, can't say as I blame you." He let in the clutch and the truck heaved itself up, moved off in a howl of worn turbos.

Five hours later, Henry dropped from the truck at the edge of the sprawling new city that had sprung up around the booming port of Pango-Ri. The driver waved.

"Good luck, pal. You ain't much company, but I'll say this fer ya—you don't talk a guy's ear off . . ." He gunned the truck. Henry watched him out of sight, then set off as quickly as his crippled knee would allow toward the shabby towers that had risen where Tent Town had been.

The crowd at the Solar Corona had changed. The

bustling women were gone; the loudmouthed
hopefuls had disappeared; the hard-drinking ad-
venturers had sought cheerier surroundings for
their dissipations.

Now half a dozen stony-faced teamsters
hunched over the shabby bar where a dyed slat-
tern poured undersized drinks from a finger-stain-
ed bottle. At a back table, a group of sullen-eyed
men nursed thick glasses. The late evening street
noises seemed remote, far away.

Henry took a seat in a booth halfway down the
room, signaled for a sealed bottle, poured an inch
of thin yellowish fluid into his glass, sat waiting.
One of the men from the table rose, walked past
Henry's table, darted a sharp look at him, went
out through a side door.

Henry finished his drink, poured a second. The
man who had gone out returned, glanced at Henry
again. Henry stared into his glass.

Three slow hours passed. The street door swung
open abruptly; a narrow-shouldered, gray-haired
man with close-set eyes and a puckered mouth
slipped in, walked quickly back to the man at the
table. He leaned close to a thick-necked coarse-
skinned redhead, muttered something. The redhead barked a question. Henry thought a scrap of
the conversation: " . . . he look like . . . ?"

Under the table, Henry gripped the butt of the
blaster, eased it from its holster, fitting his clumsy
fingers to its curve with his thumb resting lightly
on the firing stud.

The small man stepped back from the table; the
redhead rose, headed for the door, followed by the

other three men; heavy power guns bobbed at their hips. They moved up the aisle.

As they reached Henry's table, he brought the gun up into view, leveled it at the square buckle on the belt that cinched in the redhead's ample midriff. The man jerked to a halt; his freckled hand went toward his hip, paused, dropped to his side. Behind him, the third man in line dropped into a half crouch, reaching for his gun—

Henry moved the blaster half an inch, stared into the other's eyes; the man straightened slowly, raised his hands clear of his sides.

Henry motioned toward the table; his glance darted aside to take in the men at the bar; they hunched over their drinks, unaware of the byplay.

"What's the game, grandpa?" the redhead grated softly.

Henry motioned again, his eyes on the redhead's face. The other's pale eyes narrowed under bushy auburn brows.

"You tired of being alive—" he started. His expression flickered suddenly.

"Hoad!" he snapped. The man behind him moved up cautiously, stared into Henry's face.

"Ever seen him before?"

"Naw, I—" Hoad stopped. He gaped at Henry. "Jeezus . . ."

"Uh-huh," the redhead said. "O.K., pop; I guess maybe you might use the iron after all . . ." He backed slowly, his men behind him. Carefully, they resumed their seats. Henry watched them, the gun resting on the table, aimed steadily at the redhead's chest.

From his table, Henry had a good view of both the front door and the four men at the table. Slow minutes ticked past. The men muttered together. The man called Hoad rose, came carefully up to Henry, his eyes on the blaster. His tongue darted out, touched his upper lip.

"Listen," he said. He had a small, hoarse voice, like a man who had been choked too hard once. "Rusty says—he wants to make a deal . . ."

Henry looked at him with his one eye.

Hoad went on. "The deal is—a trade. You got something we want, see? And we got something you want . . ."

Henry sat in the shadowy booth, the gun butt against the table, the sights centered on Hoad's chest. Silently he waited.

"You give Rusty the tabs—and you get her back —all in one piece."

Henry's eye seemed to glitter under his shaggy gray brows.

"We got her, all right," Hoad said. He edged back from the table, eyes on Henry. "Look, I'm just delivering the message, see? I ain't the one . . ." He fumbled in his pocket, brought out a small object folded in a twist of grimy paper. He peeled the paper away, held up a large violet stone in a cage of gold wire, swinging from a delicate golden chain.

"Rusty says you'll know when you see this."

Light glinted from the swinging stone. It was a forty-karat amethyst, flawless, polished in its natural shape. Henry had seen it last on Dulcia's throat.

He stood, pushed out from the booth. Hoad licked his lip again. "So you don't want to try nothing, or—"

Henry slammed the gun barrel down across the man's collarbone; he stumbled back with a shrill yelp, fell on his back. Henry swung his foot, booted him hard in the ribs. Hoad rolled to hands and knees, scuttled under a table. The men at the bar were turning now, mouths open. Henry walked toward the table where Rusty and his two men waited. The big redhead rose, took a step toward Henry, hooked his thumbs in his belt, waiting boldly. The other two crouched back, watching the gun.

"Easy now, pop," Rusty growled softly. He took a step back as the gun moved up to within five feet of him. "We got the girl—you know that. You better play ball, hah?"

Henry stepped around the table, stood covering the door and the men at the bar.

"Put the gun up," Rusty said. "You ain't going to use it now, pop. Just lay it on the table over there, and come on with me; I'll take you to the girl." He watched Henry, his eyes narrowed. Henry stood unmoving, the gun trained on the other.

"For Chrissake, say something," Rusty grated. "You ain't going to get the kid killed, just for those lousy tabs . . ."

Henry moved suddenly; Rusty started, jerked his hands high. "Hold on, damn you—"

Henry threw the gun on the floor, turned and walked toward the door. There were quick muttered words behind him. Rusty pushed past him. The blaster was in Rusty's hand now. He was grinning as he pulled the door open; he motioned with the gun.

"For a minute there, grandpa, I thought you'd popped your hatch. Now let's go see a man that's got things to say to you . . ." Rusty's glance went to the men at the bar, watching, open-mouthed.

"You boobs didn't see nothing," Rusty grated. "That makes you lucky, get me?"

Henry followed the redhead out into the street, into a dusty old-model Turbocad. It started up and wheeled off toward the lights of the tall towers beyond the port. As it rounded the corner, Henry caught a glimpse of Bartholomew's tall figure standing on the curb, staring after it.

It was a dowdy copter hotel, with rooms strung like cardboard beads on the undersized trusswork of the open-bar frame. They went in by a side door between overflowing refuse bins, rode a noisy lift to the tenth level, walked along a slanting floor to a door before which two undesirables in loud clothes of cheap cut lounged, busy with toothpicks. Their eyes darted over Henry. Rusty pushed between them, shouldered the door open. His hand was near his hip.

"I got my eye on you, pops," he said softly. "So don't get any ideas!" It was a floridly decorated room. Polarized panels let purplish light in on high-gloss woven plastic rugs which stretched to walls hung with hand-painted color-reversal scenes of night life on exotic worlds. Shaded lamps glowed in each corner. In a high-backed contour chair done in yellow plush, Senator Bartholomew sat, buttoned into a tight business suit of conservative cut.

He glanced briefly at Henry; his mouth went down at the corners, opened—

His glance went back to Henry; his eyes widened. Behind Henry Rusty chuckled. "I told you Tasker didn't sell out—he was cut out," he said. "Some time I'd like to hear pops here tell me how he pulled it off."

"Where . . ." Bartholomew's eyes went past Henry. He clamped his mouth, gripped the arms of the chair. His jowls were pale. "Where's my boy . . . ?" he said hoarsely.

"Pops was alone," Rusty said.

Bartholomew looked at Henry, reluctantly.

"Where is he . . . ?" His voice was thin, stretched.

"Pops don't talk much," Rusty said. "Maybe he needs some encouragement . . ." He moved to Henry's side.

"No!" Bartholomew put up his hands.

"He'll talk." His eyes held on Henry's face now. "Where's Larry? He's done you no harm. Give me my boy and . . ." he swallowed. "I'll see that you're well repaid for your efforts."

"I told him we got the girl," Rusty put in. Bartholomew's face dropped into a slack mask of dismay—then tightened into fury.

"You . . . blundering idiot!"

Rusty swaggered over to the chair, looked down on the red-faced Senator.

"You may be Mr. Big back on Elderberry or wherever it is—but here, I'm the one that draws the water. Sure, I mentioned the kid. I had to." He barked a short laugh. "The old man had a blaster on me."

Bartholomew came out of his chair. "Where's my boy?" he demanded. He took out a scented tissue, wiped at his forehead. He looked from Henry to the redhead. "I have to know! Where is he?"

"Cool it, Senator. I can find out—but not by giving him lollipops."

"All right. Do—whatever you have to do." Bartholomew sank back into the chair, his eyes on Henry.

"You heard him, granddad . . ." Rusty's eyes were narrowed. "I don't like to pick on cripples, but business is business . . ."

"If you want to see the girl again—alive— you'd better speak up," Bartholomew blurted.

"Shut up, Senator," Rusty snarled. "Sometimes you give me the feeling I'm in a dirty racket." He faced Henry, scowling. "The Senator knows all about your corundum mine; you've been feeding a few nice stones into the market every year, just enough to get by on. He checked you out, found out where you'd been; he narrowed the mine down to Corazon. Then he foxed you into making the Run. He's put time and money into this deal—and he wants his payoff. You can see that, pops. So give. Where's your tabs—"

"Never mind the tabs—for now," Bartholomew cut in. "My boy—"

"You sent a guy to the Registry Office," the redhead went on. "He didn't make it—"

"He sent a man? That might be Larry—"

"Naw—this guy was a bruiser. He caught wise and smeared two of the boys and got clear—but he didn't register no tabs. Probably some timber bum that pops here met up with and worked out a split."

"Split? I'll split him—" Bartholomew pushed up to Henry. "I see it now—why you demanded that the proceeds be divided between you and—Larry. You killed him—and now you think you can steal it all—"

Rusty elbowed the Senator aside. "You get too excited, Senator. Go sit down. This is business." He sighed, looking at Henry. "Better give, old-timer. Where do you and your sidekick meet? Where's the mine located at? And just by the way, where's the Senator's kid?"

"Why doesn't he talk?" Bartholomew screech-ed. "Why doesn't he say something . . . ?"

"Maybe you make him nervous," Rusty snap-ped.

"I'll kill the girl!" Bartholomew snarled. "I swear I'll kill her—"

"Hold onto your hairpiece, Senator! Maybe this guy didn't kill your kid; maybe he's just got a natural yen to hold on to the marbles; after all, he found 'em—"

"If Larry's dead, I'll kill her!" Bartholomew pointed to a thin man standing quietly near the wall. "Bring her in; I'll show him I mean what I say—"

The thin man went through a connecting door; half a minute later he pushed Dulcia into the room. Her hands were trussed together with a wide strap; her mouth was gagged. She stared at Bartholomew, then at Henry. Tears started, ran down her face.

There was a sound beyond the hall door. A brief

*whap! whap!* Then a heavy fall. Rusty's hand darted to his hip, whipped out a 2mm needler. He plunged for the door—

Henry took a quick step, thrust out a foot, hooked the redhead's ankle, chopped hard at the back of his neck as he went down. Across the room, the thin man yelled, jumped clear of Dulcia, reaching—

She spiked his foot with a heel, threw herself at him; they went down together. As Henry turned, Bartholomew dived for a desk, snatched up a gun, whirled—

The door slammed wide. Larry Bartholomew stood in the entry a power gun in his hand. The thin man flung clear of Dulcia, brought up a gun—

Larry fired, knocked the thin man flat; he whirled on the Senator—and stood, frozen, staring at his father.

The gun in the Senator's hand jumped, a flat bark echoing in the room. Larry spun sideways, fell against the wall, blood spattering behind him. He went down on his face; his breath went out in a long sigh.

"Stand where you are," the Senator said in a high, thin voice. "You saw how I shot that man. I'll kill both of you if I have to. Now answer when I speak, or—"

A gun cracked beyond the door. Bartholomew tossed the gun from him, looking startled. His expression changed, became blank. He leaned forward, fell over the yellow chair, slammed the floor.

Heavy Joe Saggio eased his bulk through the doorway, stood, smiling gently around the room.

His eyes fell on Henry; he stared. The smile faded.
The thick tongue came out, touched his lips.

"Enrico baby. I heard you had a tough time."
From behind him, a small man in a tight jacket
and a yachting cap sidled into the room, looked
around.

"This is the kind of hotel I like," he said in a thin
nasal. "Nobody sticks their nose in, just because
they hear guns working."

Henry went past him, knelt at Larry's side,
turned him over. There was a scorched furrow
across the side of his chest. His breathing was
shallow, noisy. Unseen, Henry slipped a hand into
Larry's breast pocket, removed the red marker
tabs.

"The kid bad?" Saggio stood behind Henry,
looking down at young Bartholomew. Henry rose,
shook his head, went to Dulcia, raised her, pulled
the gag from her mouth.

"Oh, Grandpa..." She smiled, crying. He
fumbled out a knife with his stiff fingers, cut the
strap from her hands. She threw her arms around
him.

"We... thought you were dead.... It was so
long... and then Mr. Bartholomew invited me to
come with him... to try to find you...."

On the floor, the thin man sat up, whining.
Saggio jerked his head at the man in the cap.

"Take care of these bums, Johnny—and get a
medic up here for the kid."

"Listen," the thin man gasped. "I know plenty,
see? You want to get me a doc, treat me right. This
old guy's got this mine—the Senator knew about
it—"

Saggio stood by Henry. "I didn't have nothing to do with it, Enrico—you know I don't play them games . . . ."

"Listen . . . !" The thin man was babbling, fighting as the small man tugged at him. "It's a corundum mine, you got to listen! Stones like pigeon eggs! He knows where it is, I swear—"

"What's he talking?" Saggio stepped to the thin man, slammed a blow to the side of his head. The man went limp.

"Dump him in the alley. He's delirious. Then get that medic up here quick." Saggio looked at Dulcia, showed a gold toothed smile, bowed.

"I heard about the young lady, Enrico—but I don't know she's your grandbaby. Otherwise, I fix these bums a long time ago."

"Grandpa—is Larry—did he . . . die out there . . .?"

Henry nodded toward the tall, solidly built man lying on the floor. Dulcia's eyes went to him. She gasped, darted to his side.

"Larry! Oh, Larry . . . Grandpa—will he be all right?"

Henry nodded. Saggio caught his eye. "The little lady's all right now, Enrico. I get the doc here in a minute for the boy. I guess maybe you got business now, hey?" His eye went to the empty holster at Henry's side. He stooped, picked up the gun Larry had dropped, handed it to Henry.

"Maybe you need this, hah?"

Henry holstered the gun. Dulcia looked up.

"Grandpa—where are you going . . . ?"

"It's O.K.—your grandpapa, he's got a problem to settle," Saggio nodded to Henry. "I'll see she's O.K."

Henry nodded. Saggio smiled, his eyes cool.
"I see you in a little while, Enrico baby . . ."

Henry stepped out into early-evening light, looked up and down the gaudy street, spotted a glare
panel indicating a bar. Inside, he nodded toward a
bottle on the back bar, took it and a glass to the
table.

He poured a drink, swallowed it, then looked at
the half-stiff fingers of his right hand. He flexed
them; they were like rusted metal. He gripped the
pistol butt, straining to fit his fingers to the con-
tours. It was like picking up an ice block with
paper tongs.

He shoved the pistol back into the holster, had a
second drink. Then he rose, went out into the light-
strung street, walked slowly west along the plastic
boardwalk toward the square.

The wide plaza was empty, bleak under the poly-
arcs of the port, an arena ringed by the dark
mouths of deserted streets. The harsh squares of
light that were the windows of the Registry Office
threw pale rectangles across the oily pavement. A
block away, music thumped and screeched, voices
rang; here in the deserted square it was silent.

Henry moved out from the wall. Across the
square, a large shadow stirred. Heavy Joe Saggio
stepped into view, a wide pistol belt strapped
across his chest, sagging with the weight of the
heavy blaster under his arm.

"I guess we're square now, hey Enrico?" he
called softly. "You let me go one time; I help you
out just now . . . It's nice like this: Just you and
me—like the old days . . ."

Henry walked steadily toward the lighted door, half-way down the side of the plaza.

"That kid, your compadre; he's O.K.; he was talking soft words with the little lady when I go; it's a nice couple, Enrico; you should be proud."

It was a hundred feet to the office door. Henry walked slowly, not favoring the knee.

"It was a kick, seeing you here last fall, Enrico; I'm getting dumb in my old age, I didn't figure you had an angle. Corundum hey, Enrico? Nice, those gemstones. I got a real fondness for them. They're nice to look at, hah? Not like dirty money . . ."

Saggio came toward him, moving heavily—a big, thickset, powerful man, getting old now, but never soft . . .

He stopped, fifty feet away, facing Henry. Henry saw his tongue touch his lower lip, the glint of the gold tooth.

"You put up a good fight, Enrico. You make a monkey out of Tasker, I hear. That's good. I never like that guy. And you make a great hike back. It's a story I tell my grandchildren—only someplace I forget to have some . . ."

Henry came on; somewhere a night lizard called motonously.

"Look, Enrico—you make a split, now, hey? It's plenty for all, I hear. You got a right—but what about me? I win a share on points, hey?"

They were thirty feet apart now. Saggio's eyes narrowed. His shoulders tightened.

"That's far enough now, Enrico," he growled. "You don't talk much, baby—that's O.K. But you don't go through that door before you give me an answer. And I tell you, Enrico; the next word I

speak will be the big one, and the last one . . .''
Saggio's hand edged toward the shoulder holster,
fingers curled—

Henry stopped and spread his legs, braced to
draw—

"Captain!"

Henry whirled. Behind him, coming at him from
the opposite side of the square, was Larry Bartholomew, a white gleaming swathe of bandage
under his open jacket, his hands held out from his
sides. Light glinted from the polished butt of a
power pistol at his hip.

"Back off, Captain!" he shouted at Henry. "Back
off the way you came—"

Henry glanced over his shoulder at Saggio.
Saggio's hand darted toward his gun. Henry was
caught between them. He drove his stiff hand for
his own gun, glancing back to Larry. Drawing as
he ran, Larry was running to his right. Saggio's
gun coughed and the shot went wide of Henry,
toward Larry. Larry stopped; his gun was out; he
stood, a hand on his hip, sighting down the barrel
at seventy yards. Saggio's gun snarled again.
Larry's pistol jumped, racketed. Saggio leaped
back, tumbled down, his gun clattering away; he
coiled, grinding his face into the pavement; then
the big body went slack.

The sun was warm on Henry's face. Dulcia sat beside him on the pool edge, brushing her long pale gold hair. Behind her, the sunlight sparkled in the varicolored spray of the fountain.

"I'm so pleased about your hand, Grandpa," she said. "Dr. Spangler said it's almost well now. Please let him do your knee . . ."

Henry shook his head. Dulcia laughed.

"You don't have to make signs, Grandpa! Your voice is as good as new."

"Waste of money," Henry said gruffly. "Wants to graft an eye, too. What for? I can see all the foolishness I want to with this one."

"Please don't be that way, Grandpa. You should be so proud! No one else could have done what you did—a whole new universe opened up! Admiral Hayle said in his letter it was the greatest discovery of the millennium. They promoted you to Commodore—"

"Posthumous promotion," Henry growled. "And I didn't do it. Larry—"

"I'd rather we didn't talk about Larry," Dulcia said shortly. She tossed the brush aside, picked up a colored pebble from the poolside, stared into it.

"Where the devil is the boy?" Henry said. "Hardly seen him since we got back."

"Making more deals, I suppose! You should have seen him when we landed. Some of those terrible men who worked for his father were there; the big ones—Councilman Hogger—came up and started to say something about how they'd been the Senator's best friends. I wanted to tell him he ought to be ashamed to admit it. I thought Larry would tell them to stay away from him, that he

wanted nothing to do with all that crooked political dealing—but do you know what he did?"
Dulcia stared at Henry indignantly. "He started
shaking hands and telling them how glad he was to
be back in time for the big campaign, and that he
had ideas for the Galactic Council nominee . . ."

"Can't blame the boy; politics is all he
knows . . ."

"He ought to know a lot more now! He spent
nearly a year with you on Corazon, Grandpa. And
he saw what his father was really like . . ."

"Can't ask a man to turn against his father—
no matter what, Dulcie-girl."

Across the lawn, the porter chimed. Dulcia
looked up. Larry Bartholomew stood in the doorway, tall, solid, his hair neatly trimmed, a smile on
his regular features; he was dressed in the latest
mode, and the tiny broken veins just under the
skin over his cheekbones from frostbite gave him
a look of ruddy health. He carried a box in his
hand.

He came across the lawn, shook Henry's hand,
turned to the girl.

"Dulcia, I want to apologize for my neglect these
last few weeks; I've been tied up—"

"I know. Politics," Dulcia said shortly.

Larry extended the legs of a small portable Tri-
D, set it up in front of Henry. "The election results
are coming in," he said. "I wanted to be sure
you—"

Dulcia jumped up. "You know what Grandpa
thinks of your Statistical Average! No, Larry! I've
kept all that away from him! I don't want him
upset!"

"The the delegates are on the final roll call now, Dulcia! This is an important moment; Aldorado's first Galactic Delegate—"

"I don't care about that! It's peaceful here—"

"It's all right," Henry cut in, almost gently. "We can't stay shut away forever, girl. Turn it on, Larry."

"Thank you, Captain." Bartholomew twiddled the control. A voice boomed:

" . . . candidate of the new Statistical Excellence party which Lawrence Bartholomew, son of the late Senator . . .." Larry turned it down.

"It's been a hectic seven weeks, Captain," Larry said. "I arrived in the nick of time. My father's organization had been holding off their big push, waiting for his return. I jumped in and started spending money where it would do the most good the quickest."

Dulcia stared at Bartholomew. "You ought to be ashamed to admit you used your money to influence the voting!"

"Why? That's the system, after all. I learned that from your great-granddad; there's no point in waving flags; if you believe in something, go get it —any way you have to."

Dulcia threw the bright stone down, walked away.

"Dulcia—" Larry started after her.

"Let her go," Henry said. "Let's hear what's going on."

Bartholomew turned the volume up. On the small screen, a wide-mouthed man in an artificial-looking hairdo blared on:

" . . . slate of pledged delegates from their sector. And now the weight of the entire northern tier will be thrown behind the Statex candidate! It's an astonishing last-minute upset, a tribute to the organizational powers and crusading zeal of young Bartholomew! Now here's the vote from the Seaboard delegate, and yes! It's a bolt to the Statex standard! The delegates are crowding down now, all eager to get on the Statex bandwagon . . ."

Music blared up, drowning the shouting voice. Bartholomew tuned to another channel:

" . . . and it is now conceded by all dopesters that the Statex slate has taken the election by a rapidly widening margin, as delegation after delegation goes over to make this a landslide victory for the dark-horse candidate . . ."

"And yes, here it is! Provincial Chairman Crodfoller has conceded to Lawrence Bartholomew, the Statex candidate, and the crowd here at election headquarters is going mad with enthusiasm. Aldorado has a Delegate to the Galactic Council! And—hold everything, folks!"

There was a new tumult off-microphone.

"Listen, everyone!" the announcer's voice came back, babbling with excitement. "A flash, just in— Mark Hanforth, Chairman of the Galactic Council, now meeting on Terra, has just proposed a further honor for Aldorado. Speaking before the Council, just this past hour, he said, in part, ' . . . it is fitting that we take this moment in which a new world is represented on this Council to repay a debt long owed by the whole human race to a resident of that new world. I refer, Council Members, to Commodore Henry of Aldorado, who in my opinion earned the title and honors of Citizen of the Race, several generations ago—but who found it necessary to discover even newer worlds for the human race to conquer, before we laggards were reminded of the need to honor him.

"'... I propose, therefore, that without delay, and at the same time as the new Delegate from Aldorado is invested with his rank and accorded the Aeterna treatment—the prerequisite of that rank—that the treatment also be accorded to Commodore Henry, as his long-overdue wages for a long lifetime already devoted to the future of the human race ...'"

The announced babbled on. But the door of the house burst open and Dulcia came running, her face alight with joy, sparkling with tears. She threw herself at the old man.

"Grandpa! Did you hear! Now you'll get the Aeterna treatment and ... and ..." She looked toward Larry. "Larry! Why didn't you say something? You must have known something like this was in the wind! The Council President's an Expansionist, just like your new Statex party is—"

"Knew!" grunted Henry, staring over her head at Larry. "He must have been the one to arrange it —weren't you, boy? Hanforth wouldn't make a move like this just at this moment without some reason!"

Dulcia turned to stare at Larry, who laughed with a rough touch of embarrassment.

"Politics, Dulcie," he admitted. "The Expansionist and Conservative sides of the Council table are tied even. The new delegate from Aldorado was bound to break the tie. I just mentioned something about the Captain—"

"As the price of your party's alignment!" grunted Henry. "Very neat. Did you ever think of asking me if I wanted to be one of their Citizens of the Race?"

Larry looked squarely at him.

"Captain," he said, "I don't give a damn if you wanted it or not. I wasn't much good for anything until you took me on the Run; and the Run made a man out of me. But being with you on Corazon did more than just that. It shook me up and let me see things squarely for the first time in my life—and not just things about myself, but about you as well."

"Me?" growled Henry, shoving himself up from his chair.

"Sit down," said Larry, levelly. "And listen to me for a change. You can cut a rough, whitish stone into a diamond that will knock your eye out —but it has to have been a diamond to start off with. All right, I needed to be cut to shine the way I should—but I never was a diamond, Captain. Maybe a passable emerald, but that's it. I'm a politician—maybe, with luck and Dulcie's help a great one, one day—but I never was a Captain Henry!"

"What makes you think—" snapped Henry.

"I said, shut up and listen," Larry said evenly. "When I'm through you can say anything you want. I'm telling you—there's only one Captain Henry. I didn't get you the Aeterna treatment for yourself! I did it for me—for Dulcie—for all of us. You remember that poem of Kipling's about the explorer? The one you quoted, that night we went through the portal on Corazon? Well, do you remember one of the verses to it—one that goes:

> . . . Well I know who'll take the credit—all the
> clever chaps that followed—
> Came, a dozen men together—never knew my
> desert fears;
> Tracked me by the camps I'd quitted, used the
> waterholes I'd hollowed.
> They'll go back and do the talking. *They'll* be
> called the Pioneers! . . .

" . . . that's you, Captain!" said Larry. "There's hundreds and thousands of good men who can come . . . 'a dozen men together' . . . and follow up where you've blazed the trail. But there's only one man who can blaze that trail. That's you—and by God, the human race needs you!"

Larry drew a deep breath.

"I told you once, Captain, that you'd never die," he said. "And you never will, if I have anything to say about it. If you don't want to take the Aeterna treatment, I'll help hold you down myself while they stick the first needle in. Because we're not going to lose you while I have anything to say about it—and that's final!"

He swung about to the girl.

"Come on, Dulcie!" he said. "Let's leave him a while and give him time to let some common sense soak into that diamond-hard head of his!"

He turned on his heel and left. Dulcie jumped up and ran after him.

"Dulcie!" roared Henry, in outrage at her abandonment of him at the command of this brash young man. Still roaring, he heaved himself heavily to his feet—but they were already disappearing into the house. He was alone by the pool.

Snorting, he fell back into his chair.

"Hold *me* down!" he growled in white-hot fury. "Why . . ."

He stopped. Slowly, the picture he must have made blowing and roaring in protest like an overage walrus, began to grow inside him. Gradually the humor of it kindled in him, and after a long moment he threw his head back and began to laugh.

The laughter washed him clean inside. He sobered at last. Of course the young squirt was right. He'd be the worst possible sort of pouting idiot to turn down a chance at unlimited life and all the exploration that a man could dream of doing. Henry laughed—softly this time.

Hayle had made him a Commodore. Well, he'd take him up on that. He'd have a deep-space scout carted through the portal, piece by piece—and reassembled—and he'd see what lay beyond those farther stars.

He stooped, picked up the bit of colored stone Dulcia had tossed aside. It was twelve-karat amethyst of a flawless pale violet. He dropped it into the pool, watched it sink down to nestle among its brilliant fellows, stirring and sparkling in the natural spring which had washed them up from the corundum deposit far below.

Colored stones. Men had died for them, too. And on the far worlds, what unknown treasures might not be waiting . . .

If only Dulcia could have been here. But a man couldn't have everything. Life was compounded of equal parts of joy and sorrow; the trick was to savor the one while you had it—and not let the other make you forget that once life had been good—and could be good again.

Henry stood, looking down into the water, while the setting sun painted the sky in the colors of jewels.

# II

From a half million miles out, Vangard was a sphere of gray cast-iron, arc-lit, yellow-white on the sunward side, coalmine black on the other, with a wide band of rust-red along the terminator. The mountain ranges showed up as crooked black hairlines radiating from the white dazzle of the poles, fanning out, with smaller ridges rising between them, forming a band of broken gridwork across the planet like the back of an old man's hand. I watched the detail grow on the screen until I could match it up with the lines on the nav chart. Then I broke the seal on my U-beamer and sounded my Mayday:

"King Uncle 629 calling CQ! I'm in trouble! I'm on emergency approach to R-7985-23-D, but it doesn't look good. My track is 093 plus 15, at 19-0-8 standard, mark! Standing by for instructions, and make it fast! Relay, all stations!" I set the auto-squawk to squirt the call out a thousand times in one-millsec bursts, then switched to listen and waited while forty-five seconds went past. That's how long it would take the hype signal to hit the beamer station off Ring 8 and bounce back an automatic AK.

The auto signal came in right on schedule; another half a minute passed, and a cold finger touched my spine. Then a voice that sounded like I shouldn't have disturbed its nap came in:

"King Uncle 629, Monitor Station Z-448 reading you three by three. You are not, repeat *not* cleared for planet-fall. Report full detail—"

"Belay that!" I came back with plenty of edge. "I'm going to hit this rock; how hard depends on you! Get me down first and we'll handle the paperwork later!"

"You're inside interdict range of a Class Five quarantined world. This is an official navigational notice to sheer off—"

"Wise up, 448," I cut into that. "I'm seven hundred hours out of Dobie with special cargo aboard! You think I picked this spot to fuse down? I need a tech advisory and I need it now!"

Another wait; then my contact came back on, sounding tight-lipped: "King Uncle, transmit a board read-out."

"Sure, sure. But hurry it up." I sounded rattled. I pushed the buttons that gave him a set of duplicate instrument readings that would prove I was in even worse trouble than I claimed. It was no fake. I'd spent plenty to make sure the old tub had seen her last port.

"All right, King Uncle; you waited too long to make your report, you're going to have to jettison cargo and set up the following nav sequence—"

"I said special cargo!" I yelled back at him. "Category ten! I'm on a contract run for the Dobie med service. I'm carrying ten freeze cases!"

"Uh, Roger, King Uncle," the station came back, sounding a little off-balance now. "I understand you have living casualties under cryothesis aboard. Stand by." There was a pause. "You've handed me a cozy one, 629," the voice added, sounding almost human.

"Yeah," I said. "Put some snap on it. That rock's coming up fast."

I sat and listened to the star-crackle. A light and a half away, the station computer would be going into action, chewing up the data from my board and spitting out a solution; and meanwhile, the sharp boy on duty would be checking out my story. That was good. I wanted it checked. It was solid all down the line. The passengers lashed down in the cargo cell were miners, badly burned in a flash fire three months ago on Dobie, a mean little world with no treatment facilities. I was due to collect forty thousand when I delivered them to the med center on Commonweal in a viable condition. My pre-lift inspection was on file, along with my flight plan, which would show my minimum-boost trajectory in past Vangard, just the way a shoestring operator would plot it, on the cheap. It was all in the record. I was legitimate, a victim of circumstances. It was their ball now. And if my calculations were any good, there was only one way they could play it.

"King Uncle, you're in serious trouble," my unseen informant told me. "But I have a possible out for you. You're carrying a detachable cargo pod?"

He paused as if he expected an answer, then went on. "You're going to have to ride her down, then jettison the pod on airfoils inside atmosphere. Afterwards, you'll have only a few seconds in which to eject. Understood? I'll feed you the conning data now." A string of numbers rattled off to be automatically recorded and fed into the control sequencer.

"Understand, 448," I said when he finished. "But look—that's wild country down there. Suppose the cooler's damaged in the drop? I'd better stay with her and try to set her down easy."

"Impossible, King Uncle!" The voice had warmed up a few degrees. After all, I was a brave if penny-pinching merchant captain, determined to do my duty by my charges even at the risk of my own neck. "Frankly, even this approach is marginal. Your one chance—and your cargo's—is to follow my instructions implicitly!" He didn't add that it was a criminal offense not to comply with a Monitor's navigational order. He didn't have to. I knew that, was counting on it.

"If you say so. I've got a marker circuit on the pod. But listen: How long will it take for you fellows to get a relief boat out here?"

"It's already on the way. The run will take . . . just under three hundred hours."

"That's over twelve standard days!" I allowed the short pause required for the slow mental process of a poor but honest spacer to reach some simple conclusions, then blurted: "If that freeze equipment's knocked out, the insulation won't hold low-O that long! And . . . " Another pause for the next obvious thought to form. "And what about me? How do I stay alive down there?"

"Let's get you down first, Captain." Some of the
sympathy had slipped, but not much. Even a hero
is entitled to give some thought to staying alive,
after he's seen to the troops.

There was a little more talk, but the important
things had all been said. I was following orders,
doing what I was told, no more, no less. Inside the
hour, the whole Tri-D watching public of the
Sector would know that a disabled hospital ship
was down on Vangard, with ten men's lives—
eleven, if you counted mine—hanging in the balance. And I'd be inside the target's defenses, in
position for phase two.

At ten thousand miles, the sound started up: the
lost, lonely wail of air molecules being split by a
thousand tons of over-aged tramp freighter,
coming in too fast, on a bad track, with no retros
working. I played with what was left of the alti-
tude jets, jockeying her around into a trail-first
position, saving the last of my reaction mass for
when and where it would do the most good. When
I had her where I wanted her, I had less than eight
thousand miles of gravity well to work with. I
checked the plotting board, pin-pointing my target
area, while she bucked and buffeted under me and
the moans rose to howls like gut-shot direbeasts.

At two hundred miles, the drive engines cut in
and everything turned to whirly red lights and

pressures like a toad feels under a boot. That went on long enough for me to pass out and come to half a dozen times. Then suddenly she was tumbling in free fall and there were only seconds left. Getting a hand on the pod release was no harder than packing an anvil up a rope ladder; I felt the shock as the cargo section blasted free and away. I got myself into position, clamped the shock frame down, took a last lungful of stale ship air, slapped the eject button. Ten tons of feather pillow hit me in the face and knocked me into another world.

I swam up out of the big black ocean where the bad dreams wait and popped through into the watery sunshine of semi-consciousness in time to get a fast panoramic view of mountains like shark's teeth ranked in snow-capped rows that marched across the world to a serrated horizon a hundred miles away. I must have blacked out again, because the next second a single peak was filling the bull's-eye screen, racing toward me like a breaking wave. The third time I came up, I was on chutes, swaying down toward what looked like a tumbled field of dark lava. Then I saw that it was foliage; green-black, dense, coming up fast. I just had time to note that the pod locator marker was blinking green, meaning that my cargo was down and intact, before the lights went out again.

This time I woke up cold: that was the first datum that registered. The second was that my head hurt; that, and all the rest of me. It took me long enough to write a will leaving everything to the Euthanasia Society to get unstrapped and crack the capsule and crawl out into what the outdoorsy set would have called the bracing mountain air. I tallied my aches and pains, found the bones and joints intact. I ran my suit thermostat up and felt some warmth begin to seep into me.

I was standing on pine needles, if pine needles come in the three-foot length, the diameter of a swizzle stick. They made a springy carpet that covered the ground all around the bases of trees as big as Ionic columns that reached up and up into a deep green twilight. Far off among the tree trunks I saw the white gleam of snow patches. It was silent, utterly still, with no movement, not even a stir among the wide boughs that spread overhead. My suit instruments told me the air pressure was 16 PSI, oxygen content fifty-one per cent, the ambient temperature minus ten degrees Centigrade, as advertised. The locator dials said the pod was down just over a hundred miles north by east from where I stood. As far as I could tell from the gadgets fitted into my fancy harness buckle, everything there was operating normally. And if the information I had gathered was as good as the price said it ought to be, I was within ten miles of where I had planned, half a day's walk from Johnny Thunder's stamping ground. I set my suit controls for power assist, took a compass reading, and started hiking.

The low gravity made the going easy, even for a man who had been pounded by a few thousand miles of atmosphere; and the suit I was wearing helped, too. You couldn't tell it to look at it, but it had cost me the price of a luxury retirement on one of those rhodium-and-glass worlds with taped climate and hot and cold running orgies. In addition to the standard air and temperature controls, and the servo-booster that took the ache out of my walking, it was equipped with every reflex circuit and sense amplifier known to black market science, including a few the League security people would like to get their hands on. The metabolic monitor gear alone was worth the price.

My compass heading took me upslope at a long slant that brought me to the snow line in an hour. The trees continued for another few thousand feet, ended where the sea-blue glacier began. I got my first look at Vangard's sky: deep blue, shading down to violet above the ice-crowned peaks that had it all to themselves up here, like a company of kings.

I took a break at the end of the first hour, gave myself a squirt of nutrient syrup and swallowed some water, and listened to eternity passing, one second at a time. I thought about a shipload of colonists, back in the primitive dawn of space travel, setting off into a Universe they knew less about than Columbus did America, adrift for nine years before they crash-landed here, I thought about them stepping out into the great silence of this cold world—men, women, probably children —knowing that there would never, ever be any re-

turning for them. I thought about them facing that
—and going on to live. They'd been tough people,
but their kind of toughness had gone out of the
world. Now there was only the other kind; my
kind. They were pioneer-tough, frontier-tough,
full of unfounded hope and determination and big
ideas about the future. I was big-city tough, smart-
tough, rat-tough; and the present was enough for
me.

"It's the silence," I said aloud. "It gets to you."
But the sound of my voice was too small against
all that emptiness. I got to my feet and started off
toward the next ridge.

Three hours later, the sun was still hanging in the
same spot, a dazzle of green above the big top, that
every now and then found a hole and shot a cold
shaft of light down to puddle on the rust-red
needles. I had covered almost forty kilometers as
the buzzard flies. The spot I was looking for
couldn't be far off. I was feeling a little fatigue in
spite of the low G, and the sophisticated suit cir-
cuitry that took half the load of every muscular
contraction, and the stuff the auto-med was
metering into my arm. At that, I was lucky. Back
home, I'd have been good for two weeks in a recovery ward after the beating I had taken. I
cheered myself with the idea while I leaned
against a tree and breathed the enriched canned
air the suit had prescribed, and thought positive

thoughts to counteract the little lights whirling before my eyes. I was still busy with that when I heard the sound . . . .

Now, it's curious how, after a lifetime surrounded by noises, a few hours without them can change your whole attitude toward air vibrations in the audible range. All I heard was a faint, whooping call, like a lonely sea bird yearning for his mate; but I came away from the tree as though it had turned hot, and stood flat-footed, my head cocked, metering the quality of the sound for clues. It got louder, which meant closer, with a speed that suggested the futility of retreat. I looked around for a convenient sapling to climb, but these pines were born old; the lowest branch was fifty feet up. All that was left in the way of concealment was a few thousand tree trunks. Somehow I had the feeling I'd rather meet whatever it was out in the open. At least I'd see it as soon as it saw me. I knew it was something that was alive and ate meat; a faint, dogmatic voice from my first ancestor was telling me that. I did the thing with the wrist that put the bootleg miniature crater gun in my palm and waited, while the booming call got louder and more anguished, like a lovelorn sheep, a heartbroken bull, a dying elk. I could hear the thud of big feet now, galloping in a cadence that, even allowing for the weak gravity field, suggested ponderous size. Then it broke through into sight, and confirmed great-grandpa's intuition. It wasn't a hound, or even a hyaenodon, but it was what a hyaenodon would have been if it had stood seven feet at the shoulder, had legs as big around at the ankle as my thigh, a head the size of a one-man helicab, and jaws that could pick a man up like Rover trotting home with the evening paper. Maybe it was that last thought that kept my finger from twitching on the firing stud. The monster dog skidded to a halt in a slow-motion flurry of pine needles, gave a final bellow, and showed me about a yard of bright red tongue. The rest of him was brown and black, sleek-furred, loose-hided. His teeth were big, but not over six inches from gum line to needle point. His eyes were shiny black and small, like an elephant's, with crescents of red under them. He came on slowly, as if he wanted to get a good look at what he was eating. I could hear his joints creak as he moved. His shoulders were high, molded with bunched muscle. At each step his foot-wide pads sank into the leaf mold. I felt my knees begin to twitch, while what hackles I had did their best to stand on end. He was ten feet away now, and his breath snorted through nostrils I could have stuck a fist into, like steam around a leaky piston. If he came any closer, I knew my fingers would push that stud, ready or not.

"Down, boy!" I said, in what I hoped was a resonant tone of command. He halted, hauled in the tongue, let it out again, then lowered his hind quarters gingerly, like an old lady settling into her favorite rocker. He sat there and looked at me, and I looked back. And while we were doing that, the giant arrived.

He came up silently along an aisle among the big trees, and was within fifty feet of me before I saw him, big as he was.

And big he was.

It's easy to talk about a man twelve feet high; that's just about twice normal, after all. Just a big man, and let's tell a joke about his shoe size.

But twice the height is four times the area of sky he blanks off as he looms over you; eight times the bulk of solid bone and muscle. Sixteen hundred pounds of man, at Earth-normal G. Here he weighed no more than half a ton, but even at that, each leg was holding up five hundred pounds. They were thick, muscle-corded legs that matched the arms and the chest and the neck that was like a section of hundred-year oak supporting the big head. But massive as he was, there was no distortion of proportion. Photographed without a midget in the picture for scale, he would have looked like any other Mr. Universe contender, straight-boned, clean-limbed, every muscle defined, but nothing out of scale. His hair was black, curly, growing in a rough-cut mane, but no rougher than any other man that lives a long way from a barber. He had a close-trimmed beard, thick black eyebrows over wide-set pale blue eyes. His skin was weather-burned the color of well-used cowhide. His features were regular enough to be called handsome, if you admire the Zeus-Poseidon style. I saw all this as he came striding up to me, dressed in leather, as light on his feet as the dog was heavy. He stopped beside the pooch, patted his head carelessly with a hand the size of first base, looking down at me, and for a ghostly instant I was a child again, looking up at the Brobdingnagian world of adults. Thoughts flashed in my mind, phantom images of a world of warmth and love and security and other illusions long forgotten. I pushed those away and remembered that I was Baird Ulrik, professional, out on a job, in a world that had no place for fantasies.

"You're the man they call Johnny Thunder," I said.

He let that pass. Maybe he smiled a little.

"I'm Patton. Carl Patton. I bailed out of a ship." I pointed to the sky.

He nodded, "I know," he said. His voice was deep, resonant as a pipe organ; he had a lot of chest for it to bounce around in. "I heard your ship fall." He looked me over, didn't see any compound fractures. "I'm glad you came safely to ground. I hope Woola did not frighten you." His Lingua sounded old-fashioned and a little stilted, with a trace of a strange accent. My trained poker face must have slipped a couple of feet at what he said, because he smiled. His teeth were square and porcelain white.

"Why should he?" I said without squeaking. "I've seen my three-year-old niece pat a Great Dane on the knee. That was as high as she could reach."

"Come back with me to my house. I have food, a fire."

I pulled myself together and went into my act:

"I've got to get to my cargo pod. There are . . . passengers aboard it."

His face asked questions.

"They're alive—so far," I said. "I have a

machine that tells me the pod landed safely, on her chutes. The cannisters are shock-mounted, so if the locator gear survived, so did they. But the equipment might not have. If it was smashed, they'll die."

"This is a strange thing, Carl Patton," he said after I had explained, "to freeze a living man."

"They wouldn't be living long, if they weren't in low-O," I told him. "Third-degree burns over their whole bodies. Probably internal, too. At the med center they can put 'em in viv tanks and regrow their hides. When they wake up, they'll be as good as new." I gave him a significant look, full of do-or-die determination. "If I get there in time, that is. If they come out of it there . . ." I let the sentence die off without putting words to the kind of death that would be. I made a thing out of looking at the show dials on my wrist. "The pod is down somewhere in that direction." I pointed away up-slope, to the north. "I don't know how far." I shot a look at him to see how that last datum went over. The less I gave away, the better. But he sounded a little more sophisticated than my researches had led me to expect. A slip now could queer everything. "Maybe a hundred miles, maybe more."

He thought that one over, looking down at me. His eyes were friendly enough, but in a remote way, like a candle burning in the window of a stranger's house.

"That is bad country, where they have fallen," he said. "The Towers of Nandi are high."

I knew that; I'd picked the spot with care. I gave him my manly, straight-from-the-shoulder look.

"There are ten men out there, my responsibility. I've got to do what I can."

His eyes came back to mine. For the first time, a little fire seemed to flicker a light behind them.

"First you must rest and eat."

I wanted to say more, to set the hook; but just then the world started a slow spin under me. I took a step to catch my balance and a luminous sleet was filling the air, and then the whole thing tilted sideways and I slid off and down into the black place that always waited . . .

I woke up looking at a dancing pattern of orange light on a ceiling of polished red and black wood twenty feet overhead. The light was coming from a fire big enough to roast an ox in, blazing away on a hearth built of rocks the size of tombstones. I was lying on a bed not as large as a handball court, and the air was full of the odor of soup. I crawled to the edge and managed the four-foot jump to the floor. My legs felt like overcooked *pasta*. My ribs ached—probably from a long ride over the giant's shoulder.

He looked across at me from the big table. "You were tired," he said. "And you have many bruises."

I looked down. I was wearing my underwear, nothing else.

"My suit!" I barked, and the words came out

thick, not just from weakness. I was picturing sixty-grand worth of equipment and a million credit deal tossed into the reclaimer—or the fire —and a clean set of overalls laid out to replace them.

"There," my host nodded to the end of the bed. I grabbed, checked. Everything looked OK. But I didn't like it; and I didn't like the idea of being helpless, tended by a man I had business with later.

"You have rested," the big man said. "Now eat."

I sat at the table on a pile of blankets and dipped into a dishpanful of thick broth made of savory red and green vegetables and chunks of tender white meat. There was bread that was tough and chewy, with a flavor of nuts, and a rough purple wine that went down better than the finest vintage at Arondo's, on Plaisir 4. Afterward, the giant un-folded a chart and pointed to a patch of high relief like coarse-troweled stucco.

"If the pod is there," he said, "it will be difficult. But perhaps it fell here." He indicated a smoother stretch to the south and east of the badlands.

I went through the motions of checking the azi-muth on the indicator; the heading I gave him was only about three degrees off true. At 113.8 miles— the position the R&D showed for the pod—we would miss the target by about ten miles.

The big man laid off our line of march on his map. It fell along the edge of what he called the Towers of Nandi.

"Perhaps," he said. He wasn't a man given to wasting words.

"How much daylight is left?" I asked him.

"Fifty hours, a little less." That meant I'd been out for nearly six hours. I didn't like that, either. Time was money, and my schedule was tight.

"Have you talked to anyone?" I looked at the big, not quite modern screen at the side of the room. It was a standard Y-band model with a half-millionth L lag. That meant a four-hour turn-around time to the Ring 8 Station.

"I told the monitor station that you had come safely to ground," he said.

"What else did you tell them?"

"There was nothing more to tell."

I stood. "You can call them again now," I said. "And tell them I'm on my way out to the pod." I gave it the tight-lipped no-tears-for-me delivery. From the corner of my eye I saw him nod, and for a second I wondered if maybe the famous Ulrik system of analysis had slipped, if this big hunk of virility was going to sit on his haunches and let poor frail little me tackle the trail alone.

"The way will not be easy," he said. "The winds have come to the high passes. Snow lies on the heights of Kooclain."

"My suit heater will handle that part. If you can spare me some food . . . ."

He went to a shelf, lifted down a pack the size and shape of a climate unit for a five-room conapt. I knew then my trap was closing dead on target.

"If my company will not be unwelcome, Carl Patton, I will go with you," he said.

I went through the routine protestations, but in the end I let him convince me. We left half an hour later, after notifying Ring station that we were on the way.

Johnny Thunder took the lead, swinging along at
an easy amble that covered ground at a deceptive
rate, not bothered by the big pack on his back. He
was wearing the same leathers he had on when he
met me. The only weapon he carried was a ten-foot
steel-shod staff. The monster mutt trotted along
off-side, nose to the ground; I brought up the rear.
My pack was light; the big man pointed out that
the less I carried the better time we'd make. I
managed to keep up, hanging back a little to make
it look good. My bones still ached some, but I was
feeling frisky as a colt in the low G. We did a good
hour without talking, working up along the angle
of a long slope through the big trees. We crested
the rise and the big fellow stopped and waited
while I came up, puffing a little, but game as they
come.

"We will rest here," he said.

"Rest hell," I came back. "Minutes may make all
the difference to those poor devils."

"A man must rest," he said reasonably, and sat
down, propping his bare arms on his knees. This
put his eyes on a level with mine, standing. I didn't
like that, so I sat too.

He took his full ten minutes before starting off
again. Johnny Thunder, I saw, was not a man to be
bullied. He knew his best pace. I was going to have
my hands full walking him to death on his own
turf.

We crossed a wide valley and headed up into high country. It was cold, and the trees were sparser here, gaunter, dwarfed by the frost and twisted by the winds into hunched shapes that clutched the rock like arthritic hands. There were patches of rotten snow, and a hint in the sky that there might be more to come before long. Not that I could feel the edge of the wind that came whipping down off the peaks; but the giant was taking it on his bare arms.

"Don't you own a coat?" I asked him at the next stop. We were on a shelf of rock, exposed to the full blast of what was building to a forty-mile gale.

"I have a cape, here." He slapped the pack on his back. "Later I will wear it."

"You make your own clothes?" I was looking at the tanned leather, fur side in, the big sailmaker's stitches.

"A woman made these garments for me," he said. "That was long ago."

"Yeah," I said. I tried to picture him with his woman, to picture her, how she'd move, what she'd look like. A woman ten feet tall . . . .

"Do you have a picture of her?"

"Only in my heart." He said it matter-of-factly, as if it were a ritual phrase. I wondered how it felt to be the last of your kind, but I didn't ask him that. Instead I asked, "Why do you do it? Live here alone?"

He looked out across a view of refrigerated rock. "This is my home," he said. Another automatic answer, with no thought behind it. It just didn't get to this overgrown plowboy. It never occurred to him how he could milk the situation for tears and cash from a few billion sensation-hungry fans. A real-life soap opera. The end of the trail. Poor Johnny Thunder, so brave and so alone.

"Why do *you* do—what you do?" he asked suddenly. I felt my gut clench like a fist.

"What's that supposed to mean?" I got it out between my teeth, while my hand tickled the crater gun out of its wrist clip and into my palm.

"You too live alone, Carl Patton. You captain a ship of space. You endure solitude and hardship. And as now, you offer your life for your comrades."

"They're not my comrades," I snapped. "They're cash cargo, that's all. No delivery, no payment. And I'm not offering my life. I'm taking a little hike for my health."

He studied me. "Few men would attempt the heights of Kooclain in this season. None without a great reason."

"I've got a great reason. Forty thousand of them."

He smiled a faint smile. "You are many things, I think, Carl Patton. But not a fool."

"Let's hit the trail," I said. "We've got a long way to go before I collect."

Johnny Thunder held his pace back to what he thought I could manage. The dog seemed a little nervous, raising his nose and snuffling the air, then loping ahead. I easy-footed it after them, with plenty of wheezing on the upslopes and some realistic panting at the breaks, enough to make me look busy, but not enough to give the giant ideas of slowing down. Little by little I upped the cadence in an inobtrusive way, until we were hitting better than four miles per hour. That's a good brisk stride on flat ground at a standard G; it would take a trained athlete to keep it up for long. Here, with my suit's efficient piezoelectronic muscles doing most of the work, it was a breeze—for me.

We took a lunch break. The big man dug bread and cheese and a Jeroboam of wine out of his knapsack and handed me enough for two meals. I ate most of it and tucked the rest into the disposal pocket on my shoulder when he wasn't looking. When he finished his ration—not much bigger than mine—I got on my feet and looked expectant. He didn't move.

"We must rest now for an hour," he told me.

"OK," I said. "You rest alone. I've got a job to do." I started off across the patchy snow and got about ten steps before Bowser gallumphed past me and turned, blocking my route. I started past him on the right and he moved into my path. The same for the left.

"Rest, Carl Patton," Goliath said. He lay back and put his hands under his head and closed his eyes. Well, I couldn't keep him walking, but I could cut into his sleep. I went back and sat beside him.

"Lonely country," I said. He didn't answer.

"Looks like nobody's ever been here before," I added. "Not a beer can in sight." That didn't net a reply either.

"What do you live on in this place?" I asked him.
"What do you make the cheese out of, and the
bread?"

He opened his eyes. "The heart of the friendly
tree. It is pulverized for flour, or made into a paste
and fermented."

"Neat," I said. "I guess you import the wine."

"The fruit of the same tree gives us our wine."
He said 'us' as easily as if he had a wife, six kids,
and a chapter of the Knights of Pythias waiting for
him back home.

"It must have been tough at first," I said. "If the
whole planet is like this, it's hard to see how your
ancestors survived."

"They fought," the giant said, as if that
explained everything.

"You don't have to fight anymore," I said. "You
can leave this rock now, live the easy life somewhere under a sun with a little heat in it."

The giant looked at the sky as if thinking. "We
have a legend of a place where the air is soft and
the soil bursts open to pour forth fruit. I do not
think I would like that land."

"Why not? You think there's some kind of kick
in having things rough?"

He turned his head to look at me. "It is you who
suffer hardship, Carl Patton. I am at home; where-
as you endure cold and fatigue, in a place alien to
you."

I grunted. Johnny Thunder had a way of turning
everything I said back at me like a ricochet. "I
heard there was some pretty vicious animal life
here," I said. "I haven't seen any signs of it."

"Soon you will."

"Is that your intuition, or . . . ?"

"A pack of snow scorpions have trailed us for some hours. When we move out into open ground, you will see them."

"How do you know?"

"Woola tells me."

I looked at the big hound, sprawled out with her head on her paws. She looked tired.

"How does it happen you have dogs?"

"We have always had dogs."

"Probably had a pair in the original cargo," I said. "Or maybe frozen embryos. I guess they carried breed stock even way back then."

"Woola springs from a line of dogs of war. Her forebear was the mighty courser Standfast, who slew the hounds of King Roon on the Field of the Broken Knife."

"You people fought wars?" He didn't say anything. I snorted. "I'd think as hard as you had to scratch to make a living, you'd have valued your lives too much for that."

"Of what value is a life without truth? King Roon fought for his beliefs. Prince Dahl fought for his own."

"Who won?"

"They fought for twenty hours; and once Prince Dahl fell, and King Roon stood back and bade him rise again. But in the end Dahl broke the back of the King."

"So—did that prove he was right?"

"Little it matters what a man believes, Carl Patton, so long as he believes it with all his heart and soul."

"Nuts. Facts don't care who believe them."

The giant sat up and pointed to the white peaks glistening far away. "The mountains are true," he said. He looked up at the sky, where high, blackish-purple clouds were piled up like battlements. "The sky is true. And these truths are more than the facts of rock and gas."

"I don't understand this poetic talk," I said. "It's good to eat well, sleep in a good bed, to have the best of everything there is. Anybody that says otherwise is a martyr or a phony."

"What is the best, Carl Patton? Is there a couch softer than weariness? A better sauce than appetite?"

"You got that out of a book."

"If you crave the easy luxury you speak of, why are you here?"

"That's easy. To earn the money to buy the rest."

"And afterwards—if you do not die on this trek —will you go there, to the pretty world, and eat the fat fruits picked by another hand?"

"Sure," I said. "Why not?" I felt myself sounding mad, and wondered why; and that made me madder than ever. I let it drop and pretended to sleep.

Four hours later we topped a long slope and looked out over a thousand square miles of forest and glacier, spread out wide enough to hint at the size of the world called Vangard. We had been walking for nine hours and, lift unit and all, I was beginning to feel it. Big Boy looked as good as new. He shaded his eyes against the sun that was too small and too bright in a before-the-storm sort of way, and pointed out along the valley's rim to a peak a mile or two away.

"There we will sleep," he said.

"It's off our course," I said. "What's wrong with right here?"

"We need shelter and a fire. Holgrimm will not grudge us these."

"What's Holgrimm?"

"His lodge stands there."

I felt a little stir along my spine, the way you do when ghosts come into the conversation. Not that the ghosts worry me; just the people that believe in them.

We covered the distance in silence. Woola, the dog, did a lot of sniffing and grunting as we came up to the lodge. It was built of logs, stripped and carved and stained black. There was a steep gabled roof, slate-tiled, and a pair of stone chimneys, and a few small windows with colored glass leaded into them. The big man paused when we came into the clearing, stood there leaning on his stick and looking around. The place seemed to be in a good state of preservation. But then it was built of the same rock and timber as the country around it. There were no fancy trimmings to weather away.

"Listen, Carl Patton," the giant said. "Almost, you can hear Holgrimm's voice here. In a moment, it seems, he might throw wide the door to welcome us."

"Except he's dead," I said. I went past him and up to the entrance, which was a slab of black and purple wood that would have been right in scale on the front of Notre Dame. I strained two-handed at the big iron latch with no luck. Johnny Thunder lifted it with his thumb.

It was cold in the big room. The coating of frost on the purplewood floor crunched under our boots. In the deep-colored gloom, I saw stretched animal hides on the high walls, green and red, and gold-furred, brilliant as a Chinese pheasant. There were other trophies: a big, beaked skull three feet long, with a spread of antlers like wings of white ivory, that swept forward to present an array of silver dagger tips, black-ringed. There was a leathery-skinned head that was all jaw and teeth; and a tarnished battle ax, ten feet long, with a complicated head. A long table sat in the center of the room between facing fire places as big as city apartments. I saw the wink of light on the big metal goblets, plates, cutlery. There were high-backed chairs around the table; and in the big chair at the far end, facing me, a gray-bearded giant sat with a sword in his hand. The dog whined, a sound that expressed my feelings perfectly.

"Holgrimm awaits us," Johnny's big voice said softly behind me. He went forward, and I broke the paralysis and followed. Closer, I could see the fine frosting of ice that covered the seated giant, glittering in his beard, on the back of his hands, across his open eyes.

Ice rimed the table and the dishes and the smooth black woods of the chairs. Woola's claws rasped loud on the floor as she slunk behind her master.

"Don't you bury your dead?" I got the words out, a little ragged.

"His women prepared him thus, at his command, when he knew his death was on him."

"Why?"

"That is a secret which Holgrimm keeps well."

"We'd be better off outside," I told him. "This place is like a walk-in freezer."

"A fire will mend that."

"Our friend here will melt. I think I prefer him the way he is."

"Only a little fire, enough to warm our food and make a bed of coals to lie beside."

There was wood in a box beside the door, deep red, hard as granite, already split into convenient sizes. Convenient for my traveling companion, I mean. He shuffled the eight-foot, eighteen-inch diameter logs as if they were bread sticks. They must have been full of volatile oil, because they lit off on the first match, and burned with a roaring and a smell of mint and camphor. Big Johnny brewed up a mixture of hot wine and some tarry syrup from a pot on the table that he had to break loose from the ice, and handed me over a half-gallon pot of the stuff. It was strong but good, with a taste that was almost turpentine but turned out to be ambrosia instead. There was bread and cheese and a soup he stirred up in the big pot on the hearth. I ate all I could and wasted some more. My large friend gave himself a Spartan ration, raising his mug to the host before he drank.

"How long has he been dead?" I asked.

"Ten of our years." He paused, then added: "That would be over a hundred, League standard."

"Friend of yours?"

"We fought; but later we drank wine together again. Yes, he was my friend."

"How long have you been . . . alone here?"

"Nine years. Holgrimm's house was almost the last the plague touched."

"Why didn't it kill you?"

He shook his head. "The Universe has its jokes, too."

"How was it, when they were all dying?"

The big man cradled his cup in his hands, looking past me into the fire. "At first, no one understood. We had never known disease here. Our enemies were the ice wolf and the avalanche and the killing frost. This was a new thing, the foe we could not see. Some died bewildered, others fled into the forest where their doom caught them at last. Oxandra slew his sons and daughters before the choking death could take them. Joshal stood in the snow, swinging his war ax and shouting taunts at the sky until he fell and rose no more."

"What about your family?"

"As you see."

"What?"

"Holgrimm was my father."

We slept rolled up in the furs Johnny Thunder took down from the walls and thawed on the hearth. He was right about the heat. The big blaze melted the frost in a ten foot semi-circle, but didn't touch the rest of the room. It was still early afternoon outside when we hit the trail. I crowded the pace all I could. After eight hours of it, over increasingly rough ground, climbing all the time, the big fellow called me on it.

"I'm smaller than you are, but that's no reason I can't be in shape," I told him. "And I'm used to higher G. What's the matter, too rough for you?" I asked the question in an offhand way, but I listened hard for the answer. So far he looked as good as new.

"I fare well enough. The trail has been easy."

"The map says it gets rougher fast from here on."

"The heights will tell on me," he conceded. "Still, I can go on awhile. But Woola suffers, poor brute."

The dog was stretched out on his side. He looked like a dead horse, if dead horses had tails that wagged when their name was mentioned, and ribs that heaved with the effort of breathing the thin air. Thin by Vangard standards, that is. Oxygen pressure was still over Earth-normal.

"Why not send him back?"

"He would not go. And we will be glad of his company when the snow scorpions come."

"Back to that, eh? You sure you're not imagining them? This place looks as lifeless as a tombstone quarry."

"They wait," he said. "They know me, and Woola. Many times have they tried our alertness— and left their dead on the snow. And so they follow, and wait."

"My gun will handle them." I showed him the legal slug-thrower I carried; he looked it over politely.

"A snow scorpion does not die easily," he said.

"This packs plenty of kick," I said, and demonstrated by blasting a chip off a boulder twenty yards away. The *car-rong!* echoed back and forth among the big trees. He smiled a little.

"Perhaps, Carl Patton."

We slept the night at the timber line.

The next day's hike was different, right from the beginning. On the open ground the snow had drifted and frozen into a crust that held my weight, but broke under the giant's feet, and the dog's. There was no kidding about me pushing the pace now. I took the lead and big Johnny had a tough time keeping up. He didn't complain, didn't seem to be breathing too hard; he just kept coming on, stopping every now and then to wait for the pup to catch up, and breaking every hour for a rest.

The country had gotten bleaker as it rose. As long as we'd been among the trees, there had been an illusion of familiarity; not cozy, but at least there was life, almost Earth-type life. You could fool yourself that somewhere over the next rise there might be a house, or a road. But not here. There was just the snow field, as alien as Jupiter, with the long shadows of the western peaks falling across it. And ahead the glacier towering over us against the dark sky, sugar white in the late sun, deep-sea blue in the shadows.

About the third hour, the big man pointed something out to me, far back along the trail. It looked like a scatter of black pepper against the white.

"The scorpion pack," he said.

I grunted. "We won't outrun them standing here."

We did nine hours' hike, up one ridge, down the far side, up another, higher one before he called a halt. Dusk was coming on when we made our camp in the lee of an ice buttress, if you can call a couple of hollows in the frozen snow a camp. The big man got a small fire going, and boiled some soup. He gave me my usual hearty serving, but it seemed to me he shorted himself and the dog a little.

"How are the supplies holding out?" I asked him.

"Well enough," was all he said.

The temperature was down to minus nine Centigrade now. He unpacked his cloak, a black and orange striped super-sheepskin the size of a mains'l, and wrapped himself up in it. He and the dog slept together, curled up for warmth. I turned down the invitation to join them.

"My circulation's good," I said. "Don't worry about me."

But in spite of the suit, I woke up shivering, and had to set the thermostat a few notches higher. Big

Boy didn't seem to mind the cold. But then, an animal his size had an advantage. He had less radiating surface per unit weight. It wasn't freezing that would get him—not unless things got a lot worse.

When he woke me, it was deep twilight; the sun was gone behind the peaks to the west. The route ahead led up the side of a thirty-degree snow slope. There were enough outcroppings of rock and tumbled ice blocks to make progress possible, but it was slow going. The pack on our trail had closed the gap while we slept; I estimated they were ten miles, strung out in a wide crescent. I didn't like that; it suggested more intelligence than anything that looked as bad as the pictures I'd seen. Woola rolled her eyes and showed her teeth and whined, looking back at them. The giant just kept moving forward, slow and steady.

"How about it?" I asked him at the next break. "Do we just let them pick the spot? Or do we fort up somewhere, where they can only jump us from about three and a half sides?"

"They must come to us."

I looked back down the slope we had been climbing steadily for more hours than I could keep track of, trying to judge their distance.

"Not more than five miles," I said. "They could have closed any time in the last couple of hours. What are they waiting for?"

He glanced up at the high ridge, dazzling two miles above. "Up there, the air is thin and cold. They sense that we will weaken."

"And they're right."

"They too will be weakened, Carl Patton, though

not perhaps so much as we." He said this as un-concernedly as if he were talking about whether tomorrow would be a good day for a picnic.

"Don't you care?" I asked him. "Doesn't it matter to you if a pack of hungry meat-eaters corners you in the open?"

"It is their nature," he said simply.

"A stiff upper lip is nifty—but don't let it go to your head. How about setting up an ambush—up there?" I pointed out a jumble of rock slabs a hundred yards above.

"They will not enter it."

"OK," I said. "You're the wily native guide. I'm just a tourist. We'll play it your way. But what do we do when it gets dark?"

"The moon will soon rise."

In the next two hours we covered about three-quarters of a mile. The slope was close to forty-five degrees now. Powdery snow went cascading down in slow plumes with every step. Without the suit, I don't know if I could have stayed with it, even with the low gravity. Big Johnny was using his hands a lot now; and the dog's puffing was pite-ous to hear.

"How old is the mutt?" I asked when we were lying on our backs at the next break, with my trail-mates working hard to get some nourishment out of what to them was some very thin atmosphere, and me faking the same distress, while I breathed the rich mixture from my suit collector.

"Three years."

"That would be about thirty-five standard. How long . . ." I remembered my panting and did some " . . . do they live?"

"No one . . . knows."

"What does that mean?"

"Her kind . . . die in battle."

"It looks like she'll get her chance."

"For that . . . she is grateful."

"She looks scared to death," I said. "And dead beat."

"Weary, yes. But fear is not . . . bred in her."

We made another half mile before the pack decided the time had come to move in to the attack.

The dog knew it first; she gave a bellow like a gut-shot elephant and took a twenty-foot bound down-slope to take up her stand between us and them. It couldn't have been a worse position from the defensive viewpoint, with the exception of the single factor of our holding the high ground. It was a featureless stretch of frozen snow, tilted on edge, naked as a tin roof. The big fellow used his number forty's to stamp out a hollow, working in a circle to widen it.

"You damn fool, you ought to be building a mound," I yelled at him. "That's a cold grave you're digging."

"Do as I do . . . Carl Patton," he panted. "For your life."

"Thanks; I'll stay topside." I picked a spot off to his left and kicked some ice chunks into a heap to give me a firing platform. I made a big show of checking the slug thrower, then unobtrusively set

the crater gun for max range, narrow beam. I
don't know why I bothered playing it foxy; Big Boy
didn't know the different between a legal weapon
and contraband. Maybe it was just the instinct to
have an ace up the sleeve. By the time I finished,
the pack was a quarter of a mile away and coming
up fast, not running or leaping, but twinkling
along on clusters of steel-rod legs that ate up the
ground like a fire eats dry grass.

"Carl Patton, it would be well if you stood by my
back," the big man called.

"I don't need to hide behind you," I barked.

"Listen well!" he said, and for the first time his
voice lacked the easy, almost idle tone. "They
cannot attack in full charge. First must they halt
and raise their barb. In that moment are they vul-
nerable. Strike for the eye—but beware the
ripping claws!"

"I'll work at a little longer range," I called back,
and fired a slug at one a little in advance of the line
but still a couple of hundred yards out. There was
a bright flash against the ice; a near miss. The next
one was dead on—a solid hit in the center of the
leaf-shaped plate of tarnish-black armor that
covered the thorax. He didn't even break stride.

"Strike for the eye, Carl Patton!"

"What eye?" I yelled. "All I see is plate armor
and pistons!" I fired for the legs, missed, missed
again, then sent fragments of a limb flying. The
owner may have faltered for a couple of micro-
seconds, or maybe I just blinked. I wasn't even
sure which one I had hit. They came on, closing
ranks now, looking suddenly bigger, more deadly,
like an assault wave of light armor, barbed and

spiked and invulnerable, with nothing to stop
them but a man with a stick, a worn-out old
hound, and me, with my pop gun. I felt the weapon
bucking in my hand, and realized I had been firing
steadily. I took a step back, dropped the slug
thrower, and palmed the crater gun as the line
reached the spot where Woola crouched,
paralyzed.

But instead of slamming into the big dog at full
bore, the pair facing her skidded to a dead stop,
executed a swift but complicated rearrangement
of limbs, dropping their forward ends to the
ground, bringing their hindquarters up and over,
unsheathing two-foot-long stingers that poised,
ready to plunge down into the unprotected body of
the animal . . . .

I wouldn't have believed anything so big could
move so fast. She came up from her flattened position like a cricket off a hot plate, was in mid-air,
twisting to snap down at anything on the left with
jaws like a bear trap, landed sprawling, spun,
leaped, snapped, and was poised, snarling, while
two ruined attackers flopped and stabbed their
hooks into the ice before her. I saw all this in a fast
half-second while I was bringing the power gun
up, squeezing the firing stud to pump a multi-
megawatt jolt into the thing that was rearing up in
front of me. The shock blasted a foot-wide pit in it,
knocked it a yard backward—but didn't slow its
strike. The barb whipped up, over, and down to
bury itself in the ice between my feet.

"The eye!" The big man's voice boomed at me
over the snarls of Woola and the angry buzzing

that was coming from the attackers. "The eye, Carl Patton!"

I saw it then: a three-inch patch like reticulated glass, deep red, set in the curve of armor above the hook-lined prow. It exploded as I fired. I swiveled left and fired again, from the corner of my eye saw the big man swing his club left, right. I was down off my mound, working my way over to him, slamming shots into whatever was closest. The scorpions were all around us, but only half a dozen at a time could crowd in close to the edge of the twelve-foot depression the giant had tramped out. One went over, pushed from behind, scrabbing for footing, and died as the club smashed down on him. I killed another and jumped down beside the giant.

"Back to back, Carl Patton," he called. A pair came up together over a barricade of dead monsters, and while they teetered for attack position I shot them, then shot the one that mounted their thrashing corpses. Then suddenly the pressure slackened, and I was hearing the big man's steam-engine puffing, the dog's rasping snarls, was aware of a pain in my thigh, of the breath burning in my throat. A scorpion jittered on his thin legs ten feet away, but he came no closer. The others were moving back, buzzing and clacking. I started up over the side and an arm like a jib boom stopped me.

"They must . . . come to us." The giant wheezed out the words. His face was pink and he was having trouble getting enough air, but he was smiling.

"If you say so," I said.

"Your small weapon strikes a man's blow," he said, instead of commenting on my stupidity.

"What are they made of? They took my rounds like two-inch flint steel."

"They are no easy adversaries," he said. "Yet we killed nine." He looked across at where the dog stood panting, facing the enemy. "Woola slew five. They learn caution—" He broke off, looking down at me, at my leg. He went to one knee, touched a tear in my suit I hadn't noticed. That shook me, seeing the ripped edge of the material. Not even a needler could penetrate the stuff—but one of those barbs had.

"The hide is unbroken," he said. "Luck was with you this day, Carl Patton. The touch of the barb is death."

Something moved behind him and I yelled and fired and a scorpion came plunging down on the spot where he'd been standing an instant before. I fell and rolled, came around, put one in the eye just as Johnny Thunder's club slammed home in the same spot. I got to my feet and the rest of them were moving off, back down the slope.

"You damned fool!" I yelled at the giant. Rage broke my voice. "Why don't you watch yourself?"

"I am in your debt, Carl Patton," was all he said.

"Debt, hell! Nobody owes me anything—and that goes both ways!"

He didn't answer that, just looked down at me, smiling a little, like you would at an excited child. I took a couple of deep breaths of warmed and fortified tank air and felt better—but not much.

"Will you tell me your true name, small warrior?" the giant said.

I felt ice form in my chest.

"What do you mean?" I stalled.

"We have fought side by side. It is fitting that we exchange the secret names our mothers gave us at birth."

"Oh, magic, eh? Juju. The secret word of power. Skip it, big fellow. Johnny Thunder is good enough for me."

"As you will . . . Carl Patton." He went to see to the dog then, and I checked to see how badly my suit was damaged. There was a partial power loss in the leg servos and the heat was affected, too. That wasn't good. There were still a lot of miles to walk out of the giant before the job was done.

When we hit the trail half an hour later I was still wondering why I had moved so fast to save the life of the man I'd come here to kill.

We halted for sleep three hours later. It was almost full dark when we turned in, curled up in pits trampled in the snow. Johnny Thunder said the scorpions wouldn't be back, but I sweated inside my insulated longjohns as the last of the light faded to a pitch black like the inside of an unmarked grave. Then I must have dozed off, because I woke with blue-white light in my face. The inner moon, Cronus, had risen over the ridge, a cratered disk ten degrees wide, almost full, looking close enough to jump up and bang your head on.

We made good time in the moonlight, considering the slope of the glacier's skirt we were climbing. At forty-five thousand feet, we topped the barrier and looked down the far side and across a shadowed valley to the next ridge, silver white against the stars, twenty miles away.

"Perhaps on the other side we will find them," the giant said. His voice had lost some of its timbre. His face looked frostbitten, pounded numb by the sub-zero wind. Woola crouched behind him, looking shrunken and old.

"Sure," I said. "Or maybe beyond the next one, or the one after that."

"Beyond these ridges lie the Towers of Nandi. If your friends have fallen there, their sleep will be long—and ours as well."

It was two marches to the next ridge. By then the moon was high enough to illuminate the whole panorama from the crest. There was nothing in sight but ice. We camped in the lee of the crest, then went on. The suit was giving me trouble, unbalanced as it was, and the toes of my right foot were feeling the frost. And in spite of the hot concentrates I sucked on the sly as I hiked, and the synthetic pep the hyposspray metered into an artery, I was starting to feel it now. But not as badly as Big Johnny. He had a gaunt, starved look, and he hiked as though he had anvils tied to his feet. He was still feeding himself and the dog meager rations, and forcing an equal share on me. I stuffed what I couldn't eat in the disposal and watched him starve. But he was tough; he starved slowly, grudgingly, fighting for every inch.

That night, lying back of a barrier he'd built up

out of snow blocks against the wind, he asked me a question.

"What is it like, Carl Patton, to travel across the space between the worlds?"

"Solitary confinement," I told him.

"You do not love your solitude?"

"What does that matter? I do my job."

"What do you love, Carl Patton?"

"Wine, women and song," I said. "And you can even skip the song, in a pinch."

"A woman waits for you?"

"Women," I corrected. "But they're not waiting."

"Your loves seem few, Carl Patton. What then do you hate?"

"Fools," I said.

"Is it fools who have driven you here?"

"Me? Nobody drives me anywhere. I go where I like."

"Then it is freedom you strive for. Have you found it here on my world, Carl Patton?" His face was a gaunt mask like a weathered carving, but his voice was laughing at me.

"You know you're going to die out here, don't you?" I hadn't intended to say that. But I did; and my tone was savage to my own ears.

He looked at me, the way he always did before he spoke, as if he were trying to read a message written on my face.

"A man must die," he said.

"You don't have to be here," I said. "You could break it off now, go back, forget the whole thing."

"As could you, Carl Patton."

"Me quit?" I snapped. "No thanks. My job's not

done."

He nodded. "A man must do what he sets out to do. Else is he no more than a snowflake driven before the wind."

"You think this is a game?" I barked. "A contest? Do or die, or maybe both, and may the best man win?"

"With whom would I contest, Carl Patton? Are we not comrades of the trail?"

"We're strangers," I said. "You don't know me and I don't know you. And you can skip trying to figure out my reasons for what I do."

"You set out to save the lives of the helpless, because it was your duty."

"It's not yours! You don't have to break yourself on these mountains! You can leave this ice factory, live the rest of your days as a hero of the masses, have everything you'd ever want—"

"What I want, no *man* can give me."

"I suppose you hate us," I said. "The strangers that came here and killed your world."

"Who can hate a natural force?"

"All right—what *do* you hate?"

For a minute I thought he wasn't going to answer. "I hate the coward within me," he said. "The voice that whispers counsels of surrender. But if I fled, and saved this flesh, what spirit would then live on to light it?"

"You want to run—then run!" I almost yelled. "You're going to lose this race, big man! Quit while you can!"

"I will go on—while I can. If I am lucky, the flesh will die before the spirit."

"Spirit, hell! You're a suicidal maniac!"

"Then am I in good company, Carl Patton."
I let him take that one.


We passed the hundred-mile mark the next march.
We crossed another ridge, higher than the last.
The cold was sub-arctic, the wind a flaying knife.
The moon set, and the dawn came. My locator told
me when we passed within ten miles of the pod. All
its systems were still going. The power cells were
good for a hundred years. If I slipped up at my
end, the frozen miners might wake up to a new
century; but they'd wake up.

Johnny Thunder was a pitiful sight now. His
hands were split and bloody, his hollow cheeks
and bloodless lips cracked and peeling from frostbite, the hide stretched tight over his bones. He
moved slowly, heavily, wrapped in his furs. But he
moved. I ranged out ahead, keeping the pressure
on. The dog was in even worse shape than his
master. He trailed far behind on the up-slopes,
spent most of each break catching up. Little by
little, in spite of my heckling, the breaks got
longer, the marches shorter. It was late afternoon
again when we reached the high pass that the big
man said led into the badlands he called the
Towers of Nandi. I came up the last stretch of trail
between sheer ice walls and looked out over a
vista of ice peaks sharp as broken bottles, packed
together like shark's teeth, rising up and up in suc-
cessive ranks that reached as far as the eye could
see.

I turned to urge the giant to waste some more strength hurrying to close the gap, but he beat me to it. He was pointing, shouting something I couldn't hear for a low rumble that had started up. I looked up, and the whole side of the mountain was coming down on me.

*The floor was cold. It was the tiled floor of the creche locker room, and I was ten years old, and lying on my face, held there by the weight of a kid called Soup, age fourteen, with the physique of an ape and an IQ to match.*

*When he'd first pushed me back against the wall, knocked aside my punches, and thrown me to the floor, I had cried, called for help to the ring of eager-eyed spectators, most of whom had more than once felt the weight of Soup's knobby knuckles. None of them moved. When he'd bounced my head on the floor and called on me to say uncle, I opened my mouth to say it, and then spat in his face instead. What little restraint Soup had left him then. Now his red-bristled forearm was locked under my jaw, and his knee was in the small of my back, and I knew, without a shadow of a doubt, that Soup was a boy who didn't know his own strength, who would stretch his growing muscles with all the force he could muster—caught up and carried away in the thrill of the discovery of his own animal power—would bend my back until* my spine snapped, and I'd be dead, dead, dead forever more, at the hands of a moron.

Unless I saved myself. I was smarter than Soup—smarter than any of them. Man had conquered the animals with his mind—and Soup was an animal. He couldn't—couldn't kill me. Not if I used my brain, instead of wasting my strength against an animal body twice the size of my own.

I stepped outside my body and looked at myself, saw how he knelt on me, gripping his own wrist, balancing with one outflung foot. I saw how, by twisting to my right side, I could slide out from under the knee; and then, with a sudden movement...

His knee slipped off-center as I moved under him. With all the power in me, I drew up, doubling my body; unbalanced, he started to topple to his right, still gripping me. I threw myself back against him, which brought my head under his chin. I reached back, took a double handful of coarse red hair, and ripped with all my strength.

He screamed, and his grip was gone. I twisted like an eel as he grabbed for my hands, still tangled in his hair; I lunged and buried my teeth in his thick ear. He howled and tried to tear away, and I felt the cartilage break, tasted salty blood. He ripped my hands away, taking hair and a patch of scalp with them. I saw his face, contorted like a demon-mask as he sprawled away from me, still grasping my wrists. I brought my knee up into his crotch, and saw his face turn to green clay. I jumped to my feet; he writhed, coiled, making an ugly choking sound. I took aim and kicked him *hard in the mouth. I landed two more carefully placed kicks, with my full weight behind them, before the rudimentary judgment of the audience awoke and they pulled me away . . . .*

There was movement near me. I heard the rasp of something hard and rough against another hardness. Light appeared. I drew a breath, and saw the white-bearded face of an ancient man looking down at me from far above, from the top of a deep well . . . .

"You still live, Carl Patton." The giant's voice seemed to echo from a long way off. I saw his big hands come down, straining at a slab of ice, saw him lift it slowly, toss it aside. There was snow in his hair, ice droplets in his beard. His breath was frost.

"Get out of here." I forced the words out past the broken glass in my chest. "Before the rest comes down."

He didn't answer; he lifted another slab, and my arms were free. I tried to help, but that just made more snow spill down around my shoulders. He put his big impossible hands under my arms and lifted, dragged me up and out of my grave. I lay on my back and he sprawled beside me. The dog Woola crawled up to him, making anxious noises. Little streamers of snow were coming down from above, being whipped away by the wind. A mass of ice the size of a carrier tender hung unsupported a few hundred feet above.

"Run, you damned fool!" I yelled. It came out as a whisper. He got to his knees, slowly. He scooped me up, rose to his feet. Ice fragments clattered down from above. He took a step forward, toward the badlands.

"Go back," I managed. "You'll be trapped on the far side!"

He halted, as more ice rattled down. "Alone, Carl Patton . . . would *you* turn back?"

"No," I said. "But there's no reason . . . now . . . for you to die . . ."

"Then we will go on." He took another step, and staggered as a piece of ice the size of a basketball struck him a glancing blow on the shoulder. The dog snarled at his side. It was coming down around us like rice at a wedding now. He went on, staggering like a drunk, climbing up over the final drift. There was a boom like a cannon shot from above; air whistled past us, moving out. He made three more paces and went down, dropped me, knelt over me like a shaggy tent. I heard him grunt as the ice fragments struck him. Somewhere behind us there was a smash like a breaking dam. The air was full of snow, blinding, choking. The light faded . . .

The dead were crying. It was a sad, lost sound, full of mournful surprise that life had been so short and so full of mistakes. I understood how they felt. Why shouldn't I? I was one of them.

But corpses didn't have headaches, as well as I could remember. Or cold feet, or weights that crushed them against sharp rocks. Not unless the stories about where the bad ones went were true. I opened my eyes to take a look at Hell, and saw the hound. She whined again, and I got my head around and saw an arm bigger than my leg. The weight I felt was what was left of Johnny Thunder, sprawled across me, under a blanket of broken ice.

It took me half an hour to work my way free. The suit was what had saved me, of course, with its automatic defensive armor. I was bruised, and a rib or two were broken, but there was nothing I couldn't live with until I got back to base and my million credits.

Because the job was done. The giant didn't move while I was digging out, didn't stir when I thumbed up his eyelid. He still had some pulse, but it wouldn't last long. He had been bleeding from ice wounds on his face and hands, but the blood had frozen. What the pounding hadn't finished the cold would. And even if he came around, the wall of ice behind him closed the pass like a vault door. When the sob sisters arrived to check on their oversized pet they'd find him here, just as I described him, the noble victim of the weather and the piece of bad luck that had made us miss our target by a tragic ten miles, after that long, long hike. They'd have a good syndicated cry over how he'd given his all, and then close the book on another footnote to history. It had worked out just the way I'd planned. Not that I got any big kick out of having proved my cleverness once again. It was routine, just a matter of analyzing the data and then using it.

"So long, Johnny Thunder," I said. "You were a lot of man."

The dog lifted his head and whined. I switched the lift-unit built into my suit to maximum assist and headed for the pod, fifteen miles away.

The twenty-foot-long cargo unit was nestled in a drift of hard-packed snow, in a little hollow among barren rock peaks, not showing a scratch. I wasn't surprised; the auto gear I had installed could have soft-landed a china shop without cracking a teacup. I had contracted to deliver my load intact, and it was a point of pride with me to fulfill the letter of a deal. I was so busy congratulating myself on that that I was fifty feet from it before I noticed that the snow had been disturbed around the pod: trampled, maybe, then brushed out to conceal the tracks. By then it was too late to become invisible; if there was anybody around, they had already seen me. I stopped ten feet from the entry hatch and went through the motions of collapsing in a pitiful little heap, all tuckered out from my exertions, meanwhile looking around, over, and under the pod. I didn't see anything.

I lay where I was long enough for anybody who wanted to make his entrance. No takers. That left the play up to me. I made a production out of getting my feet under me and staggering to the entry hatch. The scratches there told me that part of the story. The port mechanism was still intact. It opened on command and I crawled into the lock. Inside, everything looked normal. The icebox seal was tight, the dials said the cooler units were operating perfectly. I almost let it go at that, but not quite. I don't know why, except that a lifetime of painful lessons had taught me to take nothing for granted. It took me half an hour to get the covers off the reefer controls. When I did, I saw it right away: a solenoid hung in the half-open position. It was the kind of minor malfunction you might expect after a hard landing—but not if you knew what I knew. It had been jimmied, the support bent a fractional millimeter out of line, just enough to jam the action—and incidentally to actuate the heating cycle that would thaw the ten men inside the cold room in ten hours flat. I freed it, heard gas hiss into the lines, then cracked the vault door and checked visually. The inside gauge read $+3°$ absolute. The temperature hadn't had time to start rising yet; the ten long boxes and their contents were still intact. That meant the tampering had been done recently. I was still mulling over the implications of that deduction when I heard the crunch of feet on the ice outside the open lock.

Illini looked different than he had when I had seen him last, back in the plush bureaucratic setting of League Central. His monkey face behind the cold mask looked pinched and bloodless; his long nose was blue with cold, his jaw a scruffy unshaven blue. He didn't seem surprised to see me. He stepped up through the hatch and a second man followed him. They looked around, took in the marks in the frost crust around the reefer, held on the open panel.

"Everything all right here?" the little man asked me. He made it casual, as if we'd just happened to meet on the street.

"Almost," I said. "A little trouble with a solenoid. Nothing serious."

Illini nodded as if that was par for the course. His eyes flicked over me. "Outside, you seemed to be in difficulty," he said. "I see you've made a quick recovery."

"It must have been psychosomatic," I said. "Getting inside took my mind off it."

"I take it the subject is dead?"

"Hell, no," I said. "He's alive and well in Phoenix, Arizona. How did you find the pod, Illini?"

"I was lucky enough to persuade the black marketeer who supplied your homing equipment to sell me its twin, tuned to the same code." He looked mildly amused. "Don't be too distressed, Ulrik. There are very few secrets from an unlimited budget."

"One is enough," I said. "Played right. But you haven't said why."

"The scheme you worked out was clever," he said. "Somewhat over-devious, perhaps—but clever. Up to a point. It was apparent from the special equipment installed in the pod that you had some idea of your cargo surviving the affair."

"So?"

"You wanted to present the public with a tidy image to treasure, Ulrik. Well and good. But the death of the freak in a misguided attempt to rescue men who were never in danger would smack of the comic. People might be dissatisfied. They might begin investigating the circumstances which allowed their pet to waste himself. But if it appears he *might* have saved the men—then the public will accept his martyrdom."

"You plan to spend ten men on the strength of that theory?"

"It's a trivial price to pay for extra insurance."

"And here you are, to correct my mistakes. How do you plan to square it with the Monitor Service? They take a dim view of unauthorized planetfalls."

Illini gave me his I-just-ate-the-canary look. "I'm here quite legally. By great good fortune, my yacht happened to be cruising in the vicinity and picked up your U-beam. Ring Station accepted my offer of assistance."

"I see. And what have you got in mind for me?"

"Just what was agreed on, of course. I have no intention of complicating the situation at this point. We'll proceed with your plan precisely as conceived—with the single exception I've noted. I can rely on your discretion, for obvious reasons. Your fee is already on deposit at Credit Central."

"You've got it all worked out, haven't you? But you overlooked one thing: I'm temperamental. I don't like people making changes in my plans."

Illini lifted a lip. "I'm aware of your penchant for salving your conscience as a professional assassin by your nicety in other matters. But in this

case I'm afraid my desires must prevail." The
hand of the man behind him strayed casually to
the gun at his hip. So far, he hadn't said a word. He
didn't have to. He'd be a good man with a side
arm. Illini wouldn't have brought anything but the
best. Or maybe the second best. It was a point I'd
probably have to check soon.

"Our work here will require only a few hours,"
Illini said. "After that . . ." he made an expansive
gesture. "We're all free to take up other matters."
He smiled as though everything had been cleared
up. "By the way, where is the body? I'll want to
view it, just as a matter of routine."

I folded my arms and leaned against the bulkhead. I did it carefully, just in case I was wrong
about a few things. "What if I don't feel like telling
you?"

"In that case, I'd be forced to insist." Illini's
eyes were wary. The gunsel had tensed.

"Uh-huh," I said. "This is a delicate setup. A
charred corpse wouldn't help the picture."

"Podnac's instructions are to disable, not kill."

"For a public servant doing his job, you seem to
be taking a lot of chances, Illini. It couldn't be that
the selfless motive of eliminating a technicality so
that progress could come to Vangard, the way the
Commissioner told it, is marred by some private
consideration?"

Illini lifted his shoulders. "I own an interest in
the planetary exploitation contract, yes. Someone
was bound to profit. Why not those who made it
possible?"

"That's another one on me," I said. "I should
have held out for a percentage."

"That's enough gossip," Illini said. "Don't try to stall me, Ulrik. Speak up or suffer the consequences."

I shook my head. "I'm calling your bluff, Illini. The whole thing is balanced on a knife edge. Any sign of trouble here—even a grease spot on the deck—and the whole thing is blown."

Podnac made a quick move and his gun was in his hand. I grinned at it. "That's supposed to scare me so I go outside where you can work a little better, eh?"

"I'm warning you, Ulrik—"

"Skip it. I'm not going anywhere. But you're leaving, Illini. You've got your boat parked somewhere near here. Get in it and lift off. I'll take it from there."

"You fool! You'd risk the entire operation for the sake of a piece of mawkish sentiment?"

"It's my operation, Illini. I'll play it out my way or not at all. I'm like that. That's why you hired me, remember?"

He drew a breath like a man getting ready for a deep dive, snorted it out. "You don't have a chance, Ulrik! You're throwing everything away—for what?"

"Not everything. You'll still pay off for a finished job. It's up to you. You can report you checked the pod and found everything normal. Try anything else and the bubble pops."

"There are two of us. We could take you barehanded."

"Not while I've got my hand on the gun under my arm."

The little man's eyes ate me raw. There were

things he wanted to say, but instead he made a face like a man chewing glass and jerked his head at his hired hand. They walked sideways to the hatch and jumped down. I watched them back away.

"I'll get you for this," Illini told me. "I promise you that."

"No you won't," I said. "You'll just count those millions and keep your mouth shut. That's the way the Commissioner would like it."

They turned and I straightened and dropped my hands, and Podnac spun and fired and the impact knocked me backward twenty feet across the hold.

The world was full of roaring lights and blazing sounds, but I held onto a slender thread of consciousness, built it into a rope, crawled back up it. I did it because I had to. I made it just in time. Podnac was coming through the hatch, Illini's voice yapping behind him. I covered him and pressed the stud and blew him back out of sight.

I was numb all over, like a thumb that's just been hit by a hammer. I felt hot fluid trickling down the inside of my suit, felt broken bones grate. I tried to move and almost blacked out. I knew then: this was one scrape I wouldn't get out of. I'd had it. Illini had won.

His voice jarred me out of a daze.

"He fired against my order, Ulrik! You heard me tell him! I'm not responsible!"

I blinked a few times and could see the little man through the open port, standing in a half crouch on the spot where I'd last seen him, watching the dark hatchway for the flash that would finish him. He was holding the winning cards, and didn't know it. He didn't know how hard I'd been hit, that he could have strolled in and finished the job with no opposition. He thought tough, smart Baird Ulrik had rolled with another punch, was holding on him now, cool and deadly and in charge of everything.

OK. I'd do my best to keep him thinking that. I was done for, but so was he—if I could con him into leaving now. When the Monitors showed up and found my corpse and the note I'd manage to write before the final night closed down, Illini and Company would be out of the planet-stealing business and into a penal colony before you could say malfeasance in high office. I looked around for my voice, breathed on it a little, and called:

"We won't count that one, Illini. Take your boy and lift off. I'll be watching. So will the monitor scopes. If you try to land again you'll have them to explain to."

"I'll do as you say, Ulrik. It's your show. I . . . I'll have to use a lift harness on Podnac."

I didn't answer that one. I couldn't. That worried Illini.

"Ulrik? I'm going to report that I found everything in order. Don't do anything foolish. Remember your million credits."

"Get going," I managed. I watched him back a few steps, then turn and scramble up the slope. The lights kept fading and coming up again.

Quite suddenly Illini was there again, guiding the slack body of his protege as it hung in the harness. When I looked again they were gone. Then I let go of whatever it was I had been hanging onto, and fell forever through endlessness.

When I woke up, Johnny Thunder was sitting beside me.

He gave me water. I drank it and said, "You big, dumb ox! What are you doing here?" I said that, but all that came out was a dry wheeze, like a collapsing lung. I lay with my head propped against the wall, the way he had laid me out, and looked at the big, gaunt face, the cracked and peeling lips, the matted hair caked with ice, the bright blue eyes fixed on mine.

"I woke and found you had gone, Carl Patton." His voice had lost its resonance. He sounded like an old man. "Woola led me here."

I thought that over—and then I saw it. It almost made me grin. A note written in blood might poke a hole in Illini's plans—but a live giant would sink them with all hands.

I made another try and managed a passable whisper: "Listen to me, Johnny. Listen hard, because once is all you're likely to get it. This whole thing was a fix—a trick to get you dead. Because as long as you were alive, they couldn't touch your world. The men here were never in danger. At least they weren't meant to be. But there was a change in plan. But that's only after you're taken care of. And if you're alive . . ." It was getting too complicated.

"Never mind that," I said. "You outsmarted 'em. Outsmarted all of us. You're alive after all. Now the trick is to stay that way. So you lie low. There's heat and emergency food stores here, all you need until pickup. And then you'll have it made. There was a jammed solenoid, you understand? You know what a solenoid looks like? And you freed it. You saved the men. You'll be a hero. They won't dare touch you then . . . ."

"You are badly hurt, Carl Patton—"

"My name's not Carl Patton, damn you! It's Ulrik! I'm a hired killer, understand? I came here to finish you—"

"You have lost much blood, Ulrik. Are there medical supplies here?"

"Nothing that will help me. I took a power gun blast in the hip. My left leg is nothing but bone splinters and hamburger. The suit helped me some —but not enough. But forget that. What's important is that they don't know you're alive! If they sneak back for another look and discover that— before the relief crew gets here—then they win. And they can't win, understand? I won't let 'em!"

"At my house there is a medical machine. The doctors placed it there, after the Sickness. It can heal you."

"Sure—and at Med Center they'd have me dancing the Somali in thirty-six hours. And if I'd stayed away, I wouldn't have been in this fix at all! Forget all that and concentrate on staying alive . . . ."

I must have faded out then, because the next I knew someone was sticking dull knives in my side. I got my eyelids up and saw my suit open and lots of blood. Big Johnny was doing things to my leg. I told him to leave me alone, but he went on sawing at me with red-hot saws, pouring hot acid into the wounds. And then after a while I was coming up from a long way down, looking at my leg, bandaged to the hip with tape from the first aid locker.

"You have much strength left, Ulrik," he said. "You fought me like the frost-demon."

I wanted to tell him to let it alone, let me die in peace, but no sound came out. The giant was on his feet, wrapped in the purple and green fur. He squatted and picked me up, turned to the port. I tried again to yell, to tell him that the play now was to salvage the only thing that was left; revenge. That he'd had his turn at playing St. Bernard to the rescue, that another hopeless walk in the snow would only mean that Dombeck and Illini won after all, that my bluff had been for nothing. But it was no use. I felt him stagger as the wind hit him, heard my suit thermostat click on. Then the cotton-wool blanket closed over me.

I don't remember much about the trip back. The suit's metabolic monitor kept me doped—those and nature's defenses against the sensation of being carried over a shoulder through a blizzard, while the bone chips separated and began working their way through the crushed flesh of my thigh. Once I looked into the big, frost-scarred face, met the pain-dulled eyes.

"Leave me here," I said. "I don't want help. Not from you, not from anybody. I win or lose on my own."

He shook his head.

"Why?" I said. "Why are you doing it?"

"A man," he said. "A man . . . must do . . . what he sets out to do."

He went on. He was a corpse, but he wouldn't lie down and die.

I ate and drank from the tubes in my mouth from reflex. If I'd been fully awake I'd have starved myself to shorten the ordeal. Sometimes I was conscious for a half an hour at a stretch, knowing how a quarter of beef felt on the butcher's hook; and other times I slept and dreamed I had passed the entrance exams for Hell. A few times I was aware of falling, of lying in the snow, and then of big hands that painfully lifted, grunting, of the big, tortured body plodding on.

Then there was another fall, somehow more final than the others. For a long time I lay where I was, waiting to die. And after a while it got through to me that the suit wouldn't let me go as easily as that. The food and the auto-drugs that would keep a healthy man healthy for a year would keep a dying man in torture for almost as long. I was stuck on this side of the river, like it or not. I opened my eyes to tell the giant what I thought of that, and saw his house, looming tall against the big trees a hundred yards away. It

didn't take me more than a day to crawl to it. I
did it a hundred miles at a time, over a blanket of
broken bottles. The door resisted for a while, but
in the end I got my weight against it and it swung
in and dumped me on the plank floor. After that
there was another long, fuzzy time while I clawed
my way to the oversized med cabinet, got it
opened, and fell inside. I heard the diagnostic unit
start up, felt the sensors moving over me. Then I
didn't know any more for a long, long time.

This time I came out of it clearheaded, hungry,
pain-free, and with a walking cast on my leg. I
looked around for my host, but I was all alone in
the big lodge. There was no cheery blaze on the
hearth, but the house was as warm as toast. At
some time in the past, the do-gooders had installed
a space-heater with automatic controls to keep the
giant cozy if the fire went out. I found some food
on the shelves and tried out my jaws for the first
time in many days. It was painful, but satisfying. I
fired up the comm rig and got ready to tell the
Universe my story. Then I remembered there were
still a few details to clear up. I went to the door
with a vague idea of seeing if Johnny Thunder was
outside, chopping wood for exercise. All I saw was
a stretch of wind-packed snow, the backdrop of
giant trees, the gray sky hanging low overhead like
wet canvas. Then I noticed something else: An
oblong drift of snow, halfway between me and the

forest wall.

The sound of snow crust crunching under my feet was almost explosively loud in the stillness as I walked across to the long mound. He lay on his back, his eyes open to the sky, glazed over with ice. His arms were bent at the elbow, the hands open as if he were carrying a baby. The snow was drifted over him, like a blanket to warm him in his sleep. The dog was beside him, frozen at his post.

I looked at the giant for a long time, and words stirred inside of me: Things that needed a voice to carry them across the gulf wider than space to where he had gone. But all I said was: "You made it, Johnny. We were the smart ones; but you were the one that did what you set out to do."

I flipped up the SEND key, ready to fire the blast that would sink Dombeck and crew like a lead canoe; but then the small, wise voice of discretion started whispering to me. Nailing them would have been a swell gesture for me to perform as a corpse, frozen with a leer of triumph on my face, thumbing my nose from the grave. I might even have had a case for blowing them sky-high to save Johnny Thunder's frozen paradise for him, in view of the double-cross they'd tried on me.

But I was alive, and Johnny was dead. And that million was still waiting. There was nothing back at the pod that couldn't be explained in terms of the big bad scorpion that had chewed my leg.

Johnny would be a hero, and they'd put up a nice marker for him on some spot the excavating rigs didn't chew up—I'd see to that.

In the end I did the smart thing, the shrewd thing. I told them what they wanted to hear; that the men were safe, and that the giant had died a hero like a giant should. Then I settled down to wait for the relief boat.

I collected. Since then I've been semi-retired. That's a nice way of saying that I haven't admitted to myself that I'm not taking any more assignments. I've spent my time for the past year traveling, seeing the sights, trying out the luxury spots, using up a part of the income on the pile I've stashed away. I've eaten and drunk and wenched and sampled all the kicks from air-skiing to deep-sea walking, but whatever it is I'm looking for, I have a hunch I won't find it, any more than the rest of the drones and thrill-seekers will.

It's a big, impersonal Universe, and little men crave the thing that will give them stature against the loom of stars.

But in a world where once there was a giant, the rest of us are forever pygmies.

# III

The sun could not fail in rising over the Kentucky hills, nor could Kyle Arnam in waking. There would be eleven hours and forty minutes of daylight. Kyle rose, dressed, and went out to saddle the gray gelding and the white stallion. He rode the stallion until the first fury was out of the arched and snowy neck; and then led both horses around to tether them outside the kitchen door. Then he went in to breakfast.

The message that had come a week before was beside his plate of bacon and eggs. Teena, his wife, was standing at the breadboard with her back to him. He sat down and began eating, rereading the letter as he ate.

" . . . The Prince will be traveling incognito under one of his family titles, as Count Sirii North; and should not be addressed as 'Majesty.' *You will call him 'Lord'* . . . "

"Why does it have to be you?" Teena asked.

He looked up and saw how she stood with her back to him.

"Teena—" he said, sadly.

"Why?"

"My ancestors were bodyguards to his—back in the wars of conquest against the aliens. I've told you that," he said. "My forefathers saved the lives of his, many times when there was no warning—a Rak spaceship would suddenly appear out of nowhere to lock on, even to a flagship. And even an Emperor found himself fighting for his life, hand to hand."

"The aliens are all dead now, and the Emperor's got a hundred other worlds! Why can't his son take his Grand Tour on them? Why does he have to come here to Earth—and you?"

"There's only one Earth."

"And only one you, I suppose?"

He sighed internally and gave up. He had been raised by his father and his uncle after his mother died, and in an argument with Teena he always felt helpless. He got up from the table and went to her, putting his hands on her and gently trying to turn her about. But she resisted.

He sighed inside himself again and turned away to the weapons cabinet. He took out a loaded slug pistol, fitted it into the stubby holster it matched, and clipped the holster to his belt at the left of the buckle, where the hang of his leather jacket would hide it. Then he selected a dark-handled knife with a six-inch blade and bent over to slip it into the sheath inside his boot top. He dropped the cuff of his trouser leg back over the boot top and stood up.

"He's got no right to be here," said Teena fiercely to the breadboard. "Tourists are supposed to be kept to the museum areas and the tourist lodges."

"He's not a tourist. You know that," answered Kyle, patiently. "He's the Emperor's oldest son and his great-grandmother was from Earth. His wife will be, too. Every fourth generation the Imperial line has to marry back into Earth stock. That's the law—still." He put on his leather jacket, sealing it closed only at the bottom to hide the slug-gun holster, half turned to the door—then paused.

"Teena?" he asked.

She did not answer.

"Teena!" he repeated. He stepped to her, put his hands on her shoulders and tried to turn her to face him. Again, she resisted, but this time he was having none of it.

He was not a big man, being of middle height, round-faced, with sloping and unremarkable-looking, if thick, shoulders. But his strength was not ordinary. He could bring the white stallion to its knees with one fist wound in its mane—and no other man had ever been able to do that. He turned her easily to look at him.

"Now, listen to me—" he began. But, before he could finish, all the stiffness went out of her and she clung to him, trembling.

"He'll get you into trouble—I know he will!" she choked, muffledly into his chest. "Kyle, don't go! There's no law making you go!"

He stroked the soft hair of her head, his throat stiff and dry. There was nothing he could say to her. What she was asking was impossible. Ever since the sun had first risen on men and women together, wives had clung to their husbands at times like this, begging for what could not be. And always the men had held them, as Kyle was holding her now—as if understanding could somehow be pressed from one body into the other—and saying nothing, because there was nothing that could be said.

So, Kyle held her for a few moments longer, and then reached behind him to unlock her intertwined fingers at his back, and loosen her arms around him. Then, he went. Looking back through the kitchen window as he rode off on the stallion, leading the gray horse, he saw her standing just where he had left her. Not even crying, but standing with her arms hanging down, her head down, not moving.

He rode away through the forest of the Kentucky hillside. It took him more than two hours to reach the lodge. As he rode down the valleyside toward it, he saw a tall, bearded man, wearing the robes they wore on some of the Younger Worlds, standing at the gateway to the interior courtyard of the rustic, wooded lodge.

When he got close, he saw that the beard was graying and the man was biting his lips. Above a straight, thin nose, the eyes were bloodshot and circled beneath as if from worry or lack of sleep.

"He's in the courtyard," said the gray-bearded man as Kyle rode up. "I'm Montlaven, his tutor. He's ready to go." The darkened eyes looked almost pleadingly up at Kyle.

"Stand clear of the stallion's head," said Kyle. "And take me in to him."

"Not that horse, for him—" said Montlaven,

looking distrustfully at the stallion, as he backed away.

"No," said Kyle. "He'll ride the gelding."

"He'll want the white."

"He can't ride the white," said Kyle. "Even if I let him, he couldn't ride this stallion. I'm the only one who can ride him. Take me in."

The tutor turned and led the way into the grassy courtyard, surrounding a swimming pool and looked down upon, on three sides, by the windows of the lodge. In a lounging chair by the pool sat a tall young man in his late teens, with a mane of blond hair, a pair of stuffed saddlebags on the grass beside him. He stood up as Kyle and the tutor came toward him.

"Majesty," said the tutor, as they stopped, "this is Kyle Arnam, your bodyguard for the three days here."

"Good morning, Bodyguard . . . Kyle, I mean." The Prince smiled mischievously. "Light, then. And I'll mount."

"You ride the gelding, Lord," said Kyle.

The Prince stared at him, tilted back his handsome head, and laughed.

"I can ride, man!" he said. "I ride well."

"Not this horse, Lord," said Kyle, dispassionately. "No one rides this horse, but me."

The eyes flashed wide, the laugh faded—then returned.

"What can I do?" The wide shoulders shrugged. "I give in—always I give in. Well, almost always." He grinned up at Kyle, his lips thinned, but frank. "All right."

He turned to the gelding—and with a sudden leap was in the saddle. The gelding snorted and plunged at the shock; then steadied as the young man's long fingers tightened expertly on the reins and the fingers of the other hand patted a gray neck. The Prince raised his eyebrows, looking over at Kyle, but Kyle sat stolidly.

"I take it you're armed, good Kyle?" the Prince said slyly. "You'll protect me against the natives if they run wild?"

"Your life is in my hands, Lord," said Kyle. He unsealed the leather jacket at the bottom and let it fall open to show the slug pistol in its holster for a moment. Then he resealed the jacket again at the bottom.

"Will—" The tutor put his hand on the young man's knee. "Don't be reckless, boy. This is Earth and the people here don't have rank and custom like we do. Think before you—"

"Oh, cut it out, Monty!" snapped the Prince. "I'll be just as incognito, just as humble, as archaic and independent as the rest of them. You think I've no memory! Anyway, it's only for three days or so until my Imperial father joins me. Now, let me go!"

He jerked away, turned to lean forward in the saddle, and abruptly put the gelding into a bolt for the gate. He disappeared through it, and Kyle drew hard on the stallion's reins as the big white horse danced and tried to follow.

"Give me his saddlebags," said Kyle.

The tutor bent and passed them up. Kyle made them fast on top of his own, across the stallion's withers. Looking down, he saw there were tears in the bearded man's eyes.

"He's a fine boy. You'll see. You'll know he is!" Montlaven's face, upturned, was mutely pleading.

"I know he comes from a fine family," said Kyle, slowly. "I'll do my best for him." And he rode off out of the gateway after the gelding.

When he came out of the gate, the Prince was nowhere in sight. But it was simple enough for Kyle to follow, by dinted brown earth and crushed grass, the marks of the gelding's path. This brought him at last through some pines to a grassy open slope where the Prince sat looking skyward through a single-lens box.

When Kyle came up, the Prince lowered the instrument and, without a word, passed it over. Kyle put it to his eye and looked skyward. There was the whir of the tracking unit and one of Earth's three orbiting power stations swam into the field of vision of the lens.

"Give it back," said the Prince.

"I couldn't get a look at it earlier," went on the young man as Kyle handed the lens to him. "And I wanted to. It's a rather expensive present, you know—it and the other two like it—from our Imperial treasury. Just to keep your planet from drifting into another ice age. And what do we get for it?"

"Earth, Lord," answered Kyle. "As it was before men went out to the stars."

"Oh, the museum areas could be maintained with one station and a half-million caretakers," said the Prince. "It's the other two stations and you billion or so free-loaders I'm talking about. I'll have to look into it when I'm Emperor. Shall we ride?"

"If you wish, Lord." Kyle picked up the reins of the stallion and the two horses with their riders moved off across the slope.

" . . . And one more thing," said the Prince, as they entered the farther belt of pine trees. "I don't want you to be misled—I'm really very fond of old Monty, back there. It's just that I wasn't really planning to come here at all—*Look at me, Bodyguard!*"

Kyle turned to see the blue eyes that ran in the Imperial family blazing at him. Then, unexpectedly, they softened. The Prince laughed.

"You don't scare easily, do you, Bodyguard . . . Kyle, I mean?" he said. "I think I like you after all. But look at me when I talk."

"Yes, Lord."

"That's my good Kyle. Now, I was explaining to you that I'd never actually planned to come here on my Grand Tour at all. I didn't see any point in visiting this dusty old museum world of yours with people still trying to live like they lived in the Dark Ages. But—my Imperial father talked me into it."

"Your father, Lord?" asked Kyle.

"Yes, he bribed me, you might say," said the Prince thoughtfully. "He was supposed to meet me here for these three days. Now, he's messaged there's been a slight delay—but that doesn't matter. The point is, he belongs to the school of old men who still think your Earth is something precious and vital. Now, I happen to like and admire my father, Kyle. You approve of that?"

"Yes, Lord."

"I thought you would. Yes, he's the one man in the human race I look up to. And to please him, I'm making this Earth trip. And to please him—only to please *him*, Kyle—I'm going to be an easy Prince for you to conduct around to your natural wonders and watering spots and whatever. Now, you understand me—and how this trip is going to go. Don't you?" He stared at Kyle.

"I understand," said Kyle.

"That's fine," said the Prince, smiling once more. "So now you can start telling me all about these trees and birds and animals so that I can memorize their names and please my father when he shows up. What are those little birds I've been seeing under the trees—brown on top and whittish underneath? Like that one—there!"

"That's a Veery, Lord," said Kyle. "A bird of the deep woods and silent places. Listen—" He reached out a hand to the gelding's bridle and brought both horses to a halt. In the sudden silence, off to their right they could hear a silver bird voice, rising and falling, in a descending series of crescendos and diminuendos, that softened at last into silence. For a moment after the song was ended the Prince sat staring at Kyle, then seemed to shake himself back to life.

"Interesting," he said. He lifted the reins Kyle had let go and the horses moved forward again. "Tell me more."

For more than three hours, as the sun rose toward noon, they rode through the wooded hills, with Kyle identifying bird and animal, insect, tree and rock. And for three hours the Prince listened —his attention flashing and momentary, but intense. But when the sun was overhead that intensity flagged.

"That's enough," he said. "Aren't we going to stop for lunch? Kyle, aren't there any towns around here?"

"Yes, Lord," said Kyle. "We've passed several."

"Several?" The Prince stared at him. "Why haven't we come into one before now? Where are you taking me?"

"Nowhere, Lord," said Kyle. "You lead the way. I only follow."

"I?" said the Prince. For the first time he seemed to become aware that he had been keeping the gelding's head always in advance of the stallion. "Of course. But now it's time to eat."

"Yes, Lord," said Kyle. "This way."

He turned the stallion's head down the slope of the hill they were crossing and the Prince turned the gelding after him.

"And now listen," said the Prince, as he caught up. "Tell me I've got it all right." And to Kyle's astonishment, he began to repeat, almost word for word, everything that Kyle had said. "Is it all there? Everything you told me?"

"Perfectly, Lord," said Kyle. The Prince looked slyly at him.

"Could you do that, Kyle?"

"Yes," said Kyle. "But these are things I've known all my life."

"You see?" The Prince smiled. "That's the difference between us, good Kyle. You spend your life learning something—I spend a few hours and I know as much about it as you do."

"Not as much, Lord," said Kyle, slowly.

The Prince blinked at him, then jerked his hand dismissingly, and half-angrily, as if he were throwing something aside.

"What little else there is probably doesn't count," he said.

They rode down the slope and through a winding valley and came out at a small village. As they rode clear of the surrounding trees a sound of music came to their ears.

"What's that?" The Prince stood up in his stirrups. "Why, there's dancing going on, over there."

"A beer garden, Lord. And it's Saturday—a holiday here."

"Good. We'll go there to eat."

They rode around to the beer garden and found tables back away from the dance floor. A pretty, young waitress came and they ordered, the Prince smiling sunnily at her until she smiled back—then hurried off as if in mild confusion. The Prince ate hungrily when the food came and drank a stein and a half of brown beer, while Kyle ate more lightly and drank coffee.

"That's better," said the Prince, sitting back at last. "I had an appetite . . . Look there, Kyle! Look, there are five, six . . . seven drifter platforms parked over there. Then you don't all ride horses?"

"No," said Kyle. "It's as each man wishes."

"But if you have drifter platforms, why not other civilized things?"

"Some things fit, some don't, Lord," answered Kyle. The Prince laughed.

"You mean you try to make civilization fit this old-fashioned life of yours, here?" he said. "Isn't that the wrong way around—" He broke off. "What's that they're playing now? I like that. I'll bet I could do that dance." He stood up. "In fact, I think I will."

He paused, looking down at Kyle.

"Aren't you going to warn me against it?" he asked.

"No, Lord," said Kyle. "What you do is your own affair."

The young man turned away abruptly. The waitress who had served them was passing, only a few tables away. The Prince went after her and caught up with her by the dance floor railing. Kyle could see the girl protesting—but the Prince hung over her, looking down from his tall height, smiling. Shortly, she had taken off her apron and was out on the dance floor with him, showing him the steps of the dance. It was a polka.

The Prince learned with fantastic quickness. Soon, he was swinging the waitress around with the rest of the dancers, his foot stamping on the turns, his white teeth gleaming. Finally the number ended and the members of the band put down their instruments and began to leave the stand.

The Prince, with the girl trying to hold him back, walked over to the band leader. Kyle got up quickly from his table and started toward the floor.

The band leader was shaking his head. He turned abruptly and slowly walked away. The Prince started after him, but the girl took hold of his arm, saying something urgent to him.

He brushed her aside and she stumbled a little. A busboy among the tables on the far side of the dance floor, not much older than the Prince and nearly as tall, put down his tray and vaulted the railing onto the polished hardwood. He came up behind the Prince and took hold of his arm, swinging him around.

" . . . Can't do that here." Kyle heard him say, as Kyle came up. The Prince struck out like a panther—like a trained boxer—with three quick lefts in succession into the face of the busboy, the Prince's shoulder bobbing, the weight of his body in behind each blow.

The busboy went down. Kyle, reaching the Prince, herded him away through a side gap in the railing. The young man's face was white with rage. People were swarming onto the dance floor.

"Who was that? What's his name?" demanded the Prince, between his teeth. "He put his hand on me! Did you see that? He put his hand on me!"

"You knocked him out," said Kyle. "What more do you want?"

"He manhandled me—*me!*" snapped the Prince. "I want to find out who he is!" He caught hold of the bar to which the horses were tied, refusing to be pushed farther. "He'll learn to lay hands on a future Emperor!"

"No one will tell you his name," said Kyle. And the cold note in his voice finally seemed to reach through to the Prince and sober him. He stared at

Kyle.

"Including you?" he demanded at last.

"Including me, Lord," said Kyle.

The Prince stared a moment longer, then swung away. He turned, jerked loose the reins of the gelding and swung into the saddle. He rode off. Kyle mounted and followed.

They rode in silence into the forest. After a while, the Prince spoke without turning his head.

"And you call yourself a bodyguard," he said, finally.

"Your life is in my hands, Lord," said Kyle. The Prince turned a grim face to look at him.

"Only my life?" said the Prince. "As long as they don't kill me, they can do what they want? Is that what you mean?"

Kyle met his gaze steadily.

"Pretty much so, Lord," he said.

The Prince spoke with an ugly note in his voice.

"I don't think I like you, after all, Kyle," he said. "I don't think I like you at all."

"I'm not here to be liked, Lord," said Kyle.

"Perhaps not," said the Prince, thickly. "But I know *your* name!"

They rode on in continued silence for perhaps another half hour. But then gradually the angry hunch went out of the young man's shoulders and the tightness out of his jaw. After a while he began to sing to himself, a song in a language Kyle did not know; and as he sang, his cheerfulness seemed to return. Shortly, he spoke to Kyle, as if there had never been anything but pleasant moments between them.

Mammoth Cave was close and the Prince asked

to visit it. They went there and spent some time going through the cave. After that they rode their horses up along the left bank of the Green River. The Prince seemed to have forgotten all about the incident at the beer garden and be out to charm everyone they met. As the sun was at last westering toward the dinner hour, they came finally to a small hamlet back from the river, with a roadside inn mirrored in an artificial lake beside it, and guarded by oak and pine trees behind.

"This looks good," said the Prince. "We'll stay overnight here, Kyle."

"If you wish, Lord," said Kyle.

They halted, and Kyle took the horses around to the stable, then entered the inn to find the Prince already in the small bar off the dining room, drinking beer and charming the waitress. This waitress was younger than the one at the beer garden had been; a little girl with soft, loose hair and round brown eyes that showed their delight in the attention of the tall, good-looking, young man.

"Yes," said the Prince to Kyle, looking out of the corners of the Imperial blue eyes at him, after the waitress had gone to get Kyle his coffee, "This is the very place."

"The very place?" said Kyle.

"For me to get to know the people better—what did you think, good Kyle?" said the Prince and laughed at him. "I'll observe the people here and you can explain them—won't that be good?"

Kyle gazed at him, thoughtfully.

"I'll tell you whatever I can, Lord," he said.

They drank—the Prince his beer, and Kyle his

coffee—and went in a little later to the dining room for dinner. The Prince, as he had promised at the bar, was full of questions about what he saw—and what he did not see.

"... But why go on living in the past, all of you here?" he asked Kyle. "A museum world is one thing. But a museum people—" he broke off to smile and speak to the little, soft-haired waitress, who had somehow been diverted from the bar to wait upon their dining-room table.

"Not a museum people, Lord," said Kyle. "A living people. The only way to keep a race and a culture preserved is to keep it alive. So we go on in our own way, here on Earth, as a living example for the Younger Worlds to check themselves against."

"Fascinating . . ." murmured the Prince; but his eyes had wandered off to follow the waitress, who was glowing and looking back at him from across the now-busy dining room.

"Not fascinating. Necessary, Lord," said Kyle. But he did not believe the younger man had heard him.

After dinner, they moved back to the bar. And the Prince, after questioning Kyle a little longer, moved up to continue his researches among the other people standing at the bar. Kyle watched for a little while. Then feeling it was safe to do so, slipped out to have another look at the horses and to ask the innkeeper to arrange a saddle lunch put up for them the next day.

When he returned, the Prince was not to be seen.

Kyle sat down at a table to wait; but the Prince did not return. A cold, hard knot of uneasiness began to grow below Kyle's breastbone. A sudden pang of alarm sent him swiftly back out to check the horses. But they were cropping peacefully in their stalls. The stallion whickered, low-voiced, as Kyle looked in on him, and turned his white head to look back at Kyle.

"Easy, boy," said Kyle and returned to the inn to find the innkeeper.

But the innkeeper had no idea where the Prince might have gone.

" . . . If the horses aren't taken, he's not far," the innkeeper said. "There's no trouble he can get into around here. Maybe he went for a walk in the woods. I'll leave word for the night staff to keep an eye out for him when he comes in. Where'll you be?"

"In the bar until it closes—then, my room," said Kyle.

He went back to the bar to wait, and took a booth near an open window. Time went by and gradually the number of other customers began to dwindle. Above the ranked bottles, the bar clock showed nearly midnight. Suddenly, through the window, Kyle heard a distant scream of equine fury from the stables.

He got up and went out quickly. In the darkness outside, he ran to the stables and burst in. There in the feeble illumination of the stable's night lighting, he saw the Prince, pale-faced, clumsily saddling the gelding in the center aisle between the stalls. The door to the stallion's stall was open. The Prince looked away as Kyle came in.

Kyle took three swift steps to the open door and looked in. The stallion was still tied, but his ears were back, his eyes rolling, and a saddle lay tumbled and dropped on the stable floor beside him.

"Saddle up," said the Prince thickly from the aisle. "We're leaving." Kyle turned to look at him.

"We've got rooms at the inn here," he said.

"Never mind. We're riding. I need to clear my head." The young man got the gelding's cinch tight, dropped the stirrups and swung heavily up into the saddle. Without waiting for Kyle, he rode out of the stable into the night.

"So, boy . . ." said Kyle soothingly to the stallion. Hastily he untied the big white horse, saddled him, and set out after the Prince. In the darkness, there was no way of ground-tracking the gelding; but he leaned forward and blew into the ear of the stallion. The surprised horse neighed in protest and the whinny of the gelding came back from the darkness of the slope up ahead and over to Kyle's right. He rode in that direction.

He caught the Prince on the crown of the hill. The young man was walking the gelding, reins loose, and singing under his breath—the same song in an unknown language he had sung earlier. But, now as he saw Kyle, he grinned loosely and began to sing with more emphasis. For the first time Kyle caught the overtones of something mocking and lusty about the incomprehensible words. Understanding broke suddenly in him.

"The girl!" he said. "The little waitress. Where is she?"

The grin vanished from the Prince's face, then came slowly back again. The grin laughed at Kyle.

"Why, where d'you think?" The words slurred

on the Prince's tongue and Kyle, riding close, smelled the beer heavy on the young man's breath. "In her room, sleeping and happy. Honored . . . though she doesn't know it . . . by an Emperor's son. And expecting to find me there in the morning. But I won't be. Will we, good Kyle?"

"Why did you do it, Lord?" asked Kyle, quietly.

"Why?" The Prince peered at him, a little drunkenly in the moonlight. "Kyle, my father has four sons. I've got three younger brothers. But I'm the one who's going to be Emperor; and Emperors don't answer questions."

Kyle said nothing. The Prince peered at him. They rode on together for several minutes in silence.

"All right, I'll tell you why," said the Prince, more loudly, after a while as if the pause had been only momentary. "It's because you're not *my* bodyguard, Kyle. You see, I've seen through you. I know whose bodyguard you are. You're *theirs!*"

Kyle's jaw tightened. But the darkness hid his reaction.

"All right—" The Prince gestured loosely, disturbing his balance in the saddle. "That's all right. Have it your way. I don't mind. So, we'll play points. There was that lout at the beer garden who put his hands on me. But no one would tell me his name, you said. All right, you managed to body-guard him. One point for you. But you didn't manage to bodyguard the girl at the inn back there. One point for me. Who's going to win, good Kyle?"

Kyle took a deep breath.

"Lord," he said, "some day it'll be your duty to

marry a woman from Earth—"

The Prince interrupted him with a laugh, and this time there was an ugly note in it.

"You flatter yourselves," he said. His voice thickened. "That's the trouble with you—all you Earth people—you flatter yourselves."

They rode on in silence. Kyle said nothing more, but kept the head of the stallion close to the shoulder of the gelding, watching the young man closely. For a little while the Prince seemed to doze. His head sank on his chest and he let the gelding wander. Then, after a while, his head began to come up again, his automatic horseman's fingers tightened on the reins, and he lifted his head to stare around in the moonlight.

"I want a drink," he said. His voice was no longer thick, but it was flat and uncheerful. "Take me where we can get some beer, Kyle."

Kyle took a deep breath.

"Yes, Lord," he said.

He turned the stallion's head to the right and the gelding followed. They went up over a hill and down to the edge of a lake. The dark water sparkled in the moonlight and the farther shore was lost in the night. Lights shone through the trees around the curve of the shore.

"There, Lord," said Kyle. "It's a fishing resort, with a bar."

They rode around the shore to it. It was a low, casual building, angled to face the shore; a dock ran out from it, to which fishing boats were tethered, bobbing slightly on the black water. Light gleamed through the windows as they hitched their horses and went to the door.

The barroom they stepped into was wide and bare. A long bar faced them with several planked fish on the wall behind it. Below the fish were three bartenders—the one in the center, middle-aged, and wearing an air of authority with his apron. The other two were young and muscular. The customers, mostly men, scattered at the square tables and standing at the bar wore rough working clothes, or equally casual vacationers' garb.

The Prince sat down at the table back from the bar and Kyle sat down with him. When the waitress came they ordered beer and coffee, and the Prince half-emptied his stein the moment it was brought to him. As soon as it was completely empty, he signaled the waitress again.

"Another," he said. This time, he smiled at the waitress when she brought his stein back. But she was a woman in her thirties, pleased but not overwhelmed by his attention. She smiled lightly back and moved off to return to the bar where she had been talking to two men her own age, one fairly tall, the other shorter, bullet-headed and fleshy.

The Prince drank. As he put his stein down, he seemed to become aware of Kyle, and turned to look at him.

"I suppose," said the Prince, "you think I'm drunk?"

"Not yet," said Kyle.

"No," said the Prince, "that's right. Not yet. But perhaps I'm going to be. And if I decide I am, who's going to stop me?"

"No one, Lord."

"That's right," the young man said, "that's

right." He drank deliberately from his stein until it was empty, and then signaled the waitress for another. A spot of color was beginning to show over each of his high cheekbones. "When you're on a miserable little world with miserable little people . . . hello, Bright Eyes!" he interrupted himself as the waitress brought his beer. She laughed and went back to her friends. " . . . You have to amuse yourself any way you can," he wound up.

He laughed to himself.

"When I think how my father, and Monty—everybody—used to talk this planet up to me—" he glanced aside at Kyle. "Do you know at one time I was actually scared—well, not scared exactly, nothing scares me . . . say *concerned*—about maybe having to come here, some day?" He laughed again. "Concerned that I wouldn't measure up to you Earth people! Kyle, have you ever been to any of the Younger Worlds?"

"No," said Kyle.

"I thought not. Let me tell you, good Kyle, the worst of the people there are bigger, and better-looking and smarter, and everything than anyone I've seen here. And I, Kyle, I—the Emperor-to-be—am better than any of them. So, guess how all you here look to me?" He stared at Kyle, waiting. "Well, answer me, good Kyle. Tell me the truth. That's an order."

"It's not up to you to judge, Lord," said Kyle.

"Not—? Not up to me?" The blue eyes blazed. "*I'm* going to be Emperor!"

"It's not up to any one man, Lord," said Kyle.

"Emperor or not. An Emperor's needed, as the symbol that can hold a hundred worlds together. But the real need of the race is to survive. It took nearly a million years to evolve a survival-type intelligence here on Earth. And out on the newer worlds people are bound to change. If something gets lost out there, some necessary element lost out of the race, there needs to be a pool of original genetic material here to replace it."

The Prince's lips grew wide in a savage grin.

"Oh, good, Kyle—good!" he said. "Very good. Only, I've heard all that before. Only, I don't believe it. You see—I've seen you people, now. And you don't outclass us, out on the Younger Worlds. *We* outclass *you*. We've gone on and got better, while you stayed still. And you know it."

The young man laughed softly, almost in Kyle's face.

"All you've been afraid of, is that we'd find out. And I have." He laughed again. "I've had a look at you; and now I know. I'm bigger, better and braver than any man in this room—and you know why? Not just because I'm the son of the Emperor, but because it's born in me! Body, brains and everything else! I can do what I want here, and no one on this planet is good enough to stop me. Watch."

He stood up, suddenly.

"Now, I want that waitress to get drunk with me," he said. "And this time I'm telling you in advance. Are you going to try and stop me?"

Kyle looked up at him. Their eyes met.

"No, Lord," he said. "It's not my job to stop you."

The Prince laughed.

"I thought so," he said. He swung away and walked between the tables toward the bar and the waitress, still in conversation with the two men. The Prince came up to the bar on the far side of the waitress and ordered a new stein of beer from the middle-aged bartender. When it was given to him, he took it, turned around, and rested his elbows on the bar, leaning back against it. He spoke to the waitress, interrupting the taller of the two men.

"I've been wanting to talk to you," Kyle heard him say.

The waitress, a little surprised, looked around at him. She smiled, recognizing him—a little flattered by the directness of his approach, a little appreciative of his clean good looks, a little tolerant of his youth.

"*You* don't mind, do you?" said the Prince, looking past her to the bigger of the two men, the one who had just been talking. The other stared back, and their eyes met without shifting for several seconds. Abruptly, angrily, the man shrugged, and turned about with his back hunched against them.

"You see?" said the Prince, smiling back at the waitress. "He knows I'm the one you ought to be talking to, instead of—"

"All right, sonny. Just a minute."

It was the shorter, bullet-headed man, interrupting. The Prince turned to look down at him with a fleeting expressioin of surprise. But the bullet-headed man was already turning to his taller friend and putting a hand on his arm.

"Come on back, Ben," the shorter man was saying. "The kid's a little drunk, is all." He turned back to the Prince. "You shove off now," he said. "Clara's with us."

The Prince stared at him blankly. The stare was so fixed that the shorter man had started to turn away, back to his friend and the waitress, when the Prince seemed to wake.

"Just a minute—" he said, in his turn.

He reached out a hand to one of the fleshy shoulders below the bullet head. The man turned back, knocking the hand calmly away. Then, just as calmly, he picked up the Prince's full stein of beer from the bar and threw it in the young man's face.

"Get lost," he said, unexcitedly.

The Prince stood for a second, with the beer dripping from his face. Then, without even stopping to wipe his eyes clear, he threw the beautifully trained left hand he had demonstrated at the beer garden.

But the shorter man, as Kyle had known from the first moment of seeing him, was not like the busboy the Prince had decisioned so neatly. This man was thirty pounds heavier, fifteen years more experienced, and by build and nature a natural bar fighter. He had not stood there waiting to be hit, but had already ducked and gone forward to throw his thick arms around the Prince's body. The young man's punch bounced harmlessly off the round head, and both bodies hit the floor, rolling in among the chair and table legs.

Kyle was already more than halfway to the bar and the three bartenders were already leaping the wooden hurdle that walled them off. The taller friend of the bullet-headed man, hovering over the two bodies, his eyes glittering, had his boot drawn back ready to drive the point of it into the Prince's kidneys. Kyle's forearm took him economically like a bar of iron across the tanned throat.

He stumbled backwards choking. Kyle stood still, hands open and down, glancing at the middle-aged bartender.

"All right," said the bartender. "But don't do anything more." He turned to the two younger bartenders. "All right. Haul him off!"

The pair of younger, aproned men bent down and came up with the bullet-headed man expertly handlocked between them. The man made one surging effort to break loose, and then stood still.

"Let me at him," he said.

"Not in here," said the older bartender. "Take it outside."

Between the tables, the Prince staggered unsteadily to his feet. His face was streaming blood from a cut on his forehead, but what could be seen of it was white as a drowning man's. His eyes went to Kyle, standing beside him; and he opened his mouth—but what came out sounded like something between a sob and a curse.

"All right," said the middle-aged bartender again. "Outside, both of you. Settle it out there."

The men in the room had packed around the little space by the bar. The Prince looked about and for the first time seemed to see the human wall hemming him in. His gaze wobbled to meet Kyle's.

"Outside . . . ?" he said, chokingly.

"You aren't staying in here," said the older bartender, answering for Kyle. "I saw it. You started the whole thing. Now, settle it any way you want— but you're both going outside. Now! Get moving!"

He pushed at the Prince, but the Prince resisted, clutching at Kyle's leather jacket with one hand.

"Kyle—"

"I'm sorry, Lord," said Kyle. "I can't help. It's your fight."

"Let's get out of here," said the bullet-headed man.

The Prince stared around at them as if they were some strange set of things he had never known to exist before.

"No . . ." he said.

He let go of Kyle's jacket. Unexpectedly, his hand darted in towards Kyle's belly holster and came out holding the slug pistol.

"Stand back!" he said, his voice high-toned. "Don't try to touch me!"

His voice broke on the last words. There was a strange sound, half grunt, half moan, from the crowd: and it swayed back from him. Manager, bartenders, watchers—all but Kyle and the bullet-headed man drew back.

"You dirty slob . . ." said the bullet-headed man, distinctly. "I knew you didn't have the guts."

"Shut up!" The Prince's voice was high and cracking. "Shut up! Don't any of you try to come after me!"

He began backing away toward the front door of the bar. The room watched in silence, even Kyle standing still. As he backed, the Prince's back straightened. He hefted the gun in his hand. When he reached the door he paused to wipe the blood from his eyes with his left sleeve, and his smeared face looked with a first touch of regained arrogance at them.

"Swine!" he said.

He opened the door and backed out, closing it behind him. Kyle took one step that put him facing the bullet-headed man. Their eyes met and he could see the other recognizing the fighter in him, as he had earlier recognized it in the bullet-headed man.

"Don't come after us," said Kyle.

The bullet-headed man did not answer. But no answer was needed. He stood still.

Kyle turned, ran to the door, stood on one side of it and flicked it open. Nothing happened; and he slipped through, dodging to his right at once, out of the line of any shot aimed at the opening door.

But no shot came. For a moment he was blind in the night darkness, then his eyes began to adjust. He went by sight, feel and memory toward the hitching rack. By the time he got there, he was beginning to see.

The Prince was untying the gelding and getting ready to mount.

"Lord," said Kyle.

The Prince let go of the saddle for a moment and turned to look over his shoulder at him.

"Get away from me," said the Prince, thickly.

"Lord," said Kyle, low-voiced and pleading, "you lost your head in there. Anyone might do that. But don't make it worse, now. Give me back the gun, Lord."

"Give you the gun?"

The young man stared at him—and then· he laughed.

"Give *you* the gun?" he said again. "So you can let someone beat me up some more? So you can not-guard me with it?"

"Lord," said Kyle, "Please. For your own sake—give me back the gun."

"Get out of here," said the Prince, thickly, turning back to mount the gelding. "Clear out before I put a slug in you."

Kyle drew a slow, sad breath. He stepped forward and tapped the Prince on the shoulder.

"Turn around, Lord," he said.

"I warned you—" shouted the Prince, turning.

He came around as Kyle stooped, and the slug pistol flashed in his hand from the light of the bar windows. Kyle, bent over, was lifting the cuff of his trouser leg and closing his fingers on the hilt of the knife in his booth sheath. He moved simply, skillfully, and with a speed nearly double that of the young man, striking up into the chest before him until the hand holding the knife jarred against the cloth covering flesh and bone.

It was a sudden, hard-driven, swiftly merciful blow. The blade struck upwards between the ribs lying open to an underhanded thrust, plunging deep into the heart. The Prince grunted with the impact driving the air from his lungs; and he was dead as Kyle caught his slumping body in leather-jacketed arms.

Kyle lifted the tall body across the saddle of the gelding and tied it there. He hunted on the dark ground for the fallen pistol and returned it to his holster. Then, he mounted the stallion and, lead-

ing the gelding with its burden, started the long
ride back.

Dawn was graying the sky when at last he
topped the hill overlooking the ledge where he had
picked up the Prince almost twenty-four hours
before. He rode down towards the courtyard gate.

A tall figure, indistinct in the predawn light, was
waiting inside the courtyard as Kyle came
through the gate; and it came running to meet him
as he rode toward it. It was the tutor, Montlaven,
and he was weeping as he ran to the gelding and
began to fumble at the cords that tied the body in
place.

"I'm sorry . . ." Kyle heard himself saying; and
was dully shocked by the deadness and remote-
ness of his voice. "There was no choice. You can
read it all in my report tomorrow morning—"

He broke off. Another, even taller figure had
appeared in the doorway of the lodge giving on the
courtyard. As Kyle turned towards it, this second
figure descended the few steps to the grass and
came to him.

"Lord—" said Kyle. He looked down into features like those of the Prince, but older, under
graying hair. This man did not weep like the tutor,
but his face was set like iron.

"What happened, Kyle?" he said.

"Lord," said Kyle, "you'll have my report in the
morning . . ."

"I want to know," said the tall man. Kyle's
throat was dry and stiff. He swallowed but
swallowing did not ease it.

"Lord," he said, "you have three other sons. One

of them will make an Emperor to hold the worlds together."

"What did he do? Whom did he hurt? Tell me!" The tall man's voice cracked almost as his son's voice had cracked in the bar.

"Nothing. No one," said Kyle, stiff-throated. "He hit a boy not much older than himself. He drank too much. He may have got a girl in trouble. It was nothing he did to anyone else. It was only a fault against himself." He swallowed. "Wait until tomorrow, Lord, and read my report."

*"No!"* The tall man caught at Kyle's saddle horn with a grip that checked even the white stallion from moving. "Your family and mine have been tied together by this for three hundred years. What was the flaw in my son to make him fail his test, back here on Earth? *I want to know!*"

Kyle's throat ached and was dry as ashes.

"Lord," he answered, "he was a coward."

The hand dropped from his saddle horn as if struck down by a sudden strengthlessness. And the Emperor of a hundred worlds fell back like a beggar, spurned in the dust.

Kyle lifted his reins and rode out of the gate, into the forest away on the hillside. The dawn was breaking.